The

PHARAOH'S SON

As told by:

MICHAEL J. DAHL

Published by:

Astabora Publishing Company
P.O. Box 11502
Burbank, California 91510-1502

ISBN: 0-9667244-0-2

Library of Congress Catalog Card Number: 98-73040

Printed in the United States of America

I wish to thank my family
and all the friends throughout the years.

A special thanks to Joe and Pam Crugnale
for their meticulous efforts, and valuable insights.

TABLE OF CONTENTS

Dedicated to all the troubled daughters of the world.

1

IN THE BEGINNING

This is the story of the son of an ancient Egyptian pharaoh, who by some combination of chance and destiny becomes born into the twentieth century. To begin our story we will go back in time to the day of the spring equinox in the year 1009 BC. We are in the Karnak district of Thebes—the southern capital of Egypt. We find ourselves entering a world that in many ways is similar to the world we live in today. People go to work, raise families, and pay and evade taxes. They have good days as well as bad. They attend weddings, funerals, and conduct labor strikes.

Today however, is a very special day. It is the closing day of the Grand Jubilee—a festive week long occasion in honor of Pharaoh Amenhotep IV. Foreign dignitaries have come from near and far—from the Aegean isles, Mesopotamia, and kingdoms in the Levant. There has been much feasting on deliciously prepared meats, fresh fruits and vegetables, baked bread, beer, wine, and honey. Ceremonies to honor certain gods have taken place daily. The entire kingdom has rejoiced, for this has been a time of plenty. All will soon be over, however, for the final processional march is about to begin.

Two groups of musicians take their places along the Grand Processional Walkway of the huge, multipurpose, open-air temple-complex known as the Gempaaten, as thousands of onlookers laugh and cheer. The first musicians are a group of Egyptian women playing harps, lutes, pipes, and percussions. The second group are Asiatic men playing their native instruments. The master of ceremonies delivers a speech announcing the arrival of Pharaoh. The music starts, and the procession is under way.

Pharaoh then appears in all his shining glory. He sits on a palanquin—a kind of platform with poles attached, the whole thing being born and transported on the shoulders of servants. The King is sitting straight and proud, head held up high, with arms crossed against his chest. In each hand he holds a royal scepter. On his head rests the White Crown of Upper Egypt.

The stunningly beautiful Chief Queen Nefertiti appears close behind the King on her own covered palanquin. Behind her are three smaller palanquins, each carrying a little girl. It is not the custom for royal children to participate in these processions. The little girls are stand-ins for the royal couple's three young daughters—Meryt, Meket, and Ankhesen.

As Pharaoh outwardly revels in his present glory, inwardly he recalls his childhood and how bleak his prospects seemed. As a child he was very timid, given more to the pursuit of art and poetry than to the waging of war. Moreover, he possessed peculiar physical characteristics that caused many people to treat him with reservation. He had a long, droopy face, slender neck, rather plump breasts, a pot belly, and fat thighs tapering down quickly to skinny ankles. People constantly made comments about him behind his back. Once, he accidentally overheard a conversation between two of his father's officials, both agreeing that it would be a sad day for the Empire if little Neferkheprure-Waenre, the 'Royal Embarrassment' ever stepped up to the throne.

He thinks next of his older brother Prince Thutmose, first in line and the one everybody thought would become king. The elder son died prematurely however, and left the half-bewildered Neferkheprure to prepare for kingship and assume the royal name of his father. His mother, Queen Tiye who showed the most confidence in him was never very far from his side.

Towards the end of the of the processional march Amenhotep sees a group of his local officials. Among them is his southern vizier Ramose, a man with whom relations seem terribly strained at times. This has caused the King much distress, since Ramose was one of the few men from his father's regime that he felt he could ever trust. Not far from Ramose stands the Priest of Amen—a man Pharaoh despises thoroughly.

The King knows that today is not the proper time to dwell on such things, but he finds it difficult to avoid. He has a tendency to be compulsive about things that concern him. Today should be his day of triumph, but even among the throngs and cheers and waving arms of the adoring crowds he can not rid his mind of what he perceives as the 'evil' that lurks around him.

Soon the processional march comes to an end. Four bowmen position themselves along an outer perimeter, each facing one of the four cardinal points. They each shoot an arrow high in the air. This act symbolizes the ever increasing boundaries and influence of the Empire. The jubilee now officially ends.

Amidst the euphoric support of the people following the jubilee, Amenhotep spends the following months overseeing the various projects that are underway in Karnak. One day after inspecting the temples under construction, he visits the studio of the Master Sculptor Bek.

"Greetings my lord," Bek says nervously as Amenhotep enters.

Bek is of the old school, accustomed to creating in the traditional style. Amenhotep has encouraged him to pursue a freer style of art. Bek has tried to follow his pharaoh's inspiration, but is not at all certain how Amenhotep will react. He escorts Pharaoh to one of the back rooms to show him his latest creation. Amenhotep gazes at a larger than life-size statue for what to Bek seems like an eternity. The statue looks like Amenhotep, except all of his least flattering physical features are grossly exaggerated—his long, thin face, his pot belly, even his hips are so wide as to appear feminine.

"Excellent! You are truly a genius." Akhenaten finally proclaims. Bek is instantly relieved. Pharaoh continues, "You have managed to completely detach yourself from the vanities of the past, and in so doing, you have reached a higher level of artistic expression. This time will be remembered as the beginning of a renaissance . . . an age of innovation . . . and you, Bek, will be remembered as the father of the new art."

"Thank you my lord. It does my heart good to know that you are pleased with my work." Bek then recalls a message he was to deliver to Pharaoh. "Ramose was here earlier hoping to find you my lord. He asked that I remind you of the meeting you agreed to have with him."

Akhenaten's expression suddenly changes from a smile to reluctant acknowledgment. "Oh yes. I have been avoiding him lately. I suppose I should keep the appointment this time . . . Well Master Bek," Pharaoh sighs, "I will return on another day when we can spend more time together."

Amenhotep goes to the palace and finds Ramose there waiting for him. Ramose is a proud elder statesman who displays the dignity befitting a man of his stature. Small and wiry, he dresses simply in the traditional tunic of the vizier.

"My lord." Ramose begins. "There are urgent matters I need to discuss with you. The Hittites are acting up again. They are posturing themselves for an attack against the Mitanni. We have just recieved another plea from The King of Mitanni for our help."

"As I have told you in the past . . . the Hittites only want back what was theirs to begin with."

4

"But they won't stop just there my lord. They want to build an empire to rival ours."

"I don't believe that. I believe they should be left alone to work out their problems."

"The Mitanni are our allies my lord."

"They are not allies we need under such circumstances."

"With all due respect . . . I believe they are."

Pharaoh looks disapprovingly, then asks impatiently, "Was there anything else you wanted Ramose?"

"Yes my lord. There is one other thing. The Habiru are wreaking havoc raiding the villages of the eastern desert. We need to step up our military presence in those areas."

"I'm sure these are only isolated incidences. I will deal with that problem in a different way." Inwardly, Pharaoh has plans of bringing the settled Habiru of the Levant into his fold. He does not wish to jeopardize his relations by attacking their less civilized nomadic cousins of the eastern dessert. "Is there anything else?" Pharaoh asks again.

Ramose tightens his jaw, visibly upset then responds, "No my lord."

Several months pass and tensions continue to rise between Amenhotep and certain high ranking people, notably, the Priest of Amen. This situation climaxes one morning when the priest awaits Pharaoh outside his private Re-Herakhte temple.

The Priest is a slightly rotund man with a shaved head, and an intense, humorless face. He wears a garment of white cloth, with a leopard skin over his shoulders.

"Pharaoh." calls the Priest as Pharaoh leaves the temple.

Amenhotep turns around, irritated that his deep thought has been interupted. "What do you want?" he demands.

"We need to talk."

"We have nothing to say to each other."

"You are making some serious mistakes. I should remind you that Amen is the supreme god of the land, and the reason for all of Egypt's successes."

"The Cult of Amen has gained influence steadily from the time of my conquering ancestors. It was my great-great grandfather Thutmose III who made this empire what it is today."

"Amen was the god of Thutmose III."

"True, but you are not Amen. You simply crave wealth, prestige, and power to rival my own . . . and that I cannot allow."

"I repeat. You are making some serious mistakes. I should remind you Amen is the resident god of this city. You can not simply replace him with Re-Herakhte on a whim. You are placing both yourself and the country you claim to rule in grave danger."

"The country I *claim* to rule? How dare you question my authority!" Pharaoh walks close to the priest. "I hereby relieve you of your duties as the Priest of Amen."

The priest is stunned, but quickly recovers, his eyes, narrow and calculating. "Very well then. Just remember . . . all actions have consequences."

After the disgruntled priest has sauntered off, Amenhotep's anger cools. He feels disheartened, for part of what the priest said rang true. There is a silent majority in Thebes still sympathetic to the old beliefs.

As time passes, many people in the land become unhappy with Pharaoh's radical, pacifist policies—reality is sinking back in—the Jubilee after all is a thing of the past. The King's Mother Queen Tiye councils her son about the mounting problems over dinner one evening.

"How are you feeling this evening my son?" Tiye asks as she looks thoughtfully and lovingly into her son's troubled face.

"Rather depressed Mother. The corruption angers me, and the resistance to change is great . . . even for a Pharaoh. It is all so overwhelming at times."

"Your father was not very happy about the situation either, but he did what he felt he had to do in order to hold things together."

"My father was a patient man. He usually found a way to win people over to his way of thinking, but not when it came to the Cult of Amen." Pharaoh adds.

"This is a new time and you might find the way yet. It is time that the power of the Cult of Amen be broken. Perhaps we should go to Memphis for a while. A brief stay in the northern capital might give you a different perspective," suggests Tiye.

"Memphis would probably not be much different from here . . . but I do find the thought of going to the city of On appealing."

"The resident city of our god Re-Herakhte! I think that would be an excellent idea. Perhaps there you can gain enlightenment in a way that you can not anywhere else."

After many days of preparation, the journey to On begins. It is a cool, crisp fall morning. A patch in the eastern sky has warmed to a red glow. The flotilla has already assembled when the King and his family board the Royal Vessel. They say a prayer, then the boats break water.

As the boats drift away from Thebes, Amenhotep feels a great burden lifting from his soul. The sun continues to rise, cutting a dramatic pattern through the date trees growing along the banks of the River Nile amidst a luxuriant green blanket of successful agriculture. Farmers lead their ox-drawn carts into the fields as they ready for the work of the day. Thick clumps of papyrus shoot up from the water occasionally along the banks. Lotus flowers float on the water's surface, creating a rich variety of form, color, and texture. A bright, thick blanket of fog hugs the fields. As the sun burns the topmost layers away, Pharaoh marvels at how each droplet catches the light and sparkles with the radiance of the sun. The lush green fields, the date trees, the mist, the light—it is a truly magical morning. Pharaoh's two oldest daughters, Meryt and Meket, climb up on their father's lap as the nurse hands the youngest, Ankhesen, to Nefertiti.

The King's mother sits in a comfortable chair nearby. A servant inverts a scented ointment jar on the top of her coiffure—tightly braided hair thrown to the back and sides of her head, cut short at the neck. Her facial expression conceals the delight she feels toward this happy family scene, for her mouth possesses a downward cast seeming to suggest a perpetual state of sadness. What might be mistaken for sadness, though, is really pride—pride in her ancestry as a descendent of the house of the southern princes. Her father, who was of Asiatic extraction, was Captain of the Chariotry during her husband's reign. Born near Akhmin, she inherited the dark skin of her Nubian mother and is especially popular in the southern reaches.

The first few days of the journey pass without notice. Each vessel manned by thirty oarsman gliding swiftly downstream by day as navigators constantly test the river's ever changing depth with long poles. Pharaoh spends most of his time writing poetry and dictating letters. Just before twilight on the evening of the fifth day, the women and children have already retired to their quarters. Only Pharaoh and Parennefer, the King's Cupbearer remain on deck. In childhood, Parennefer was the King's playmate. A close relationship developed between the two over the years. In fact, at times when they are alone, they seem almost as brothers. The King confides things to Parennefer that he will to no one else. As they drink beer from jars through reed straws Pharaoh makes a confession.

"Yes Waenre!" answers Parennefer, his mouth dropping open in amazement.

There is an intense glow near the horizon in a northeasterly direction, unlike anything either of them has ever seen before.

"What can it be?" wonders Pharaoh.

"Perhaps it is an omen." suggests Parennefer.

The King orders the boats stopped for the night. He is so wrought with anticipation he can hardly sleep. The following morning, anticipation turns to disappointment, for as daylight gathers in the sky, before him to the east lies a vast expanse of land—barren, save for a few scrub bushes here and there. Beyond the expanse, a range of low mountains form a cliff at one point. Pharaoh might very well have dismissed the whole thing, except for Parennefer, who convinces him they should stay a bit longer. This proves to be fateful advice.

"Look! The way the sun rises. This must be a second omen." declares an excited Pharaoh. There is a break in the mountains and as the sun rises it fills the break in a way that suggests the hieroglyphic sign for 'horizon'.

The two leave the boat and climb up the steep bank to a more level surface. They walk some distance on the white, gravelly ground. As Pharaoh ponders the situation, things become clear to him.

"Don't you see Parennefer?" Pharaoh begins. "The special way in which the sun had risen through the break in the mountain signifies its importance as the source and the power of life. The sun itself is supreme—not the human form of Re-Herakhte, but rather the crown that rests on his head."

"I understand Waenre. Without the sun we are nothing."

"A new capital city shall be erected over this expanse! I dedicate this new city to the solar disc . . . the 'Aten'. Like the rays of the sun, the influence of this new city will reach far and wide. It will become the spiritual center of the entire world!"

Amenhotep never reaches the city of On. Instead, he returns to Thebes full of enthusiasm, ordering the cessation of all ongoing construction projects, and redirecting those resources to the construction of the new city he names Akhetaten, which means 'The Horizon of the Aten' or 'The City of the Horizon'. By the year 1007 BC he changes his name to Akhenaten, which means 'He Who Serves the Aten'.

The vizier Ramose voices opposition to the ultra radical changes now taking place and is promptly dismissed. Pharaoh replaces him with a young upstart named Nakht. Parennefer is elevated to the highly exalted rank of Pope or 'Chief Overseer Of The Prophets Of The Gods'.

Later in the same year Akhenaten returns to the site of the new city. Workers have already set up temporary tent dwellings for the King's entourage, including the Royal Family. Things are

9

going on at a frantic pace. Stone is being cut and brought in from the quarries in massive quantity. Gold, silver, and copper pour in almost daily. Ground plans are being laid, and the soil is being prepared for cultivation on the west side of the river.

One afternoon, Pharaoh is in his private tent discussing theology with Parennefer and the Chief Servitors of the Aten Cult, Meryre and Tutu, when the steward informs him the mayor of the city, Sekheprer, and Mahu, the chief of police are calling and have urgent news for him. Pharaoh recieves the two men.

"The surveyors have found something of a mysterious nature at the top of the cliff!" the mayor exclaims.

"We do not know what it is, but it is quite large, and the color of silver . . . perhaps some sort of vessel, but with no openings." Mahu adds.

"I would like to see it." Pharaoh replies without hesitation.

The only easy access to the site is by first going to the northern extreme of the city, and then following the gradual ascent of the mountain ridge southward to the point where the cliff rises. The King arrives at the site, accompanied by the two officials and Parennefer. He is amazed at what he sees—a huge object, round in shape, but flattened out at the top and bottom, with three legs extending from the bottom to provide support and balance. Akhenaten, standing at the top of the cliff turns east towards the river and realizes this is the same direction from which he saw the glowing light in the sky earlier on while traveling downstream. A sense of calm overcomes him. He knows in his heart this strange object—this huge disc is somehow related to the first omen. Suddenly, he feels inspired by a sense of higher purpose. Energy surges through him as new truths unfold to consciousness. Standing at the top of the cliff, arms outstretched toward the sky, he declares, "My father the Aten, the only true God, has delivered me! I am the son of the sun—the realization of God on earth. His rays reach out like arms through the heavens to strengthen me. The City of the Horizon is the home I shall never leave. This is truly the dawning of a new age!"

The others, especially Parennefer become so excited by the tremendous burst of energy from the usually somber King they feel swept away. When the fervor dies down Akhenaten gives the order to close off the area.

Pharaoh returns daily to the sight for prayer and meditation. Three weeks later he has been kneeling before the vessel, praying for hours, when he hears a faint humming sound. His heart quickens as he watches part of the lower half of the vessel opening down to the ground, yielding a flight of stairs. Moments pass and nothing more happens, then a figure appears at the top of the stairs. The figure is humanoid in appearance, but definitely not human, moving with an almost supernatural grace and agility as he descends the walkway. He is tall and sinewy, with large slanted eyes, and a small nose and mouth that seem arranged too closely together given the size of the head, but not unpleasant in appearance. The being is hairless and has small, slightly pointed ears. He stares into the eyes of Pharaoh and raises his right hand as a sign of greeting.

Pharaoh does not immediately respond. He is motionless and speechless, as if frozen to the ground on which he stands. Finally he manages to overcome his awe, and returns the greeting.

"Where do you come from?" Akhenaten asks.

The being does not understand Pharaoh and responds in a very peculiar tongue—one combining syllables, pitch, and tone in a singularly melodic fashion. The sounds suggest a highly efficient language, yet rich in meaning and shades of meaning. The being beckons Pharaoh to follow him up the stairs of the vessel. Pharaoh enters the vessel and sees two other beings, similar in appearance to the first, working over a table. One of the beings holds what appears to be a metal sphere, about the size of a fist. Setting the sphere to the side, he motions reassuringly for Pharaoh to lie on the table. The King, convinced that these beings have something to do with his god, easily submits. They remove his crown, and place a device having the shape of a visor over his eyes.

Soon, Akhenaten melts away into a state of trance. He has a vision of relaxing in a cool, beautiful oasis. There is a pond of water. In the middle of the pond stands a beautiful blond woman wearing a sheer white gown. The King's heart fills with passion and he walks out on the water towards her. She disrobes and they embrace to make love while floating weightlessly somewhere above the water. The woman and the King reach orgasm together as the world turns into a shower of sparkling gold mist. Pharaoh comes out of the trance state and wakes up feeling light and airy, but disappointed that the beautiful woman has disappeared.

In the days that follow, Akhenaten arranges for tents and canopies to be raised around the vessel. Servants bring food and other offerings. The beings up to that point had subsisted on low bulk, concentrated nutrients, and are grateful to have 'real food' for a change. The King visits them daily, and they soon learn ways of communicating with each other.

The beings who come to be known as the 'Sky People', came from a planet on the other side of the galaxy. They evolved into their present humanoid form eons ago from a cat-like predatory creature. In a world teaming with predators and a shortage of prey, some of these creatures gradually adapted to a vegetable diet, living in trees, and evolving hands for grasping branches and handling fruit. As the planet entered an ice age, many of the creatures returned to the ground, supplementing their diets with the flesh of animals. Once again, becoming predators, but perfecting their skills to a higher level with the development of tools and the evolution of a bipedal gait.

During the course of their evolution, the Sky People developed a technology allowing them to accelerate a space vehicle to a speed approaching that of light. They found in theory and proved in practice that when more acceleration is applied, the vehicle not only increases its mass, but eventually, it traverses the curvature of three dimensional deep space, entering the middle regions of fourth dimensional space-time. As dimensional shift occurs, the vehicle attempts to align with a frame of reference compatible with its increased mass. This causes it to adjust its direction toward a fifth dimensional straight line course to its destination. An analogy to this might be finding a tunnel to travel straight through a mountain, rather than going around it. It was a trick of nature allowing them to effectively exceed the speed of light without actually doing so.

Travel through deep space came closer to reality, but the journey could still take hundreds of years, and no one would still be alive. To solve this problem they developed a technique of suspended animation, causing the aging process to slow down tremendously.

The three Sky People who landed on earth were scientists on a mission of discovery to aid in the survival of their race. They knew that a certain star near their home planet was destined to become a uper nova, and destroy their home world. The hope was to find a planet capable of supporting life, but devoid of intelligent beings.

The aliens, upon finding intelligent life on earth, would have continued their search after collecting samples for scientific research purposes, but had problems with their propulsion system. To avoid the heat of the day, they worked nights, attempting to repair the faulty equipment with the aid of artificial lights—and these lights were the source of the glow in the sky that Pharaoh had seen from the river on his Royal Vessel.

Politically, the next three years are very difficult ones for the King. One morning in 1005 BC, as Pharaoh lounges on a couch in his new palace writing poetry, Nefertiti returns from her morning ride along the Royal Road.

"What are you writing?" Nefertiti asks.

"I'm putting the finishing touches on the *Hymn to the Aten*. It will be the creed of the faith."

"Word came today that the King of Hatti has crushed the Empire of Mitanni." she informs Akhenaten solemnly.

"At last that issue can be laid to rest." replies Pharaoh, sounding relieved.

"Do you think it is best that things turned out as they did?"

"It was perhaps the only reasonable solution. Are you having doubts?"

"It seems we have moved from a known situation into an unknown one that could have been prevented." Nefertiti responds.

"The power of the Aten provides guidance in these matters."

"Doesn't the Aten also provide us with the ability to reason and the power to act?"

"I have reasoned that sometimes the best action is nonaction."

"As you wish . . . There is also another message. The King of Assyria has asked to open diplomatic relations with us."

Akhenaten displays obvious delight.

"You realize that he is an opportunist . . . taking advantage of the situation with the Mitanni, don't you?" admonishes Nefertiti.

"This is the beginning of a new era for mankind. It is time we all set our past differences aside. When can he send a delegation?"

"As soon as we send our approval."

"Make it so."

"Very well then." replies Nefertiti reluctantly.

As time passes, Pharaoh becomes less popular than ever with his people. Egypt is losing her grip on the empire and living conditions are poor for the majority. The worse things get the more time he spends praying, meditating, and visiting the Sky People. One evening under the tents surrounding the vessel, Akhenaten tells them, "Everywhere, people seem to prefer war and bloodshed over peace and beauty. They can not seem to grasp the truly important things in life . . . and they continue to resist my reforms."

The Sky People take great interest in what he has to say, but try not to influence him. They are cautious about how they answer his questions. This is out of a desire to not interfere with human society. They do care however, and on occasion give him philosophical advice. The most talkative of the three aliens seems to act as spokesman for the others. He tells Pharaoh, "Your people by nature hold high convictions for the things they believe. High conviction can be constructive, but it can also cause stagnation. One would do well to remember that things do constantly change, nothing remains the same. You should forever search for a more perfect truth."

"I agree and I will. My greatest fear is that the work will not be competed in my lifetime. I need a son to succeed me, but the Queen only gives me daughters . . . six children and not one boy."

Soon, the Sky People present Pharaoh with a gift. It is a clay tablet, round at the top, with a raised image of the solar disc. Rays fall down on an image of Pharaoh, in contemporary Aten style. Below the image is a phonetic glyph inscription.

The spokesperson for the aliens tell Pharaoh, "This is a very special tablet . . . keep it as long as you can, then give it to someone else and tell them to do the same."

"But what makes it so special?" Pharaoh asks.

"Let us just say it provides the possibility of a wish fulfilled." answers the alien.

"Thank you." replies the King as he accepts the tablet. "I promise to do as you ask." Akhenaten places the tablet carefully to the side before continuing:

"I have noticed the three of you not looking well lately. Are you ill?"

"We are becoming weary like you, but for different reasons. Our problems are difficult to explain. It has to do with the differences between our worlds." the alien answers.

Being from a less massive planet, they suffer from the intense gravity of the earth. Extra effort has to be made to overcome the effects of sheer weight. The world they come from has longer days, shorter years, lower average temperatures, and higher humidity. Here, they become lethargic from the heat of the day if they leave the vessel for any length of time. They are subject to rapid dehydration, fatigued by gravity, and have problems synchronizing their biological clocks. They have been unsuccessful in their attempts to repair their vessel, and face the prospect of spending the rest of their lives on Earth.

Lurking in the shadows are the former High Priest of Amen, the former vizier Ramose, and Maia, the deposed Envoy to Philistine. They meet secretly, one moonlit night, in the underground vault of an obscure Amen temple in the outskirts of Thebes. The room is dimly lit with flickering candles that reveal stone walls adorned with bas-reliefs of the god Amen—one of the few places where such images have not been obliterated. Sitting at a table in the middle of the room, the three malcontents express their grievances.

"Brothers," Ramose begins. "The state of affairs of the empire is urgent to say the least. We are made to endure one embarrassment after another. Bad enough our Pharaoh would even consider diplomatic relations with the likes of the Assyrian King, but when the delegation does arrive, he insists the meetings be held out of doors under the rays of his glorious Aten. They were in the sun so long that one of the poor devils collapsed from heatstroke."

The others look disbelievingly.

"I have right here a copy of a scathing letter from the Assyrian King to that effect." Ramose declares as he places the scroll on the table in support of his argument. "But that is a trivial matter when compared to the plight of poor Maia."

"Yes. I had no choice but to follow his orders against the better judgment of myself and the King of the Philistines. Pharaoh insisted that David be made vassal King of Hebron. He said David would be an asset to us. Now he has turned against his benefactors and seized the throne of Jerusalem." Maia explains, disheartened.

"Our ruler had used poor judgment, but of course, a Pharaoh can never be wrong and someone had to take the blame." Ramose adds.

"I have always served my country well . . . it was my life." Maia sighs.

"And what does Pharaoh do? In a weak show of retaliation he reluctantly exiles a few Habiru from the eastern desert to Nubia." Ramose interjects disgustedly.

"He was deluded into believing he could convert the cursed Habiru to his faith. David catered to the deviant's sick vanity with his high praise of the defiled *Hymn to the Aten*." the Priest adds.

The group is silent momentarily as they each weigh the severity of the problems. The High Priest's anger builds as he thinks of the heavy losses his once powerful Cult of Amen has been forced to endure.

"The people will never accept his idea of God. Even in his own city I've heard that the poorer classes hide statues of Bes and Het-heru in their dwellings. His most loyal followers seem to be the ones he gives the most gold to. It is a pathetic situation and he is a pathetic creature. He doesn't act like a king, and he certainly doesn't look like a king. If a man was dragged through the swamps of Kush for forty days, he would come away fairing better than our dilapidated King in all his slothful splendor. I often ask myself what our Pharaoh would have been in life had he not been born into royalty . . . a starving poet? A wandering, half-crazed priest? My only consolation is that he does not have a son to perpetuate this reign of madness."

"I think we all agree there is a problem. Now the question: what is to be done?" inquires Ramose.

"I say death to the heretic!" exclaims the Priest vehemently.

"That is indeed one possible solution. It would not be the first time, but such an act carries with it consequences that can not easily be foreseen." Ramose warns.

"But he is a madman whose infirmities will spell the end for us all." the Priest insists.

"Perhaps there is another way." Maia suggests. "I have heard rumors of a strange race of people . . . well three of them anyway. The King spends a considerable amount of time with them . . . too much in fact. I don't know what kind of influence they have on him, but if we did something about them, maybe he would come to his senses."

"For the derilect to come to his senses is to expect Set to make ammends with Osiris." the Priest insists.

"Where do these people come from?" Ramose asks.

"No one knows for sure . . . except perhaps Pharaoh himself, but it is a place very far away." answers Maia.

"This is something we should investigate further." states Ramose. "If there is anything to it, we can take action. If not, there is always the other solution." turning to the High Priest who begrudgingly agrees.

Together, they rally the financial support of people of who have fallen from royal favor, but still of great wealth. They send spies into the City of the Horizon to learn all they can of the mysterious 'foreigners'. Finally, the hour of action is close at hand.

One evening, at twilight, the Sky People sit out in the open enjoying the coolness, when Nubian bowmen masquerading as royal soldiers overcome the guards with their arrows. Immediately after, Bedouin fighters rush in to finish off the surviving guards, while the bowmen seize the Sky People, bind them and hand them over to the Bedouins. The aliens might have been put to death, had it not been considered a bad omen. Instead, they are taken deep into the Sahara desert and banished.

Akhenaten, upon hearing the news of the disappearance of the Sky People goes into a state of deep depression. He is never quite the same again, preferring to withdraw to the confines of the Royal Palace. The King's mother dies not long after, and he withdraws further. The rift between Akhenaten and Nefertiti widens. She moves to the Northern Palace.

Pharaoh spends more time with Kiya, a lesser Queen who holds the title 'Royal Favorite'. There is beauty that can delight the eye, and beauty that can arouse the passions. The two beauties are not always identical. Queen Kiya is an attractive woman with a slightly childlike face. Her soft brown eyes, and full luscious lips emit a fire, and arouse passions in the King in a way that Nefertiti never could. For better or for worse, she is submissive, caring, and supportive of her pharaoh's every whim—in sharp contrast to Nefertiti's sophistication and intellect. The two become virtual hermits in his palace, surrounded by indoor pools of cool water, and walls beautifully decorated with hieroglyphs formed by inlaying richly colored stones into backgrounds of contrasting colors—rich red quartzite and green agate set against obsidian black.

Kiya, though, has not the credentials to bear him a son that would have any hope of ever ascending the throne. Akhenaten's daughters, however, do have the necessary credentials. The King takes his second daughter, Meket, and impregnates her. Meket dies in childbirth, but leaves a daughter behind.

Akhenaten continues his downward spiral. He turns his attentions to his eldest daughter, Meryt and her husband, Smenkhare. The King's anima or female part of his psyche, while always considerable, seems to become more dominant than before and in constant turmoil with his male counterpart. He courts the affections of Smenkhare, who also happens to be his half brother, then takes his daughter Meryt as his Chief Queen.

In 996 BC Akhenaten contracts a mysterious illness. Pharaoh calls his closest confidant, Parennefer to his bedside, giving him specific instructions regarding his burial, and what to do with the vehicle that had belonged to the Sky People. Parennefer, with tears in his eyes listens. Pharaoh signals his steward to bring forth the clay tablet given to him by the Sky People. He passes it over to Parennefer telling him to keep it as long as he can, then give it to someone else and tell them to do the same. Akhenaten also gives his 'brother' a wealth of gold, silver, and lapis lazuli stones. He instructs him to use the wealth to take the true believers of the Aten faith away to a place where they can enjoy peace and happiness if they do not find it here. Parennefer unhesitatingly agrees to his wishes.

Pharaoh becomes weaker and less coherent. He gathers strength briefly as he recalls an event that happened in the first year of his reign. A solar eclipse had occurred just before sunset over the Ugarit—a clear sign that the Aten would show disfavor to the lands of the disbelievers. The solar disc seems now darkened over Pharaoh, and he wonders if his god has forsaken him.

Before the rising of the sun of the next day, Akhenaten, Pharaoh of Egypt is dead—and so ends the reign of the most enigmatic, and controversial monarch in the history of dynastic Egypt: Neferkheprure-Waenre, may he rest in peace.

2

THE SECOND EXODUS

Nearly fifteen years have passed since the death of Akhenaten. Parennefer, now fifty, has had time to think. He realizes his Pharaoh might have behaved peculiarly at times, perhaps he might have made a better priest, poet, or sculptor, than a head of state—but he was Pharaoh, and Pharaoh is God. Besides, is the message not more important than the messenger? Parennefer feels the time has come to gather the loyal followers and find a new land. His resolve is reinforced by the omens: the darkening of the solar disc over the Ugarit in the first year of Akhenaten's rule, the rising of the sun over the break in the mountains, and the coming of the Sky People.

Parennefer next has to decide where to go. It has to be someplace far away from the influence of Egypt—a place where people might be tolerant of the Aten faith. After many days of pondering, he chooses the Kingdom of Punt as his destination, and has next to decide how to get there. A month long sail, south on the Eritrean Sea is the usual and easiest mode of travel, but would require heavy armaments. The risk of being robbed and killed by desperate pirates is high. The land route to Punt, while also dangerous, seems the better alternative. They might be attacked and outnumbered by unfriendly tribesman, but at least they would not be outarmed.

The loyal followers are not all in total agreement about making the move and emotions run high. They come mostly from the middle class—merchants, craftsman, and skilled workers—the ones who lived the good life within the bubble that was the City of The Horizon—the ones who poured their very hearts and souls into the new doctrine, and cannot now believe it is all ending. The reality is that the once grand City of the Horizon is all but completely deserted. It is only a shell of its past grandeur. The country's abandonment of Akhenaten's reforms is, for all practical purposes, complete. Harumhab, a General in the army, is about to ascend the throne.

The day comes to begin the journey. The followers are in a flurry making last minute preparations. They number four hundred and fifty, with beasts of burden loaded with food and supplies. Near the front of the caravan two poles attached to an ebony chest rest on the shoulders of eight men, four in the front and four in the rear. The chest is covered with a white cloth. Inside is the Clay Tablet of Aten. In the absence of Akhentaten the tablet has become a sacred object for the followers and the focal point of the cult's worship. Standing ahead of this portable altar is Parennefer, in the rear is Meryre, the High Priest of the Aten cult.

The pilgrims travel along the west bank of the Nile through known territory, veering away from the river at times as the banks give way to limestone cliffs. In about two and a half month's time they arrive at Buhen, a town in Nubia. Here they stop to rest, and trade some of their supplies for fresh meat and vegetables with the Nehasyu river dwellers. They pay for transport to the east bank, then continue in a southeasterly direction, bypassing the meandering part of the river to meet up with it days later.

As they penetrate deeply into the land of Kush, the character of the land changes dramatically to swamp and jungle. Crocodiles appear in great numbers sunbathing on the riverbanks, and snapping in the water. Eventually they reach the place where the Nile and Atbara Rivers meet. They now follow the Atbara. The jungle becomes denser. They find themselves unwelcome strangers by the local people, who appear ocassionally at a distance amidst the thick jungle growth, then suddenly disappear. This increases in frequency over a number of days. At night, the sound of drums and chanting makes sleeping difficult. Each night, the chanting and drum beats increase in intensity. The stress brought on by lack of rest shatters the nerves of many.

One day, as they push painfully forward, a fight erupts among several people. Parennefer and others try to stop the fighting when suddenly spears rain down on them from all directions. Twenty people die, including Meryre the High Priest, and many more suffer from wounds. The ambushers disappear into the thick growth without a trace. The survivors care for the wounded as best they can before continuing. Their spirits are low, and they doubt if they will ever reach their destination—many never do. People continue to die from fever and the inability to hold food. They languish over the prospect of their dead bodies left in this wilderness to decay, denying them the promise of eternal life.

The journey becomes an uphill climb. Frequent rests are necessary—with maybe only three or four hours per day of travel at best. Parennefer uses every ounce of his inner strength to provide his people a hope that he himself is not sure he has. The fact that the Clay Tablet of Aten is still intact offers some condolence.

By the fifth month the land levels, and a sight unlike anything they have ever seen unfolds before their eyes—a vast expanse of beautiful rolling hills, complemented by lush, green exotic plants growing to huge size. There are palm trees, cycads, ferns, and myrrh trees with bromeliads shooting forth handsome flowers. The growths are thick, but forgiving also—yielding at times to green, rolling meadows. Parennefer recalls stories about his people originally coming from the 'Land Beyond The Crocodiles of The Divine Beings', and he wonders if he has not found the place.

Travel is easier now. They see people again. Not like the warrish tribes of the swampy jungle, but people who cultivate the land, who raise goats, sheep, cattle, and fowl. They live in round structures with thatched roofs. With each passing day they notice more people, and larger flocks and herds. Mornings are especially enchanting as vertical rays of light dramatically accentuate the mountainous countryside. Women and children fetch bundles of wood on their heads as they return home to build the first fire of the day.

Soon, a large group of people approach who turn out to be a company of soldiers. Parennefer explains as best he can to the officer-in-charge that they are refugees looking for a better life. The officer, who does not understand, studies him suspiciously. He orders them searched and their weapons confiscated, then takes them away. The pilgrims become nervous, not knowing what to expect. Many legends exist about this natural fortress kingdom, but few have any first hand knowledge, save for the traders, and even they never venture far from shore.

In two days time they reach Amu, the capital. Darkness falls as the city assumes its night character. Musicians produce sounds strangely familiar. The instruments are somewhat crude by Egyptian standards—but the sounds wrought from them, combined with the voices of the gifted singers create a level of emotion that penetrates deep into forgotten memories.

Passing through the city, they see flames flickering from pots of burning animal fat and shadows leaping upon the ground. Curls of smoke rise in the air from the burning of incense everywhere. An old woman sits on the ground in front of a shop, throwing bones—a form of divination. Most of the women are beautiful, and broad-hipped, with naturally shadowy eyes—a trait many women in other lands try to imitate. They adorn their bodies with much gold—bracelets, neckwear, and finger rings—all with elaborately detailed designs. The men are tall, muscular, and handsome. They sit in groups in front of shops drinking traditional beer and *mes*—a concoction made from fermented honey in cups carved from the horn of cows. The scent of incense intermingles with the aroma of meat eaten raw with exotic spices.

The newcomers are in awe of the deep, mysterious energy that abounds, and well they should be. This is Ta-Aamit: the 'Land of The Mother Goddess Het-heru', the 'Garden in The South', the Great Plateau from which the first humans evolved to fashion their first tools and people the earth. Amu is a city whose traditions are preserved on the very ground on which they were originally conceived.

The military escorts stop just short of the Royal Complex at the opposite end of town. A steward appears and escorts Parennefer into the palace. They pass through a walled entry that opens up to a courtyard. Ahead, is another wall enclosing a second courtyard, and beyond that, the palace.

Parennefer enters the palace, and follows the steward down a long hall to the official reception room. King Tewasia sits on his throne in full formal attire—a robe finely decorated with brilliant, colorful feathers, and a gold crown encrusted with stones of red agate, black obsidian, clear crystalline quartz, and blue lapis lazuli. He is a large and imposing figure, with a deep resonating voice—everything one would imagine a king to be. The steward motions Parennefer to step forward and kneel.

What has brought you here?" King Tewasia asks.

Parennefer is surprised that the king has some knowledge of the Egyptian language.

"We are religious refugees in search of a new home." He answers with his head bowed to the ground.

"What is your religion? the intrigued King inquires.

25

"We are the Cult of Aten."

The King's eyes widen. "You knew Akhenaten?"

"Yes your majesty . . . We were as brothers."

"Please rise. You seem weary." He has many questions, but knowing they are tired, he orders accommodations for the night.

Early the next morning, King Tewasia comes to greet the visitors. He finds them praying around the ebony chest.

"What is in the chest?" the King inquires of Parennefer.

"It is something sacred to the Cult of Aten. Something that was brought down from the heavens by angels, and handed to Pharaoh himself." answers Parennefer.

"I have heard conflicting stories about Akhenaten from traders, but knew not what to make of them. May I see the contents of the chest?" The King asks, unable to contain his curiosity any longer.

Parennefer is no more in a position to refuse now, than he was when the soldiers searched them on the road—he shows the tablet. The King stares at it for a good while, almost in a trance, rubbing his chin, but makes no comment. Finally he turns to Parennefer on a different subject.

"I would like to invite you all to attend a reception held in your honor in the Temple of the Mother Goddess. There will be much food, drink, music, and beautiful dancers."

The next day is the official day of rest. In the evening, they gather in the Temple. There is a huge stone likeness of the Mother Goddess in the center of the temple, surrounded by a circle of fire. Within the circle incense burns sending curls of smoke up into the air playing with the light of the flames. In earlier times, the Mother Goddess was a real woman—one they would overfeed and keep fat. She wore a crown with two cow horns attached, and had servants to attend to her every need. A happy, well fed Mother Goddess would cause the land to flourish. Offerings to her were said to return three fold—and that indeed seemed to be the case.

The people gather around and begin chanting softly—a primordial chant representing the 'first cause', chanting not words, but sounds; the sounds of vowels, very precisely ordered and executed—the very same sounds they believe occurred when the world was first created. A man dressed in white comes forward. He holds a fistful of fresh green grass in one hand, chanting a different chant, but blending with the primary chant. He sprinkles grass on the people. The drums start and the chanting becomes more rhythmic. Next, a man comes out playing a whatta, a single stringed instrument resembling a violin. The chanting becomes more melodic. The drums increase in intensity.

A woman comes forth. The priestess gives her a cup carved from horn containing doma—a drink with hallucinogenic properties prepared from the sap of a tree that grows near the ocean. She drinks the doma, then opens a large basket and pulls out a live snake—the primeval Snake God. She raises the snake with arms outstretched over her head and begins to move her hips, eyes closed. As the doma takes effect she breaks out into a wild, erotic dance. Her energy builds, and the people chant more wildly than ever. The involvement is total. At the climax, she collapses and has a vision. The chanting now rises to a booming crescendo, ending with shouts of joy and happiness. The worshippers are thus reborn. Parennefer marvels at the sense of oneness the people seem to possess. He can not help but feel swept away. The rest of the evening is spent as a celebration of life, with much feasting and entertainment.

In three days' time King Tewasia must depart to Port Zula. From there he will sail across the Eritrean Sea to the Province of Saba. Parennefer, hoping to find business opportunities for his people joins the King as far as Zula. It is an eight day journey, giving the two much time for conversation. Parennefer tells everything he can of his faith, and of the Pharaoh he knew.

The King asks many questions and listens intently. He meditates for some time before commenting: "When a child is sick, it does her heart good to have the comfort of a parent. When the child grows up, she still craves a protective hand in difficult times."

Parennefer appears confused as the King continues.

"Such a god as yours will not do for most people. When your people pray, is it the sun they pray to, or is it your dead King?"

"He has returned to his Father, and in a sense they are the same." replies Parennefer.

"So then your King becomes the very image of God?"

"I suppose in a sense he does."

"Do you still follow the teachings *of* Akhenaten or the teachings *about* him?" Tewasia continues.

"I must admit over time we talk less about the teachings of Him and more about Him." relinquishes Parennefer.

"I think that his ideas were good, but I doubt people are ready for it. They still need the loving mother or father of childhood. I believe your King was ahead of his time, and for that I admire him . . . It is a shame that the one who brings the word is made to suffer the spear and battle-ax of condemnation. Do not despair. Another will come."

Parennefer says little, but thinks deeply.

They reach the Port of Zula on schedule. It is a busy, thriving center of international trade. The King controls the movement of all goods between the deeper parts of Africa and the rest of the world. Punt exports incense, myrrh trees, ivory, rare woods, animal hides, gold, monkeys, and slaves. Wine, olive oil, glassware, cloth, clothing, jewelry, knives, and axes are imported. The general character of the people is different near the shore. They seem almost impoverished, and not as tall and straight as the inlanders. The huts are smaller, shabbier, and built on piles. Scrawny jack-asses, coat-hanger cows, and emaciated-looking goats wonder about the pathetic looking heaps. Even the local chieftain who sees that the King gets safely on board the boat has an air of desperation about him—a veritable camouflage for the treasure that is the city of Amu.

Parennefer remains in Zula until the King returns from Saba. Together they return to Amu. Upon arrival Tewasia gives

28

Parennefer permission to place the Clay Tablet of Aten in an auxiliary room of the Temple of the Mother Goddess where it will be safe, perhaps also believing it to possess magical power that might be imparted to him and his kingdom. Parennefer graciously accepts.

The pilgrims prosper in the following years as shippers of exotic goods. When King Tewasia dies, his daughter Makeda becomes Queen of Punt. Parennefer lives to a ripe old age. On his deathbed he entrusts the Clay Tablet of Aten to Makeda, asking her to keep it as long as she can, then pass it on to someone else. The Aten faith never takes root, however, or rather elements of it are absorbed into the Mother Goddess cult.

Over the course of the next three hundred years, the Sabaens, who carry a strong Semitic trait, and speak a different dialect, are attracted by the pleasant climate and increased economic opportunities in Ta-Aamit. They immigrate there in great numbers. The people of the two culturally different provinces marry and over time a new culture emerges along with a new language called Ge'ez.

The Mother Goddess religion is absorbed into the Sabaen faith. The circle of fire that surrounds the Mother Goddess becomes the Circle of Shams, or Shamash the Sun God. The Mother Goddess herself becomes the Crescent Moon of Almouqah, and the Snake God is cursed as an evil serpent by all but a few who stubbornly retain the old beliefs and go into relative isolation. The name of the capital city changes to Saba. Makeda Queen of Punt, also known as the Queen of Saba, is believed by many to be the Queen of Sheba.

By the end of the first century AD, the Kingdom of Punt has evolved into the Axumite Empire. In the fourth century AD the Axumite ruler, Ezana, converts the region to Christianity. Pagan religions are now no longer tolerated. The Temple of the Mother Goddess is converted to a church, and all pagan items, including the Clay Tablet of Aten are stored away as relics of the past.

By the seventh century AD, the Axumite Empire collapses. Muslim countries surround Ta-Aamit, effectively isolating it from the rest of the world almost as a time capsule. The Clay Tablet of Aten remains stored in a forgotten place, and there it rests for the next one thousand years.

3

THE MARCH OF TIME

The tide that was upon the world was one that would sweep the continent of Africa out of mainstream existence. The European monarchs found in Christianity a useful device to control the masses, who up until that time practiced varied and loosely organized systems of belief. Once people accepted the new Christ, the monarchs had only to put the 'savior of mankind' in a church; then whoever controlled the church, controlled the people. The Age of Africa arguably ended at about the same time as the coming of Christianity. Her children in the North had grown up, and the parent was becoming old. The torch of humanity passed on as mankind entered into the Age of Eurasia—a time period during which art, philosophy, science, and technology would reach heights never before dreamed.

The advent of Christianity may have been Europe's making, but it was in part the Axumite Empire's undoing. Many of Axum's exports, notably incense, are no longer in great demand. It is the Pagans who use such things in high quantity, and few of them are left. She even assumes a name that is not of her own invention. The Greeks had always referred to the lands south of Egypt as 'Ethiopia', which means 'land of the people with burnt skins'. Now, the once powerful Ta-Aamit becomes the sole inheritor of this generic term. Perhaps the greatest irony is that Ethiopia is the world's oldest surviving Christian nation.

In the year 1434 AD, Zera Yaqob becomes Emperor of Ethiopia. He is a wise and progressive thinking monarch, realizing the need for establishing relations with the rest of the Christian world. The Crusades are by now a welcomed thing of the past. Friction still exists between Christian and Muslim, but passage through Muslim occupied territory, while strictly regulated, is at least possible. In 1441 the Emperor sends a delegation to the ecumenical Council of Churches in Florence, Italy, where they are warmly received. The Emperor has hopes of acquiring European technology for the purposes of strengthening his military capabilities and improving his country's now dwindling agricultural production. The Europeans, while willing to cooperate, express justifiable concern regarding the safeness of travel through hostile territories. As an inducement, the Emperor sends a collection of artworks and artifacts retrieved from ancient storage vaults, including the Clay Tablet of Aten. The Europeans respond to the gesture by sending a delegation, but only a few artists and craftsmen are ever able to pass through the Egyptian dominated territories.

The artifacts are publicly displayed in 1442 in Florence, Italy. An unscrupulous art dealer visits the exhibit and recognizes the Clay Tablet of Aten as strangely Egyptian and of great antiquity. Soon after, the tablet disappears into the underground market for private collectors. It exchanges many hands before resurfacing in Paris, France where a French nobleman purchases it in the year 1775. By 1799 the tablet is in the possession of the nobleman's son, who upon hearing rumors that Napoleon is receiving the Louisiana Territory back from Spain, strikes out for New Orleans with all his worldly possessions, and a dream of building a lucrative shipping business.

Three years later, Napoleon, Emperor of France, in desperate need of funds to finance his wars, sells the Louisiana Territory to the United States of America. The nobleman's son, while disappointed, is heavily invested in the New World and chooses to remain. During the war of 1812, the British send an invasionary force to New Orleans. Fearing the possibility of looting and pillaging, the nobleman's son hides his valuables. The Clay Tablet of Aten is hidden behind a wall in his house. The nobleman's son dies in a duel, and the tablet, still hidden behind the wall, falls into total obscurity.

4

A NEAR IMMACULATE CONCEPTION

One hundred and fifty years later, in 1953, Dr. Stanley Du Bois, a young history professor purchases the house once owned by the French nobleman's son. The interiors are old and worn, and the plaster on the walls, badly cracked. Du Bois decides to undertake an extensive remodeling project using his own labor. One day as he knocks loose plaster away from the walls with a hammer, an unusually large piece falls to the floor. In the wall he sees something wrapped in a course, brown material so badly dry rotted it falls apart as he touches it. Intrigued by his find, he carefully removes the bundle from within the wall and places it on the floor. He pulls away some of the dry rotted material, and there it is—the Clay Tablet of Aten. It is in good condition except for a crack near the top. Du Bois has seen this style of artwork before, and knows it is from the 'Amarna' period, as it is now called. The professor also considers the possibility of it being fake. He needs someone with more specialized knowledge, and that someone is his friend, Peter Mallinger, the son of a wealthy planter over in Mississippi. Peter has a degree in archeology and a passion for ancient Egypt.

Du Bois takes the tablet to him on the following day. Peter's wife, Marilyn greets him at the door. She is an attractive woman, a veterinarian by profession, who shares her husband's interest in Egyptology.

"Hello Stanley. Come right in. Peter is waiting for you." Marilyn escorts Du Bois through the house to the laboratory where Peter is working. He is a proportionately built, dark-haired man of medium build. He and his wife seem a well-matched couple, a handsome pair, but otherwise not strikingly different from a great many others of their class.

"Well, hello stranger. Is that your great archeological find you have there?" asks Peter.

"That's for you to tell me." Du Bois answers, clutching a blanketed bundle in his arms. He walks over and carefully lays it on the work bench. He then unwraps it to reveal the tablet. Peter and Marilyn find it difficult to believe that such an article would show up in the middle of New Orleans, but are intrigued.

"I must hurry back to teach an afternoon class. Sorry I have to run. Give me a call."
says Du Bois, waving them good-bye.

Peter begins work on the translation of the inscription. When he completes the task, he finds the result confused and garbled. It seems to have a peculiar syntax, causing him to question its authenticity. "Here Peter, let me play around with the words. Maybe I can apply some of my literary talents and make something of it." Marilyn suggests.

After some rearranging of phrases, and substituting with words of similar meaning, she manages to come up with the following verse:

The son of Aten aspires to glorious life

A Near Immaculate Conception

Or descends to troubling strife
The heir remains in a world of tranquillity
A world within a world of cold and remote possibility
Till the time of the unseen sight
And the lost words are found once more
The abscess of darkness will open the door
Then in the season of fertility
There will emerge a radiant light

"What do you suppose it means Peter?"

"I'm not sure, but it is not at all in character with any of the Amarna writings that we've come across. It seems almost a riddle or a puzzle to be solved."

"Could it be a joke that someone is playing on us?"

"Well, I suppose that anything is possible, but you have to remember the tablet evidently was hidden in the wall of Stanley's house for a very long time—even the wrappings are rotted. The Amarna period has only come to light in recent times. The first westerners did not stumble on the tombs until the 1820's. A prankster would in all likelihood base his creation on information more accessible to him." then Peter reconsiders, "On the other hand maybe I'm just seeing things the way I want to see them."

"Well, whichever the case, I imagine we'll just have to treat it seriously for the time being." reasons Marilyn.

The couple spend hours pondering over the riddle of this simple slab of clay, about four inches in thickness, rounded at the top, with the inscription on the lower half. Above the inscription are two human figures reaching up into the rays of the sun that shine down upon them. One of the figures is an unmistakable likeness of Akhenaten, the other, of a woman. The woman is not wearing the crown of a queen, and therefore not Nefertiti. The tablet is in excellent condition except for the crack near the top passing through the raised image of the sun. "*A world within a world*", Peter thinks to himself as he stares at the image of the sun.

"Let's take it to Dr. Webb's office tomorrow and have it X-rayed." he suggests.

"Do you think that will tell us anything?"

"Maybe. Maybe not. I just have a funny feeling. I think it's worth a try."

They X-ray the tablet the following morning. Three different exposures yield the same result, a circular area beneath the raised image of the sun impervious to penetration by the rays. Excitedly, they return home. Working at the laboratory bench, Peter gingerly and painstakingly works the cracked portion away. Finally it breaks free in his hand, and there imbedded in the clay of the main section he discovers a ball or sphere of some type.

"Well now, what do you make of that?" queries Peter.

"I don't know. It doesn't look like any Egyptian artifact I've ever seen. Try to lift it away from the clay."

After gently working the ball free, Peter holds it in his hand. It is about three inches in diameter, and extremely light in weight. He isn't sure if it is metallic, ceramic, or plastic. It is milky white in color, with silvery highlights that seem to come alive when held up to the sunlight streaming in through the window. Peter and Marilyn stare at it for quite some time, hypnotized by its strange luminescence. Marilyn thinks she sees something in it. "Here, let me take a closer look." she says, taking the ball from Peter. She examines it carefully until she sees what she thinks is a faint line or seam through a circumference of the ball. She grasps the ball and tries turning and twisting it this way and that as if to unscrew the two halves, but fails.

Peter tries, and has the same results. He tries again with all his might. Suddenly, a strong hissing sound ensues from the ball. Startled, Peter jumps back and drops the ball from his hands onto the laboratory workbench. The hissing gradually decreases before stopping, and the ball separates into two perfect halves. From inside the ball falls a smaller sphere that is otherwise identical to the first. It was apparently suspended within the center of the first sphere by six very thin, needle like projections. Marilyn picks it up and examines it closely, noticing that it too has a faint line running around it. She tries unscrewing it and finds it comes apart more easily than the first. Something like vapor rises into the air from within the smaller sphere. They soon realize the contents are extremely cold, in fact, frozen, and the vapor is the condensation of moisture in the surrounding air.

"But how can this be?" asks Peter.

"The outer sphere must have contained an intense vacuum. You see, heat is nothing more than the vibration, or kinetic energy of molecules and atoms. A vacuum would imply an absence of gas molecules, and therefore no transference of heat from the outer sphere to the inner one—except through these little pins." Explains Marilyn. "Here, let me try something." She lights a Bunsen burner and exposes the exterior of one of the outer half-spheres to the flame. "See, just as I thought—virtually no transfer of heat!" She exclaims as she feels the inner surface and the protruding pins with her finger. "The combination of a near total vacuum, combined with the low heat conductivity of the material could, in theory, allow the sample to remain frozen for a long time."

"In other words, acting as a super efficient thermos bottle." adds Peter as the idea becomes clear to him.

"Yes, that's it exactly."

Peter then refers back to the line in the verse: "*A world within a world of remote and cold possibility.*" He reads aloud, then turns back to Marilyn, "You know, this is becoming stranger by the minute."

Marilyn can hardly argue with him. The frozen material eventually comes to room temperature. It is viscous, and off-white to slightly yellowish in color. She places a small amount of the material on a glass slide to view under her microscope, and as she does so, another line of the verse—*Till the time of the unseen sight*—comes to Peter's mind—"the microscope allowing the eyes to see the unseen." he thinks.

As Marilyn focuses the sample, a puzzled and doubtful look comes over her face. She prepares another slide—this time using a dye to improve the contrast. She brings the second sample into focus and can hardly believe her eyes. "Oh my God!" She shouts. "It's alive!"

"It's the heir." explains a resigned Peter.

"The heir?" questions a weakly incredulous Marilyn.

"Yes . . . the heir . . . the heir of the 'son of Aten' . . . the heir of Akhenaten!"

Marilyn is able to match the living images viewed through her microscope with those of human sperm cells found in her reference books. The two find themselves confronted with the problem of what to do with their amazing and most unexpected discovery.

It is nearing dinner time, and Mary, the live in cook and housekeeper will be upset if they do not take their meals promptly. Not much is said during dinner. They are each in their own world of thought, at times glancing at each other in the hope of reading what the other is thinking.

Mary is a slightly plump, kind, sensitive old woman with an unpretty face faintly suggesting a hound dog. Her eyelids droop at the corners, seeming to convey sadness or disappointment, but her eyes glow with a gentle warmth and light sparkle. She had also worked for Marilyn's parents, practically raising Marilyn. The life she has unregrettingly settled for is mostly an extension of her young charge now grown. She knows something is wrong, but also knows better than to mention anything about it just yet. After dinner, Peter invites Marilyn to sit with him on the front porch for a while. The sun is nearly down and the neighborhood is quiet. Peter places his arm around his wife as they rock gently on the swinging bench.

"How long do you think it will remain alive?" inquires Peter.

"Under ideal conditions up to several days, but under the circumstances, coming out of a deep freeze and all . . . who knows?"

"You know, this has got to be the first time in history something like this has happened to anyone. You just can't help but wonder what such a child would be like."

"Part of me would do it, that is, with your support, but another part of me is afraid—afraid of what we might be getting ourselves into. This after all, is a human life we're talking about."

"I would support anything you decided to do, sweetheart. There's got to be a reason for this . . . and if we don't act on it soon, it will be too late, and the chance will be lost forever."

"I know, and that's what's bothering me . . . having to make such a major decision in such a short period of time."

Marilyn paces the house nervously the rest of the evening, weighing the reasons why she should, and the reasons why she shouldn't—then walks into the laboratory, just to remind herself that the sample is really there, and not just a hallucination. She retires later than her usual bedtime, and finds sleep not easy to come by, tossing and turning frequently. She arises and goes back downstairs to the laboratory, then feels overcome by confusion, turns around, and returns up the stairs. She reaches the door of the bedroom, but stops before passing through the doorway, then she thinks to herself: "Even if I go through with it, it probably would not lead to a pregnancy—so why not do it, and at least say that I tried, rather than regretting it later?"

Holding that last thought in her mind, Marilyn goes back downstairs to the laboratory, finds a syringe, and draws the sample into it. She lies on the floor, knees up, and introduces the sample to her womb, staying there in the same position for perhaps the next hour. She then returns to the bedroom, gets into bed, and calls her husband.

"Peter?"

"Yes?"

"I did it!" she whispers.

He embraces her and they both go to sleep.

The following weekend, Peter and Marilyn take the drive into New Orleans to return the tablet to Stanley Du Bois. They are reluctant to tell him anything over the telephone, and still do not quite know what to say. When they arrive, an anxious Stanley greets them at the door. Most of the house is in disarray due to the remodeling, so Stanley shows them to his makeshift study, where Peter places the wrapped tablet on a table. The couple first show him the direct translation, then their interpretation of the inscription on the tablet.

After carefully reading the materials, he turns to them. "You know, this is very curious, yes, very curious indeed . . . but what does it mean?"

Peter and Marilyn turn to look at each other, then Peter asks "Do you remember the crack that was in the tablet?"

"Yes I do." answers Stanley.

"Well, the cracked section came free, and we found this inside." responds Peter as he withdraws the spheres from a cloth bag.

An intense expression that Stanley is known to assume when something fascinates him, comes over his face as he holds the spheres, examining them carefully. "I'll be! It doesn't look quite like any material that I've ever seen."

"It's obviously the product of some advanced technology, but how it became available to the Egyptians, we are at a loss to say." adds Peter.

"It must have had some purpose or meaning attached to it." comments Stanley wonderingly.

"It was designed to keep the contents frozen for a long time." adds Marilyn.

"Contents? What contents?"

Peter and Marilyn again look again at each other, searching for the words, then Marilyn continues. "We felt there just wasn't much time! Something had to be done quickly before they died!"

Stanley looks at the two of them in disbelief, as if they are two deranged people. Peter decides to relieve his wife of the difficult task: "You see Stanley, that smaller sphere contained the living seed of Akhenaten, and Marilyn has . . . well . . . she has received it, I guess you might say."

"Promise you will never tell anyone!" pleads Marilyn. There is a long silence as Stanley stares far beyond the walls of his house. Finally, words come to him.

"You're talking about the possibility of human life here, not some laboratory experiment that either succeeds or fails, or a curiosity to be studied and gawked at. I honestly don't think the two of you really have a grasp of what you've done! You have no right to take such matters into your own hands! You are not God! Your are my friends. I trusted you." Peter and Marilyn are lost for words. Du Bois manages to partly regain his composure as he continues. "Don't worry, I'll keep your secret for the child's sake, if there is a child . . . and I hope to God there isn't."

Stanley's words echo in their minds as they drive homeward. Children were never a priority during the three years of their marriage, and now here they are, faced with the possibility of having one—wondering how much of their motivation for having it is genuine, and how much of it is simply a desire to satisfy their intellectual curiosity. Marilyn wonders if she really would have gone through with the 'experiment' if she knew for sure that it would be successful. These issues might just as well be laid to rest for the time being, they decide, since all is now in the hands of fate.

A month and a half later, Marilyn has no doubts as to her maternal status. She had indeed conceived a child. Family and friends are delighted to hear the news. There are the usual congratulations and baby shower. The ever present Mary now assumes the role of 'great mother', caring for the mother-to-be, and advising her on all matters pertaining to a successful pregnancy: adequate rest, proper diet, and what to expect during labor— forgetting completely that as a veterinarian, Marilyn is fully aware of these things. The idea of his wife actually being pregnant by another man nags Peter, but he seems to overcome these feelings, realizing how ridiculous they are under the circumstances.

Marilyn goes through a normal pregnancy, giving birth to a healthy baby boy in the late spring of 1954. It is a sunny morning when Peter and Mary come to the hospital to check out Marilyn and the baby. Peter and an attendant bring the two patients out to the car where Mary is waiting. Mary holds the baby as Marilyn gets into the car.

"Lord have mercy, just look at him!" Mary exclaims as she follows Marilyn into the back seat. "He's beautiful! Have you decided what to name him yet?"

"Yes we have Mary. We've decided to name him Christopher." answers Marilyn.

"Christopher! Now that's a fine name." adds Mary. She then holds the baby up a little higher, turning him side to side, and studying his face for a good, long while.

"Is something wrong, Mary?" Peter asks as he notices the studied look on her face through the rear view mirror.

"Oh no, nothing, nothing at all." replies Mary as if coming out of a daydream.

The following months are happy ones in the Mallinger household. The arrival of little Christopher adds a new dimension to the sterile existence of the veterinarian and the archeologist. Mary is delighted to have the opportunity to help raise another child—something she had not the pleasure of doing in years. Every now and again, however, Mary studies the child with an increasingly worried look on her face. On one such occasion, Marilyn walks in unexpectedly and sees her.

"Mary! Why do you look at Christopher like that?"

"I don't know—I guess because he's such a beautiful child." answers Mary, a bit startled and slightly embarrassed as if her innermost thoughts are being discovered.

"Well, if you say so." replies Marilyn, not quite convinced, but accepting of the answer.

Eventually, the reasons for Mary's behavior become apparent to all. The neighbors, family, and friends notice something totally unexpected about the child. He has physical traits not found in either of his 'parents'. The child's lips are rather full, his hair is becoming a bit kinky, and his skin possesses a darkish cast. People begin to gossip. They say the Mallinger baby is part Negro. Some say Peter or Marilyn or maybe both of them have Negro blood that no one knows about. Others speculate perhaps Marilyn had an affair with a Negro—possibly the 'buckra' who works down at the veterinary clinic. The rumors spread like wildfire. They start receiving anonymous telephone calls—nasty, ugly calls—the harassers say a house full of niggers don't belong in the neighborhood; that Marilyn is a nigger lovin' whore, a bitch, a slut; some of the callers suggest she does things with the animals she cares for at the clinic.

Peter becomes distant and withdrawn as he searches his confused mind for answers. Deep down inside, he knows the origin of the Egyptian Empire. He knows its founders came from the South, up through the Sudan, settling along the thread of life that is the River Nile, building great monuments first in the South and then working northwards; only later did the descendants of the Mesopotamians, and much later the Greeks, Romans, and Persians come from the North and commingle with the indigenous Africans. He knows the racial identity of the ancient Egyptians is obscured by that fact, and largely a matter of what part of Egypt you are talking about, and at what particular point in time of its nearly four thousand year existence.

Peter, however, like most of his contemporaries tricked his mind into believing these ancient people were at all times more like him, than the people his great-grandfather before him held as slaves—and now he is becoming painfully aware of the reality in the form of a living child. As a proud southern gentleman entrenched in the social dogma of his time, it is no easy matter to resolve these inner conflicts that lead him into frustration, resentment, and eventually anger.

Marilyn suffers from pressures as well, but her concerns are different from Peter's. She, as the mother, conceived, carried, and gave birth to little Christopher. Her capacity to love is not conditioned upon racial considerations in the way that it is with Peter. Marilyn feels as close to Mary as her own mother, and maybe even closer. It was Mary who bathed Marilyn as a baby, who cooked her meals, played with her, then kissed and bandaged her skinned knees when she was older. Marilyn's concerns are primarily for her child, his safety, and his chances of living a normal life. She sits with her infant son in the evening for hours, rocking him, and nursing him.

On one such evening, Peter is having an especially difficult time with himself, and probably one too many drinks of bourbon. He passes by the nursery, pauses at the door, and sees Marilyn nursing the baby. A rage that has been building overwhelms him, and he can hold it in no longer.

"My God! Just look at you!" Peter shouts disgustedly as he walks into the room. "A white woman . . . my wife, nursing a black child. Can't you let Mary feed him with a bottle or something? Don't you realize what's going on around here? What are you in, some kind of dream world or what?"

Marilyn is deeply hurt and looks at Peter in disbelief. "So this is what it's come down to? THIS IS MY CHILD YOU BASTARD! I thought he would be our child. You know, I don't think *you* realize what's going on around here. These threatening phones calls are not just going to go away, and you can't drink them away either. So maybe I'll just have to take MY child away from this place and away from you so he can have a chance to be something in life."

Peter by now is laughing wildly. "Be something? Do you really think he could ever amount to anything?" he adds sarcastically, then an idea finds its way through his intoxication. "Wait a minute! I got it! I got an idea!" he says excitedly, then pauses to assume a demeanor of mock seriousness. "You know, they *all* seem to have excellent natural musical ability, if nothing else. So what the hell." now boisterous. "We'll just buy little Chris here the best guitar money can buy, and he can become a great blues singer. Imagine that . . . our son the blues singer!" Then he starts laughing wildly again.

"I never realized you were so blind and stupid." Marilyn retorts angrily. "We took our black people away from their countries, their land, their homes, and forced them to live by rules that we made up for them. We wanted them physically strong so they could do our labor, yet docile so as not to turn against us, and stupid enough to take our orders without question. So whenever we, that is, your forefathers and mine found one like that, we used him to breed fifty others just like him. Oh yes, we had it all! We had hens bred to lay plenty of eggs, cows bred to give plenty of milk, and slaves bred to do our toil.

"Then suddenly we decided one day they are more human than animal. So we set them free, and told them to go out into the world and make it on their own, and when many of them failed, we said it was their fault . . . they lacked the intelligence . . . they had little ability and no ambition . . . they were lazy and childlike. Yes, we say all of these things, even today to ourselves, and to each other, while at the same time keeping a heavy hand upon them . . . and do you know why? Because we need to feel we are better than they are, and our greatest fear is that they will overcome the damage we have caused them and become our competitors."

Peter stands motionless, feeling weak and impotent. Marilyn, sensing her moment of triumph continues: "There is a woman downstairs named Mary who I love dearly. She might be poor and uneducated, but she has the wisdom and common sense of ten other people I know, not to mention a capacity to love that I could only hope for. I don't want her to ever hear you talk that way! Now please leave us alone."

On the next evening, Marilyn is sitting in the nursery, as usual holding Christopher, rocking him, but now weeping softly. She thinks perhaps she is feeling a bit sorry for herself, and shakes it by talking to her son. "You know my precious little one, we should go to New Orleans and see Stanley Du Bois, but I'm not quite sure how he would receive us. He hasn't called in all this time, so maybe that is not such a good idea." Just then, there is a tapping on the closed door to the nursery. "Yes, come in." Says Marilyn, a bit apprehensive that it might be Peter coming to upset her further—but it isn't Peter, it's Mary.

"Hello child. I thought I heard you talking to some one, but I know the Mister is not up here. So I just thought I would check on you. Is everything all right?"

"No, I don't guess it is." answers Marilyn.

"Don't you think it's time you talk to old Mary?"

A smile now comes across Marilyn's face. "Please come in and have a seat." Marilyn then pauses to search for the words. "You've known that there was something different about Christopher for quite some time, before any of the rest of us. Haven't you?"

"Well maybe, but I really wasn't quite sure at first, and then when I was sure, I didn't quite know how to say it . . . or even if I should say anything at all." Mary replies.

Marilyn then explains the whole thing to Mary as best she can. Mary finds it difficult to believe such a thing is possible, but also knows Marilyn would not lie.

"As you can see, Peter is not taking this very well. Things are at the point where I am going to have to take Christopher away from this place. Will you come with us?"

"Oh child, of course I will. You'd better not leave me behind, but where would we go?" asks Mary.

"I'm not sure yet, maybe up North, or out West. But there's one other thing." Marilyn recalls as she reaches into her purse on a nearby table. "This is a key to a safe deposit box down at the bank. There is enough money in the box to live on for quite a while. I have my own key, and I want you to keep this one. If anything happens to me, get the money and take Christopher away from here."

"Nothing is going to happen to you. Everything will work out just fine. But I'll tell you what, just to make you happy, I'll take this key and tie it up in a handkerchief, and then tie it around my wrist—the way I used to do for you when you were a little girl, so that you wouldn't loose your money. Do you remember?"

"Yes, I remember." Marilyn replies as she recalls the pleasant memories of a happier and far less complicated time in her life. "You do that Mary. That will make me feel real good." Then the telephone rings. "Oh God, I hope it isn't another one of those calls. Do you know they're threatening to drive us out of town or worse now?" Marilyn sighs.

Mary is worried deep down inside, but tries not to show it. "Here, why don't you let me take little Christopher. I'll stay with him. You look really tired. Try to get some rest." she says.

"Yes, I guess I should. Well, you call me if you need me. Good night." Marilyn says as she hands the baby to Mary, then gives her a kiss.

"Good night child."

Marilyn, tired and exhausted, stumbles off to her bedroom and readies herself for sleep. She has difficulty blocking her thoughts to the point that sleep will come. Just as she is dozing off, Peter comes through the door. He is sober, but looking worn and weary, with lines beginning to cut into his face, and dark circles forming around his eyes.

"I need to talk to you." Peter says apologetically. Marilyn offers him silent acknowledgment. Peter continues. "I just want to say I'm sorry about last night. I've been doing a lot of thinking, and I want to try to make things work between us."

"But Peter, there's no trying about it. It either works well or not at all. Whatever we do at this point will have a serious effect on any chance of happiness in the future for us, and for Christopher. If we continue in a bad relationship, not only are we miserable, but we could scar him psychologically for life. To cause this little baby to be born into the world, and then to corrupt his life by feeding him our emotional garbage would be to commit the greatest sin. It would be much easier to end our relationship now, rather than later, if that is the way that it has to be."

"Yes, I know. It's just that so much has happened in such a short space of time . . . and it takes some getting used to. This after all, is my home. It is the town I was born in. It's practically my life. Now it seems we are not wanted here, and it hurts. I got angry, and I took it out on you." confesses Peter, head hung low.

"Things did not turn out quite the way I expected either, but things happened as they did, and it is too late to turn back. You have to realize the little baby I gave birth to, and all that he is and represents, will stare you in the face every day of your life, and I'm not sure you are ready to accept that fact. I know I will be leaving soon, but as for the two of us . . . well, I love you deeply, you know that, but I just think we should give it some more thought."

"One of the things I've always loved about you is your insightfulness. It might also be one of the things that helps to tear us apart. I'll sleep in the guest room for the time being, until we figure things out." Peter then walks towards the door. "Goodnight sweetheart."

"Goodnight Peter."

Marilyn spends the next few days placing ads, and otherwise searching for another veterinary doctor to assume her practice. The disposal of the home is the other major item, but since she and Peter have not come to a firm agreement concerning their future relationship with each other, any action, such as listing the property for sale, is put temporarily on hold. Peter keeps deluding himself into believing the scandal will blow over, and they will somehow return to the life they had.

As Mary is in the kitchen preparing dinner the following evening, she realizes she does not have any tomatoes for the salad. She knows a maid who works in a household about a block away that has plenty of ripe tomatoes growing in the backyard, and would be more than happy to give some of them away. Little Christopher is playing with stuffed animals in his playpen in the den, within eyesight of Mary. Mary takes the child upstairs for his mother to watch while she goes down the alley to get the tomatoes, but Marilyn is bathing. Peter is upstairs in the guest bedroom, but knowing of the problems that exist between the couple, Mary decides it is best to take Christopher with her. When they arrive at the rear of the neighbor's house, Mary's friend is already in the backyard picking tomatoes and placing them into a paper bag.

"My, my! Just look at that baby! He's so pretty!" Betty exclaims. Then after some reflection she shakes her head, and says: "You know Mary, that child is going to run into a lot of problems."

"I know." Mary replies. "We'll just have to make sure we raise him to be strong."

"Well, I suppose, but if you ask me, the Misses has been doing a little creeping around. I don't believe any of those stories about Negro blood running in either of their families."

"I already told you Betty. It's not the way anyone is thinking."

"Well how is it then?" asks Betty.

"I can't really say."

"All right then. Well look here . . . I want you all to enjoy those tomatoes. You hear?"

"Thank you Betty."

As Mary returns to the Mallinger home, holding Christopher in her arms, with the bag of tomatoes dangling from one hand, she notices two men standing in the alley near the home. When the men notice Mary coming towards them they leave. After dinner, Mary goes to Marilyn's room to tell her about the incident. Marilyn seems depressed, so much so, that Mary decides it best not to add to her worry and instead urges that they move as soon as possible.

"By the end of the week Mary. I promise." Marilyn answers.

5

THE GREAT ESCAPE

"You look like you had another bad day." Mary tells Marilyn in the evening exactly one week later. "I'll take Christopher with me for a while. When he gets hungry I'll bring him back so you can nurse him." Mary then takes Christopher down to her room and readies them both for bed.

Late that night, a crackling sound awakes Mary from her sleep. She gets out of bed and opens the door of her bedroom to find the rest of the house filled with smoke. Her first thoughts are of Marilyn and Peter upstairs. She tries to get to them, but the smoke and rapidly growing flames in the living room make it impossible for her to reach the stairs. She shouts out to them and thinks she hears a reply. Then her thoughts turn to little Christopher who lies in the bed still sleeping. She throws on her robe and wraps Christopher in a blanket.

Fortunately, Mary's room has its own side entry door. She opens the door partially, but finds the fire has already begun to engulf the jambs. Quickly, she drenches a blanket with water from her bathtub and throws it over herself and Christopher before leaping through the flames outside her door way.

Once outside, she can see the entire house is almost completely engulfed in flames. She quickly moves herself and Christopher away to avoid injury. As she does, she notices a small crowd of people gathering in front of the house. Mary's first thought is to seek their help, then it occurs to her that among these people might be those involved in the starting of the fire. This thought sends a chill down her spine. Instead, she slips away through the back yard toward the alley. With tears streaming down her face, she holds on to Christopher tightly, as if he might disappear from her at any moment. When she reaches the alley, she turns once toward the house, hoping with all her heart it is all just a nightmare that will go away, but the dream is still all too real. A feeling of panic sets in, causing her to clutch her chest. She feels weak in the knees, and her head is dizzy, but she continues on, wishing with all her heart that Marilyn and Peter manage to escape the inferno.

Mary finds her way to the Negro section of town where her niece lives. Here, she and Christopher spend the rest of the night.

The next morning, Mary hears rumors the fire was started with gasoline poured around the house, causing the big wood frame structure to go up in flames almost instantly, but even worse, Peter and Marilyn never made it out. Now of necessity, she quickly begins to gather her wits about herself. She is fortunate that at least the safe deposit box key is still tied to her wrist. Her niece's boss, a man who takes kindly to Negroes, escorts Mary to the bank to help insure she gains access to the safe deposit box. The man helps assemble a few articles for her and Christopher, then takes them to the train station. She has hardly an idea where they will go. A train is leaving soon, bound for Chicago and making some stops along the way. The main thing is to get out of town and on to safer ground. Chicago seems as good a choice as any, so she buys the ticket. The train pulls out, and as Mary peers through the window, she sees the only life she has ever known pass before her eyes. The thought of the big, unknown world that lies ahead scares her, but she is a strong woman and will endure.

The long train ride proves to be soothing for Mary, giving her time to think. She has second thoughts about living in Chicago. The cold, bitter winters there do not appeal to her. She considers cutting her trip short in St. Louis where she has relatives, but she has not maintained contact with them over the years. They would be difficult to find, and besides, the winters are cold there as well. By the time she does arrive in Chicago, she decides Los Angeles will be her final destination. The weather is warm, and many of her people, seeing it as a land of opportunity, have been migrating there since the beginning of World War II. Mary knows not a soul there, but weather aside, she thinks it the best place for Christopher to start out his life.

Mary and Christopher board a train bound for Los Angeles on the same day they arrive in Chicago. The journey is sometimes depressing to her. The railroad tracks lead into endless stretches of flat, monotonous, sparsely populated land. The train makes a stop in Cheyenne, Wyoming, which has a certain romantic appeal. From the window unfolds a world not unlike the one she has seen in the western movies. Men walk around dressed in western style suits, shirts with string neckties, cowboy hats, and boots. Women wearing cotton blouses colorfully printed in checks or plaids with ruffled shoulders, tight waistlines, and full skirts, accompany the men.

The buildings are of wood in the traditional western style. Wagon wheels lean against the facades here and there as adornment. Hitching posts, rough hewn from logs, border the sidewalks. After the brief stop, the train continues the long, slow climb through the Rocky Mountains, then descends into another vast expanse of land, more desolate than the first. Where before there were farms, now there is only barren desert.

Mary is not impressed with this 'no man's land', preferring instead to concentrate her attention on Christopher. It is a challenge trying to keep him amused in the unchanging environment of a passenger train. When he cranks up badly, she walks him from car to car. He is at the tactile stage of his development, and she is constantly finding new objects to keep him occupied—paper, spoons, cups—whatever. At other times, the rhythmic rocking motion of the train tends to lull him to sleep.

Finally, they arrive at Union Train Station in Los Angeles. Like the Chicago station, it is a busy, bustling place—far removed from Mary's home town in Mississippi, and enough to make her head spin. After a bit of wandering through the station, she buys a newspaper, with the idea of finding an apartment for rent in the classifieds. She discovers there are many places available for rent and does not know where to start. Mary sees a light complexioned, middle-aged Negro gentlemen dressed in a brown suit with a matching brimmed hat standing near the exit. He is not doing anything in particular, just watching people go back and forth. She decides to approach him.

"Excuse me sir." The man acknowledges her with a smile. "My grandson and I have just arrived in town and need a place to stay. I was wondering if you could tell me which area is for colored folks."

"Why certainly ma'am, I'd be happy to." He takes the paper from her hand, looks at the headings for a moment or two, then rubs his chin as an idea comes to him. "I happen to know of a place for rent . . . nice little place not far from where I live, and not very far from here either."

"Do you think they would show it to me if I went over there right now?"

"Well, I was headed back there in a little while anyway. I usually walk, but that takes a while. We can ride a bus or taxi if you like. Oh, and by the way, my name is Mr. Thursday . . . well that's not my real name, but that's what everybody knows me as."

"I'm very pleased to meet you Mr. Thursday. My name is Mary Campbell, and this here is Christopher."

"He certainly is a handsome child! May I ask where you're coming from?"

"We just arrived from Chicago . . ." replies Mary with a pause, as Mr. Thursday waits to hear more: ". . . but really we're from Mississippi."

"Judging from the way you talk, I figured you came from somewhere like that. You know, it seems that once colored folks come up North or out West, they start looking down on folks in the South. They start forgetting where they came from or where their mothers or fathers came from and I don't think there's anything wrong with it. These colored folks here, no matter how bad they want to talk about the South, they still eat their greens and neckbones and cornbread."

"I never gave it much thought until I left home. Things just seem so much more . . . sophisticated here." declares a slightly bewildered Mary.

"It might seem that way on the surface, but underneath the differences are not all that great. People are basically the same wherever you go. A lot of things here are like down South, but there's some differences also. Just like in the South, there are all white areas, and all colored, but here, there's a few areas where white and colored live side by side. Now, most of the whites who live in these areas are either down on their luck and trying to save money, or stubborn old goats who didn't want to move out of their old neighborhoods with the rest of the whites. That's the kind of area I live in and that's what I would be taking you to."

"My, my! Imagine that! White folks and colored folks living next door to each other! That's something I surely would want to see before I die."

They hire a taxi for the ten minute ride to the Echo Park District. Along the way Mr. Thursday tells a little of his life. He explains he is originally from New York, served time in the military as a career soldier, and now retired on a disability discharge. The taxi courses around Echo Park—a manmade suburban lake bordered by a paved walkway. Surrounding the walkway are trees and grass. On the far end of the lake is a dock where rowboats can be rented for pleasure.

Dwellings are nestled in the hills that rise from the park, creating a pleasantly picturesque effect. The taxi turns off the main road on to one of the streets leading up into the hills. Shortly they reach their destination, a small wood frame apartment building. On the right side of the building is a man—a white man. He is rather short in stature, with olive skin, dark hair, and somewhat Asiatic eyes. He wears the white overalls and duck bill cap of a painter, and is apparently doing some type of work. Mary pays the taxi driver, and Mr. Thursday leads her along with Christopher over to the man.

"Good afternoon Mr. Hancock." Mr. Thursday says in greeting.

"Well, hello there Mr. Thursday. And how are you today?" Mr. Hancock flashes a broad, genuine smile that is one of his trademarks.

"I'm just fine, thank you. I have here a couple of possible tenants for you. This here is Mary Campbell, and her grandson Christopher. They just arrived in town and need a place to stay."

"I do have one available. It's only one room, but it has a bathroom, stove, and refrigerator—and it's ten dollars a week. Do you think that might do for you ma'am?" inquires Mr. Hancock.

"Yes sir, I believe it might."

Mr. Hancock leads them up the short flight of stairs to a front porch enclosed by knobbed wooden banisters, then through the front door leading into a hallway. The apartment is the first one on the left side of the hall. It is a clean room with linoleum covered floors and two windows. Mary is pleased with the room, and also very tired. She rents it on the spot.

This is a friendly neighborhood and everyone takes kindly to Mary and Christopher. Mr. Hancock can always be relied upon for a warm smile and a willingness to keep things in perfect repair. He is frequently seen in his painter's outfit with paintbrush in hand. It seems he is always painting something or other—a flight of stairs, banisters, a course or two of siding.

The neighbors are naturally curious about the background of Mary and Christopher, who share no family resemblance. They ask no questions, figuring Mary probably has a daughter somewhere, and Christopher is the daughter's unwanted bastard son by some white man.

It soon becomes apparent how Mr. Thursday got his name. Every Thursday morning or afternoon he brings many bunches of greens—usually mustards or collards, and gives them away to the neighbors. Mary finds herself waiting in anticipation of his weekly rounds, then she cooks a big pot to share with all.

As Christopher graduates to eating solid food, Mary takes him on little picnics in Echo Park. She prepares tuna sandwiches, and fresh squeezed lemonade in a gray thermos jug. They spend many afternoons on the grass under a shade tree near the lake. When Christopher is not eating the sandwiches and washing them down with the cool lemonade, he marvels at the ants inviting themselves for a share of the meal, or feeds the birds the crusts of bread he prefers not eating. At other times he begs Mary to tickle him, then rolls down the grassy slope laughing wildly. In their more tender moments, Mary hugs and kisses Christopher, telling him he is Grandma's special one, and he will be a 'great man' one day.

One day, at around noontime a fire erupts across the street in a house occupied by an old, bald-headed white gentleman. The fire trucks and ambulance arrive as Christopher and Mary watch the flurry of activity from their front porch. Fortunately, the man is rescued from the fire and escorted to an ambulance; the house is all but lost. Christopher is enthralled by the scene, but for Mary, the fire serves as a grim reminder of an all too recent disaster that changed the course of events for her and her 'grandchild'.

The fire excepted, life is pleasant in this neighborhood, but Mary is of an advanced age, and the hilly ground is proving to be too much of an obstacle for her. It so happens that Mr. Hancock manages another set of apartments several miles to the southwest on more level ground. When Christopher is two and a half years old, they move into one of these apartments on St. Andrews Place. People refer to these apartments as 'courts', because all the units open up to a common courtyard. Inside there is one room, a bathroom, and separate kitchen. The kitchen has cabinets, a refrigerator, a gas stove with a nonfunctioning pilot that requires matches for lighting, and a built in wooden booth for eating meals. There is a back door leading to clotheslines for drying laundry.

Next door to them lives an extremely old lady everyone knows as Miss Pearl. She claims to be over a hundred years old, and to have worked on the fields in the South as a slave. One can always find Miss Pearl sitting in a chair on the small area of her front porch, toothless and grinning, spitting the juices of her snuff into a tin can, and eager to engage in conversation with anyone who is willing to spare the time. She and Mary, who also worked the fields during the earliest years of her life have much in common. They spend hours talking about life on the plantation— discussing the finer points of picking cotton, corn husking parties, digging up potatoes, and roasting yams on top of hot coals. To these ladies, food somehow always seemed to taste better on the plantation, even something as simple as crumbled up cornbread, mixed with green peas, and topped off with 'ham gravy'.

Miss Pearl tells of some of her more unpleasant experiences as a slave child. These have left a deep impression on her memories. She would be forced to watch the men folk being horse whipped for stealing a chicken, or even a single potato to supplement their wanting diets. The overseer delivered the punishment with a passion that suggested a sick, deviant form of sexual arousal. Then she speaks of the 'good masters' she heard about who never beat their slaves, and even helped the bondsmen establish lives for themselves after the institution of slavery ended.

As for little Christopher, he looks forward to his wake up call each morning—the tooting horn of the bakery truck, from which cakes and donuts can be bought practically from the doorstep. In the afternoon he hears the whistle of the ice cream truck as it passes by, creating another level of excitement as Mary hurries to give him a nickel or dime before the truck gets away.

When Christopher is about four years old, Mary realizes that their one room apartment is too small, and Christopher should have his own room. Mr. Hancock, not wanting to lose a good tenant tells her of a place he has coming up for rent soon on West Adams Boulevard. Mary feels she knows Mr. Hancock fairly well by now. He has always treated her with dignity and respect. She is not the type of person who likes to do business with strangers, and agrees to see the apartment.

The apartment is actually a converted attic in a huge, two story house once owned by a wealthy doctor. In later times the house was divided into nine separate living units. Mary is not particularly fond of the attic apartment, or the many stairs she has to climb to reach it. It has a curious floor plan, and low ceilings sloped to conform to the pitch of the roof. To make matters worse, the bathrooms are on the first and second floors, and must be shared with the other tenants. Mr. Hancock entices her by offering the place at a substantially reduced rate if she agrees to help him by keeping the common areas clean. There are three bathrooms and a service porch to be mopped and scrubbed, hallways to be vacuumed, and woodwork to be polished. Mary, always concerned her money will one day run out, has been thinking about finding part time work once Christopher starts school anyway. She decides that the advantages of living here outweigh the disadvantages and takes the apartment.

With regard to the new house, Mary might be wrought with reservation, but Christopher is filled with wonder. To him, the house is like a huge play box full of interesting things—obstacles to overcome, cubbyholes to hide in, and things to be discovered. His favorite activity, when Mary has her back turned, is to slide down the long, stair banister between the first and second floors. The ride is always fun, but never long enough.

Christopher finds the attic apartment an excellent vantage point from which to view the world, and in time, Mary learns to appreciate this aspect as well. The two often sit and enjoy a bird's eye view of automobiles speeding up and down the boulevard, and the activities at the gasoline station directly across the street. Christopher becomes thoroughly familiar with the routine of the attendants, neatly outfitted in blue trousers, white shirts with bow ties, and service hats, as they pump gas and wash windshields.

Two doors away is a home for invalids. There is a certain woman living there, who Mary and Christopher see passing by often. The woman's tongue hangs out of her mouth. Her entire body is twisted, and she seems barely able to walk, but walk she does, and several times a day. When Christopher comes to the age of asking many questions, he wants to know why the lady is the way she is. Mary explains that she is sick with a disease called epilepsy. Christopher feels very sorry for the lady and wishes there was something he could do for her. Mary lends some comfort by assuring him the lady is being cared for, and that one day she will be with god and her sickness will go away.

A couple of the tenants in the rooming house stay for the long term, but most come and go at a rapid rate. Mary takes on the additional responsibilities of collecting the rents and showing the rooms to prospective tenants in exchange for free and clear rent.

The time comes for Christopher to start kindergarten. On the appointed day, Mary takes him to enroll in school. As they walk through the hallways of the school, Christopher sees many other children, most older than himself. Then he turns to Mary and asks, "Grandma?"

"Yes?" Mary responds.

"When I get bigger will I look like them?"

Mary feels struck by the question, not sure she knows what he means, and then again knowing exactly what he means. The suddenness and unexpectedness of the question leaves her bereft of an answer as she turns away and looks down at the ground, then responds incorrectly with a weak, "yes."

The Great Escape

On Sunday mornings they go to church and attend a lively service held in the southern Baptist tradition. Afterwards, Mary sometimes treats Christopher to one of his favorite meals—tacos sold at a neighborhood Mexican delicatessen. Two twenty-five cent beef tacos, stuffed with crisp lettuce, ripe tomato, and delicious cheese, along with a ten cent soda, and Christopher is half way to paradise—a small cup of orange sherbet and vanilla ice cream completes the journey.

On some Sunday afternoons, Mary prepares a big meal while listening to church programs on the single radio station in Los Angeles catering to Negro tastes. She does not care much for the usual fare of rock and roll tunes offered throughout the rest of the week. There is an occasional blues tune, or ballad that catches her ear, however.

In particular is a certain song by a young, up and coming balladeer, with whom she absolutely falls in love. She buys the record and plays it on her small phonograph for hours on end, sitting at a window facing towards the east, allowing the rich voice to strike an emotional chord deep within her, and perhaps to invoke the memory of a love, lost somewhere in the distant past. The music blends in perfectly with the broad, low expanse of Los Angeles skyline as seen from the high perch that is the attic dwelling. There are only two tall buildings that stand out prominently from the downtown area. One is an office building with red lights bordering the top, the other is in the 'space needle' style, built by a petroleum company, and bathed by soft, blue light. The distant lights twinkle in the night air. Even Christopher goes through the house mouthing the words to the music.

One day, there is a news bulletin on the radio. The singer has been killed in an automobile accident, and the singer's wife, who was also in the car, is in critical condition. The singer's wife dies days later. A heartbroken Mary, and a saddened Christopher pay their final respects by attending the public viewing at a mortuary, which happens to be not very far from where they live. A long line of people extend out of the doors, and moves slowly, but no one complains. All is quite and solemn. Inside, there are two caskets. The singer is on the left. He is dressed in a dark suit. His pretty wife is on the right. She wears a pink dress. As Mary passes the singer's casket, she stops, then extends her hand and touches his forehead—her way of bidding her beloved balladeer . . . goodnight.

Christopher completes kindergarten, then advances to the first grade. Mary decides to teach him how to come home on his own, and the safe way to cross the streets just in case she is one day unable to pick him up, but Christopher is afraid and responds by asking

"What if I get lost, Grandma?"

"I'm going to tell you a little story." Mary begins. "Once upon a time there was a little boy who wandered away from home and got lost. After wandering around for a long time, he became very thirsty and said to himself: 'I wish I had some water'. He kept saying this to himself over and over again, until finally he found his way home and got his water. If you ever get lost, just say the magic words, 'I wish I had some water', and just like that little boy, you will find your way home."

Reinforced by the confidence this little story gives him, his fears melt away, and he has no problems walking home on his own when it becomes necessary to do so.

He makes friends in the neighborhood and soon after engages in the devilish antics boys are apt to do. They raid the neighbor's fruit trees, steal soda pop bottles to take down to the five-and-ten-cents-store to exchange for candy bars, and divide into teams for rock fights. Each team has the protection of a picket fence at opposite sides of a neutral neighbor's back yard. The adversaries throw small rocks back and forth at each other. Rarely do any of the rocks hit anyone. The fights are generally held just before dinner time. The first mother within earshot who makes the dinner call is also the signal to call a truce, then all go in for the evening meal, and return for more antics afterward, if daylight permits.

The Great Escape

On one such after dinner excursion, Christopher and one of his buddies execute a plan they had devised earlier for travel to the moon. They removed from hiding, a lead pipe about three inches in diameter and maybe six to eight feet long. This they prop up against a high fence and point towards the moon. They stuff rolls intended for toy cap guns into the bottom most end of the pipe. The two would-be space voyagers then mount the lead pipe as if on horseback. Christopher's buddy is the older, and is the one who lights the match that will ignite the propulsion system. He holds the lit match to the end of the pipe, but nothing happens. They decide to add more cap gun rolls, but again, nothing. In desperation they add all the remaining cap gun rolls, including the ones intended for the return journey from the moon. To consume the fuel intended for the journey home is not as foolhardy as one might think. You see, they have a theory that once on the moon, they can eat the cheese the moon is made of, and then fly back to earth under their own powers. Unfortunately, their last ditch efforts fail as well, and they are forced to return to their homes for the evening to rethink their theories.

Sometimes, Christopher and his friends sneak down to the site of the Santa Monica Freeway, about three blocks away. At this time, it is nothing more than a wide strip of graded dirt that seems to go on forever, but to these boys, it looks like another world. It becomes a favorite place to ride bicycles, and play ball. Occasionally, they find ladies' stockings and girdles half buried in the dirt. The most perplexing problem of the day, second only to building a functioning rocket ship, is how these items ended up in the present location.

On a typical evening after the sun goes down, Mary and Christopher sit near the window overlooking the boulevard. Stray light from the street lamps and filling station wanders in and bounces off Mary's animated eyes as she spins her tales Christopher sits listening to, spellbound:

"Once upon a time . . ." Mary begins. ". . . very long ago there was a great man named Moses who lived in Egypt. Moses was unhappy, because Pharaoh who was the king of Egypt made slaves of his people. One day, Moses came to Pharaoh and asked him to let his people go, but Pharaoh said 'No.' Moses got angry and told Pharaoh: 'If you do not free my people, then God will punish you by killing the first born of every woman and beast in the land, starting with your own son!' Pharaoh did not believe Moses, and had a hard heart besides. Then one night, the Angel of Death came down upon the land of Egypt, killing all the firstborn. All that is, except the firstborn of Moses and his people. You see, God told Moses and his people to paint the sides and tops of the doorways to their houses with the blood of a lamb. If they did this, then no harm would come to them. It took all that for Pharaoh to finally let Moses and his people go."

"But Grandma, what about all the little kids who had to die? They didn't do anything to hurt anyone." Christopher reasons.

"Well baby, I suppose that's true . . . but God is the giver of life and the only one who can rightfully take it away. Sometimes He does things that are hard for us to understand. We just have to take what He gives us and try to make the best of it. Now that story I just told you teaches us we should try to not be mean or cruel to other people. Do you understand?"

"Yes, I think so." yawns Christopher.

"It's getting pretty close to your bedtime. Why don't you go down and brush your teeth, and when you come back, Grandma will tuck her big boy in bed."

When Christopher returns, he changes into his pajamas, says his prayers, then Mary tucks him in bed.

"Tell me one more story . . . please Grandma?"

"Well all right, but a short one though . . . When I was a little girl growing up, there was a mysterious mother and daughter who used to roam the countryside. They didn't seem to live anywhere, and probably all they owned was carried on their backs. Every now and then, in the late evening, they would appear at someone's back door and ask to use the kitchen. The people living in the house would usually go to bed, leaving them in the kitchen cooking food they had brought with them. By morning, the mother and daughter would be gone, and the kitchen would be left cleaner than it was before they came. No one ever knew their names, or where they were from. Then one day they stopped coming around to anyone's house . . . just disappeared . . . never to be seen or heard from again."

"But didn't the lady have a husband?" asks Christopher.

"No one knew enough about them to say one way or the other. Life was hard there for some folks in those days, and men would sometimes give up on their families." expresses Mary.

"Maybe he died . . . like my mommy and daddy."

A feeling of hurt comes over Mary as she wonders if maybe she has told the wrong story.

"Grandma, I'm glad we have beds, and our own kitchen, and I love you very much."

Mary now smiles, and her heart is lightened. "I love you too, child." she says, then gives him a hug and a kiss.

One morning in the spring of 1961, Christopher awakes from his sleep. Mary has not yet stirred. "Good." he thinks to himself. "Maybe I won't have to go to school today." He has to use the bathroom however, and manages to sneak downstairs to relieve himself, then back again, feeling very triumphant he has not awakened her. Another half hour or so passes, and he is becoming hungry. Again he rises from his bed, and goes to Mary's room calling, "Grandma," but she does not answer him. He comes closer, and shakes her shoulder, but still no response. "She seems so very, very still . . . just like the singer, and his wife." Christopher thinks to himself. He knows there was something very final, and very permanent about the singer and his wife, and that creates an uneasy feeling within him. He thinks he hears something move near the window and now becomes frightened. "Grandma! Please wake up Grandma! Please!" screaming louder, and louder, trying to reach the part of her that is somehow missing. Tears now roll down his cheeks. He sees the telephone next to her bed, and uses it to call the operator. "My grandma is sick!" he tells the operator. "She needs a doctor!" The operator asks for the address. Christopher knows the address, and gives it to her. The ambulance arrives and the attendants find Mary lying on her side, with most of her face buried in her pillow. One of the attendants turns her face up, and notices a small amount of blood on the pillow. The blood apparently trickled from her nose, by now deformed by the effects of rigor mortis. Mary had passed away some time during the night of an apparent stroke.

6

THE WONDER YEARS

The police arrive on the scene soon after the ambulance, and take charge of little Christopher. There are no relatives he can be traced to, and even if there were, it is doubtful they would want him. The police, while sympathetic, have no choice but to take him to the police station, buying him ice cream along the way. The county authorities shuttle him off to a child care facility, where he finds himself among many other children in similar situations. Christopher is especially unsuited to the institutional lifestyle, being of a rather introspective nature, and not accustomed to functioning around large groups of people for extended periods of time—preferring the personal moments, such as those spent in the evening with Mary. Every night he cries himself to sleep, praying that Mary returns to him.

After a hearing, the court officially makes Christopher a ward of the state, and places him in a foster home. Most of his classmates in the new school he now attends are loud and unruly. They run about the classroom uncontrollably, screaming and throwing things at each other. Christopher likens the teacher's lectures to the stories Mary used to tell him, and wants to hear what she has to say. He has trouble understanding why his classmates behave as they do.

Home is no better. In fact, it is worse. His foster parents force him to stay in the house most of the time, the only stimulation for him being a television set, and even that at times, proves a failed escape. Christopher sits on the floor close to the television, legs crossed, watching shows depicting the American ideal of family life. Father goes to work every day in a suit and tie, and comes home in the evening with a smile, a hug, or a kiss for everyone; Mother keeps the house spotless, and seems always to be baking cookies or cakes; Junior's crisis of the day might be figuring out whom to take to the school dance, while his little sister worries that the tooth fairy might not really come.

The idyllic existence portrayed on the picture tube is in sharp contrast to the life of Christopher. There are no cookies baking in the oven—it contains the stinking carcass of a rotting chicken, and the tooth fairy is dead.

On some weekdays, the foster father might leave the house, then return late at night, drunk and ill-tempered. When he returns, he and his wife usually start arguing loudly. The arguments usually end only after he has beaten her.

On weekends, the foster father usually disappears completely, while his wife leaves Christopher home alone for several hours at a time, especially on Friday and Saturday night. The foster mother returns late at night with some man other than her husband. Christopher then awakens to the sounds that pass easily through the thin wall that separates him from the activity in the adjacent room—the sounds of drunk, empty laughter, the rustling of sheets, bumping and grinding, loud moans, and heavy breathing.

One Friday night when Christopher is home alone he has a nightmare. In his dream an evil witch stands before him holding a broomstick in her hand. Christopher tries to run away, but something keeps pulling him back. The harder he tries to run, the harder it is to get away. In his dream he turns around to see if he has gotten any farther away. The witch lets out a wicked laugh, waves her broomstick in the air, and seems to magically draw him closer to her. Christopher wakes up terrified and sobbing uncontrollably. He finds the telephone and dials the number he still remembers. A lady answers.

"Hello, is this my grandma?" asks Christopher with the kind of hope possible only for a child.

"I'm sorry. This is not your grandmother." comes the reply. "Where are your parents? Do they know you are on the phone?" the lady continues.

Christopher tells the lady good-bye, and hangs up the telephone. Still crying, he returns to his bedside, drops to his knees, rocks back and forth with his eyes closed, and says a prayer:

"Please God, make Grandma come back to me. If you do, I'll be good . . . I promise. I don't like it here. It smells bad. The people make me use the bathroom in a bucket, and it stinks . . . They're mean to me . . . The other day I dropped a piece of bread on the floor and the lady slapped me. If you let Mary come back, I'll be extra good . . . and I won't drop anything . . . I promise. Please God! Please . . ."

God must have provided Christopher with some measure of relief. Sometime during his praying, he falls asleep, and sleeps until morning.

At school, the annual May Day Dance draws near and the students spend part of each day practicing their routines. Everyone's parents will be there proudly watching their sons and daughters perform. Christopher has no desire to attend, and wonders if he can figure out a way to avoid it. In the back yard of the dingy little house where he lives is stored a large, wooden cabinet. On May Day, Christopher pretends to go to school, but instead hides all day in the wooden cabinet. This is the first time he has ever ditched school, but it is not the last.

The cabinet becomes a refuge for him whenever the insanity of his classmates becomes too great to endure. Sometimes, while walking down the alleys he finds comic books thrown away as trash. These, he collects and reads while hiding out in the cabinet. Later on he graduates to more sophisticated magazines. Without realizing it, he teaches himself reading skills superior to those of his classmates. In a similar way, by reading the mail order advertisements, and calculating the total cost of merchandise, including taxes, shipping and handling in his head, he sharpens his ability to think mathematically.

The magazines provide some escape from the pain of his ugly life, but at other times the pain is so great, he thinks he will die. Rather than living with these feelings, he learns to shut off and shut down emotionally. He now speaks very little to anyone, and hardly ever laughs or plays with other children. The world becomes distant—almost abstract to him—a make believe land of petty wants and desires that people leave behind when they die. He feels more an observer or spectator, than a participant. The world is to Christopher an imperfect and painful place, and he longs to return to something akin to a mother's womb, but until that time comes, remaining distant and not getting close to anyone ever again is his only guarantee of protection.

In a way, it would be wrong to say that Christopher becomes completely friendless. He has friends, but they are what we would generally consider as being of an imaginary type. At night, figures appear near his bed. They dance around in the dark, inviting him to come and play with them, and provide him with entertainment. A man Christopher calls the Magician appears almost every night. The Magician likes to stand in the doorway, waving his hands through the air eloquently, while Christopher watches with great interest. Sometimes, Christopher flies away with the Magician to a place far away—a place that cannot be described with words; then almost instantly, as if traveling faster than the speed of light, the Magician brings him back to his bed. In time, Christopher learns to fly on his own—hovering over rooftops, traversing great distances of land, or soaring to incredible heights, high above the clouds. Night time and being alone are no longer things to fear, but rather an adventure to look forward to with joy!

The foster parents are not content imposing themselves, and doing their damage to one child. The county allows them to have two more. They are brothers, one and two years older than Christopher. The foster parents tricked the county into believing that the brothers would share a separate room, but jammed them both into the same small room occupied by Christopher. The brothers have very dark skins, and enjoy taunting their roommate for being different, but the thing troubling Christopher most is that his imaginary friends no longer appear to him at night.

One morning, some time after the brothers arrive, Christopher stands before the mirror in the bathroom, and breaks out in tears. "Grandma was wrong." he thinks to himself. "I'm never going to look like the other kids." It was the only time she had ever let him down. It is the first time he cries in over a year, and would be the last for a long time. He becomes angry at God, and learns to hate Him. Soon, he stops thinking about the past, blocking all memory of Mary, her death, and life before the foster home. He adopts the unruly behavior he once despised in his classmates, and becomes impossible to deal with, challenging authority at every opportunity. To Christopher's benefit, the foster parents reach the conclusion that his behavior is not worth the monthly check they receive from the county, and so send him away.

Christopher is now placed in a foster home run by very nice people—too nice, in fact, for a kid already corrupted by the ills of the system. After a brief stay with the nice people, he is transferred to a special group home. There he lives with eleven other boys—some approaching adolescence like himself, and some older. The home is staffed with an administrator, child care workers, and a cook. Occasionally, there is a visit from a social worker or therapist. The home has its benefits, but also drawbacks—the major one being the younger boys' tendency to be influenced by the older ones who often have a history of getting into more serious kinds of trouble.

During puberty, emotional forces emerge that are in conflict with Christopher's psychological mind-set to maintain a certain distance from everyone. He does not always realize what he is doing, or the reasons why. It is simply the result of a now forgotten, subconscious fear of getting hurt. With the other guys at the group home and even at school, this does not present any problems for him. A hard and insensitive exterior can be an asset, a valuable survival tool, but the conflicting forces within can cause problems, as he will later come to realize.

During World War II, the demand for labor in the factories of southern California spawned a mass immigration of people of all races throughout the forties and into the fifties, creating a population that causes the system to bust at the seams in the sixties. The practice of racial discrimination tipped the limited number of opportunities in favor of the whites, while creating a pressure cooker effect in the Negro community. The Watts Riot is the result of the exploded pressure cooker.

The boys of the group home, and others like them feel the tension of the streets during the rioting, and the fear and uncertainty it evokes, without fully understanding why it is happening. They are after all, merely the petty pawns of a system within a system, the workings of which they can not even begin to fathom—casualties, with little chance of ever knowing the promise of opportunity. Their impotence prompts them to create an illusion of power.

Christopher, in a way becomes the ultimate casualty. With the dubious distinction of being a minority within a minority, and the closest approximation to their oppressor they dare to take shots at—he haplessly assumes the role of 'White Boy', 'Honkey', 'Cracker', 'Peckerwood', and whatever other abuses the boys can manage. One night as he gets into his bed, he finds mustard spattered all over the sheets.

On the other hand, there are the girls, who start to take an interest in Christopher, and he in them. Most girls, however, want emotional, not just physical involvement. This causes Christopher to pull away, though frustrated that his lust has not been satisfied. He learns to single out those girls who are most lustful, not necessarily the most beautiful or desirable, but simply the ones who will give him what he wants for the least amount of emotional investment.

In high school he masters the practice of deceit, playing with the tender emotions of girls to satisfy his desires, and then casting them aside. Christopher becomes the king of the one night stand—sayonara, adios, hasta la vista, arrivederci baby—the master of slambamthankyouma'am. He considers any guy who allows himself to become emotionally involved as weak and gullible.

He and a couple of other like minded guys from the group home start running together. The relationship between them is more of casual companions who can only be half trusted, than it is of friends, but that's okay with Christopher. Together they find adventure on the streets, slipping into pool halls, persuading winos to transact liquor purchases for them, smoking weed, and chasing girls.

There is a small neighborhood store run by a cheap, miserly old lady whom everyone calls 'Chickaboo'. She sells nearly rotted produce, stale bread, old canned goods, beer, wine, and other assorted items to the locals at exorbitant prices. She even cheats little children by giving them less candy than their money should buy, telling them, "You don't need all that candy. It's no good for you."; or by giving them only two cents on the deposit of a soda bottle when the going rate is three.

The two guys get the idea to burglarize Chickaboo's store, and ask Christopher to join them. Christopher at first agrees, but thinks better of it later, and stays behind. The police catch the apprentice burglars, and they end up in juvenile hall. Christopher somehow manages to graduate from high school, turns eighteen and goes out into the world.

7

INTO THE WORLD

Christopher sees his manumission from the child welfare system as the beginning of a new life—a chance to leave his troubled past behind and realize dreams that were all but impossible until now. He pictures himself as becoming a new person living the American ideal of a normal life. As a step toward accomplishing this goal he decides to seek employment within a business environment for the time being, and maybe attend college a little later.

After some searching, he obtains a temporary position in a bank with the help of an employment agency. This job involves doing nothing more than filing canceled checks for eight hours a day, five days a week, but Christopher figures it is at least a foot in the door to greater opportunities.

An opportunity of another type becomes available to Christopher. Each morning, after he has begun his work, an attractive young girl passes his way. They at first acknowledge each other from a distance with only a smile. Soon though, Christopher positions himself within closer proximity so they may exchange 'good mornings', and other small talk:

"My name is Chris."

"I'm Laura."

"Have you been working here long, Laura?"

"I just started this summer. I'm hoping they'll keep me on part time after school starts."

"College?" asks Christopher.

"Yes. It will be my first year."

"What are you majoring in?"

"I'm thinking about nursing, but that might change."

"I plan to go to college myself, but not until maybe next semester." He doesn't want to explain his need to save money for college, and feels lost for any other words to fill the void. "Well, it was nice talking to you." he finally manages. "Don't work too hard."

"I'll try not, it was nice talking to you also."

One morning, Christopher asks Laura out to lunch, and she accepts. They go a Chinese restaurant. Christopher, not accustomed to dining out, feels awkward and uncomfortable, but tries not to show it. Laura on the other hand is self assured. She handles the menu with ease, running through her order as if she has done it a million times before. She has a warm, pleasant smile, and like most of the other people in the bank, an attitude free of any negativity—traits not commonly found in the impoverished and otherwise disenfranchised people of Christopher's usual environment. He tries to reciprocate with the same positive attitude, avoiding the 'street slang' he is so accustomed to using. He emulates Laura's table manners, handling his napkin and silverware as she does.

The two young people start having lunch together on a regular basis. In the coming weeks, they meet outside the work environment on an increasingly regular basis. They go to the movies, the park, and even museums occasionally. Laura opens

Christopher's eyes to a whole new world. It is the first time he has spent so much time with one girl, without trying to take her to bed. "Why am I holding back?" he asks himself. The answer to that question is near at hand. In his heart he feels he is not good enough for her—perhaps the whole thing is just a little bit over his head—and the relationship is just some impossible charade he should end so they can each go back to a normal existence.

This attitude intensifies, causing Christopher to become aloof and distant. He starts making excuses for not having lunch with Laura, or going places with her. Laura is confused and upset over his unexpected behavior. One Saturday afternoon she calls him at home.

"What's happened between us? I don't understand why you're acting this way. Is it something I've done?"

"No. It's nothing you've done."

"Then what is it? I just need to know." asks Laura, almost pleading.

"It's nothing you've done, and nothing you can do anything about. It's just the way things are, that's all." he answers, not wishing to go any deeper into the subject.

"I thought you were special . . . and I believed you thought the same about me."

"You don't know me . . . maybe you think you do, but you don't really . . . and maybe we should just leave it at that." replies Christopher.

" It doesn't matter much that you don't want to meet my parents, or you don't like talking about yourself. I figured in time that would all take care of itself. Just tell me why you changed so suddenly."

Christopher struggles to find words for a reply. He softens up a bit and responds by saying, "I think you're special also . . . maybe too special."

"What on earth do you mean? How can a person be too special?"

"I don't know . . . Maybe I'm just a little crazy or something. Look, why don't we go to a movie and talk about it more a little later."

"Well . . . only if you really want to."

"I want to. I want to. See, I'm down on bended knees."

"Sure you are."

Laura picks Christopher up that evening and they head out to Hollywood. In the theater Christopher pays little attention to the action on the screen. The thought of Laura caring so much for him gives him a definite sense of power. His feelings of inferiority seem to melt away. About half way through the film, Christopher turns to Laura, places his arm around her, and kisses her on the cheek. He then gently tilts her face towards his and kisses her on the lips. It is a warm, tender kiss. Laura is at first startled, and not altogether relaxed, perhaps from inexperience, but surrenders nevertheless.

After the show they spend time strolling down Hollywood Boulevard, window shopping and watching the interesting people. Afterwards, Laura drives Christopher back to his apartment. When they arrive, he invites her to stay for a while.

"But my parents will be expecting me to be home soon." she explains.

"You don't have to stay that long. Your house is probably only about fifteen or twenty minutes from here, and you haven't seen my apartment yet. It's not exactly View Park, but it's home for me . . . you want to know exactly where I live, don't you?"

"All right. I'll come up, but only for a while."

Christopher leads the way to the rear of a well-kept house, then up some stairs alongside a garage to a tiny one bedroom apartment. "Well, here it is." proclaims Christopher as he motions Laura to have a seat. He then places a record on the phonograph player.

"This isn't so bad. It's small, but it seems comfortable." remarks Laura.

"I suppose."

They sit on the sofa and talk for a while. Christopher now kisses her more passionately than in the theater. The surroundings are more intimate and Laura, sensing this, is less surrendering than before. She gives in momentarily, but pulls away.

"What's the matter?" asks Christopher.

"Why did you really invite me up here?"

"To show you my place . . . and also since I like you so much, I want to make love to you."

"Like? Is that all there is to it? You just *like* me?"

"No. I didn't really mean just 'like'. I meant to say love. You see, I have never loved anyone before . . . so it's not a word I have ever used. Do you understand?"

"I suppose, but I don't think you understand. You see, I have never done anything like this before."

"You mean you're a virgin?"

"Yes, I guess that's what I mean. I don't know . . . it's very difficult and scary . . . it has to be with someone special."

"You said you thought we were special."

"Yes I did, but after the way you've been behaving, I'm not so sure anymore."

"I thought I already explained. You are more special than anyone I have ever known. There is no reason to be afraid, you have me with you, and I will take care of you." Christopher assures her, then kisses her again. Laura is now more yielding than before. He leads her into the bedroom, caressing the skin of her neck with his lips. The subtle scents of rich bath oil, and fine perfume fills his nostrils. Her golden skin and auburn hair radiate magically from the low light of the living room as her clothing falls away and she experiences her first ecstasy.

From this point forward, Christopher feels more acutely than ever, the conflicting signals emanating from his brain. He is emotionally more deeply involved than ever with Laura, yet at the same time his old defense mechanisms subconsciously kick in; to care for anyone is to leave oneself vulnerable to hurt and disappointment. He manages to control these impulses for a while.

Soon, the bank lays him off his job, which was only temporary in the first place. The employment agency is able to find him only sporadic employment—a day or two here and there, but it is not enough for him to maintain himself. He begins a massive search for another job, submitting applications to businesses of all kinds—banks, department stores, warehouses, and whatever else he can think of—all dead ends. Employers consider him unfit, or not the 'right type' for the more menial jobs. Regarding the better jobs, he either has not the qualifications, or is made to suffer the indignity of racial discrimination. For example, the state employment department refers him to an electronic supply store. When Christopher arrives, the proprietor looks at him with obvious distaste, refusing to shake his hand. Christopher nevertheless goes through the motion of filling out the application, but feels certain it will be thrown into the trash can.

Meanwhile, Laura continues working for the bank, and readying herself for college. She suggests Christopher seek the help of her father, a successful businessman, in obtaining a job. Christopher however has an ill placed sense of pride that does not allow for such a thing. His inner doubts regarding his worthiness to Laura resurface and become more acute than before. He longs for the familiar old ground of the streets, where little is expected of him, and almost anything goes—a place where he can speak and act in a way that comes most naturally to him.

Christopher starts hanging out in the old areas, spending time in the pool halls, sharpening his game, and hustling a few dollars here and there. He finds the sale of drugs—mostly marijuana and speed, to be another viable source of income.

Then there are the homosexuals who cruise the streets in search of young guys to proposition for sex in exchange for money, but Christopher finds this too distasteful. One persistent homosexual tries repeatedly to gain favors from Christopher, and ends up with a brick flying through the windshield of his car. He has an acquaintance however who earns his living that way for five dollars a pop. Christopher continues to see Laura, but knows it is only a matter of time before it must end. He leads Laura into believing he sells office products for a living.

One day Christopher is in the pool hall practicing his game alone, when a man he has never seen before enters. The stranger stands near the door, with his hands in his pockets, just looking around as Christopher studies him through the corner of his eye between shots. The man is slightly built, with a small round face and eyes that seem slightly out of focus. He wears a baseball cap, a short-sleeved plaid shirt of the drug store variety, and corduroy pants. His big, shiny belt buckle is nearly the size of a saucer. "He looks like he just came off a farm. Should I try to hustle him?" Christopher thinks to himself. "I'd better not. That crazy get-up of his might be a front. He's older, and probably has a lot of experience." Just then the man walks over to the table.

"Would you like to play a friendly game?" the man asks, smiling.

Christopher thinks to himself: "A friendly game? Who's he trying to kid? There is no such thing as a friendly game. Everyone tries to make money off of everyone else. This guy must take me for a silly, young fool . . . What the hell . . . I'll play him a game or two just to see what he's about." "Okay." answers Christopher, reaching down under the table for the rack.

"Here, I'll rack." the stranger offers. He then clumsily fumbles the balls into the rack, and seems to struggle to arrange them properly.

Christopher runs a couple of balls after the break, then misses the third purposely. The man talks constantly as they play:

"My name is Geronimo. That's not my real name, but that's what they call me because I was brought up on an Indian reservation in Oklahoma. My mother was Apache Indian. She died when I was ten years old. Then I went to live with my father's relatives in the city. That's where I got the name Geronimo. They got tired of me, I guess, and sent me back to the reservation."

"So when did you leave the reservation?" Christopher asks as he sizes up his next shot.

"Well, when I was about your age, or maybe a little younger, I married a girl named Dorothy. I had a good, steady job working on the oil fields. We lived in a shack provided by the company. It wasn't much, but it was a roof, and we always ate. I used to work like a dog, but I didn't mind, because I knew at the end of the day, my Dorothy would be at home waiting for me. The best feeling in the world was when we'd snuggle up in that little old shack in the winter time with a good heat going in the wood stove. Of course, we didn't have much wood. We mixed coke and coal together, then sprinkled a little gasoline over it to get it started. Well anyway, one day I came home and Dorothy wasn't there. I guess what we had wasn't enough for her, so she went skipping down the yellow brick road. It drove me crazy. I started drinking. I lost my job.

"That sounds pretty rough." adds Christopher.

"You damn right it was. After that I just wandered around a lot—hopped freight trains, hitchhiked, walked when I had to. I picked up odd jobs here and there to pay for liquor. I remember passing through Nebraska, I think it was, where I found some work on a small farm. When the job was done, the lady of the house invited me into the kitchen to have some food. A child was sitting at the table. The lady prepared a plate for me, and I ate as the child watched. The lady asked me if I would like a cup of coffee, and I told her 'yes please'. The child's mouth dropped open, and her eyes were wide with amazement. Then she said to her mother: 'Mommy! The monkey eats with a knife and fork—and he even talks!" Geronimo now laughs.

"How can you laugh?" asks Christopher, forgetting the game at this point.

"Hell, she was only a child. She never saw a black man before . . . and besides, lets face it . . . I ain't exactly pretty."

Christopher, now confused thinks to himself: "If this guy who calls himself 'Geronimo' is really trying to hustle me by throwing me off guard with these stories, then it is one hell of a hustle. No one would talk about their self like that and mean it. Or would they?"

Christopher sinks the eight ball in a corner pocket and wins the game. Geronimo pays the pool hall operator fifteen cents for the game he lost, then racks the balls again. He does not talk as much as before. Christopher is curious and wants to know more about him.

"So what brought you to Los Angeles?"

"I thought California might be a nice place to live, so I just kept heading west. I lived up in Oakland for a while . . ." Geronimo seems pained when he mentions Oakland, but he collects himself, and continues, ". . . then I headed out for Los Angeles, doing odd jobs along the way in the Central Valley . . . mostly agriculture. I even picked some cotton. Can you imagine that? Coming all the way to California for a better life, and wind up picking cotton! I made it to Los Angeles in 1957, and I've been here ever since."

"I haven't seen you around here before." comments Christopher.

"That's because I've been living on the East Side for the past seven years. Things are getting too crazy over there, so I decided to move back to my old running ground."

Christopher loses his concentration on the game. He miscues and sinks the eight ball accidentally, losing the game. "Well, I guess you won that one Geronimo."

"You're a good player. I'm not really that good. I just like the game." adds Geronimo.

"When I first saw you come in, I thought you might be a hustler."

"I wish." replies a laughing Geronimo. "Well, I better run. Maybe I'll see you around again sometime."

"I'm in here almost every day about this time. If you don't see me, just ask for Chris."

Geronimo comes down to the pool hall whenever there is no construction work available for him, which seems to be most of the time. He and Christopher usually shoot a couple of games, then they might drive around in Geronimo's car for a while, taking in the meager sights. Geronimo loves recalling the good old days as he cruises down the boulevard and lesser streets:

"I remember when this place was jumping. I had a nice little gardening business . . . owned my own truck and equipment. I had four people working for me . . . had more money than I could spend. Every night after work, we would all go down to the Normandie Club . . . used to be right over there next to that thrift shop. When we got tired of that, there was always the Quarter Horse down on Vermont. A little later on, there was the Pink Poodle, and the Jazz a Go-Go. You can't find places like them anymore." Geronimo sighs longingly. "Everything seems to be locked up tight. Of course, in those days, people didn't do all the crazy things they do now, so the police keep a tighter hold on things. In the summertime, we would go to the beach and sit up all night long drinking beer, and smoking weed. You can't do that any more."

"No, you sure can't . . . but now that you mention it. I've got some weed at home. Why don't we pick up a six pack of beer, and go listen to some music at my house for a while?" suggests Christopher. They stop at a nearby liquor store and as they walk into the store a woman's voice calls out from down the street:

"Hey baby, hey, wait up!"

"Who's that?" asks Geronimo.

"Her name's Angela, I'll tell you about her later. Excuse me for just a minute." Christopher walks down the street, meeting her halfway.

"You got anything for me?" inquires Angela anxiously.

"No sweetheart, not until late this evening."

"Why don't I come over to your house later on then?"

"You know I don't conduct business from my house." replies Christopher.

"Now baby, who said anything about business?"

"You know, the way you've been talking lately, if I didn't know better, I'd say you were looking for some professional management."

"Oh I see, and I guess you think you're a professional." remarks Angela, smiling slightly.

"I didn't say that I was, but listen up. I've got my friend with me right now. I'll meet you back out here at eleven o'clock tonight, with your stuff, and we'll go from there."

"Well, if I'm not tied up, or laid up, I guess I'll be here."

Christopher rejoins Geronimo. They purchase the beer, and while Geronimo drives, Christopher satisfies his curiosity.

"She's a prostitute. She works mostly in the Hollywood area. Her thing is 'red devils', and she was calling me because I'm supposed to have some for her today. It's a funny thing how women get so caught up in that stuff. All it does for me is put me to sleep."

"Her hair sure is long, and her cheek bones are high. I'd say she has a little Indian in her."

"Well I guess you're right, seeing how Mexicans are part Indian. You see, her mother's black, and her father's Mexican . . . Well, enough of her. I'll deal with that later on tonight. We'll just kick back for a while."

Later that night, Christopher goes back down to the liquor store to meet Angela. "Come on, let's go to my house." he says. She follows, and along the way, starts laughing.

"What's so funny?" Christopher inquires.

"I was just thinking what kind of pimp you'd make with no car . . . walking around all the time."

"Haven't you ever heard of a tennis shoe pimp?"

"A tennis shoe what?"

"A tennis shoe pimp. With a pair of tennis shoes on my feet I can get anywhere I need to go." They both start laughing.

"Did you bring the 'reds' with you?" she probes.

"No, I forgot and left them at home."

Soon, they reach the house.

"Okay now be quiet, and walk quietly up the stairs. I don't want to wake the landlady up."

While Angela is tiptoeing up the steps, she stumbles, then starts giggling uncontrollably, placing her hand over her mouth to muffle the sound.

"What is it now?" asks Christopher.

When Angela has finally settled down she says, "here I am, tiptoeing up the steps of a tennis shoe pimp, because he doesn't want to wake his landlady up. Don't you think that's funny?"

"Hilarious." answers Christopher as he fumbles for his keys, then searches for the keyhole.

"What's the matter?"

"I can't find the hole."

"I hope this isn't a sign of things to come." says Angela with more giggles.

After some more fumbling: "Okay, I got it open." They go inside and close the door.

"All right, where's my reds?"

"Hold on, not so soon."

"Come on now baby don't start playing around."

"I see you're not laughing anymore. What happened to your sense of humor?" Angela is now visibly irritated.

"I'll give you just one right now" offers Christopher. "I don't want you falling out on me."

"And why not?"

"Because."

"Because what?" quizzes Angela, smiling seductively.

"Because we have things to do." Christopher answers as he wraps his arms around her, and she around him. He reaches into his shirt pocket and pulls out a red capsule.

"You had them all along!" Angela exclaims.

Christopher pops the capsule in her mouth and says, "I have to watch your consumption. I can't let you get too carried away and do yourself in . . . now can I?" They kiss, and as they do so, thoughts of Laura come into his mind. Such thoughts are, at the moment, unwelcome. He quickly dismisses them, kissing Angela more deeply, more passionately, and slipping farther away from the world of Laura.

Christopher finds Angela wild and uninhibited. She does everything to him—everything. He seems to go around the world and back again within the confines of his tiny bedroom. Much later in the night, the intensity dies down, and both lie sprawled out—wet, panting, and speechless. When they are finally able to catch up with themselves, they pull the covers up over them, and curl up into each other.

"I hope you realize I don't do this with my tricks. With them, I just lie there and pretend. I don't feel anything with them at all. When its over, I collect my money, wash myself, and then I'm gone. But with you, its different. With you, it's real. I need to have that. Do you understand?"

"Of course I do, baby, I'm going to give you that and more. We are going to move up in this world. We'll make more money together, than we ever could alone."

"I was laughing before, but I wasn't really laughing at you, or maybe I was laughing at the both of us. You see, I'm really no better off than you are, but the truth is, I like your style. I like the way you handle yourself. You don't say a whole lot. You keep a low profile. You get along with everybody . . . and they all seem to . . . respect you." Angela is speaking slowly and fragmented as the long day catches up with her.

Christopher mutters some nonsensical words, as people half asleep are apt to do. He yawns and pulls her closer to him. The new lovers now drift off to sleep.

From here on, Christopher and Angela spend their mornings and early afternoons together. Angela works from early evening till late into the night. Christopher continues hustling pool, but earns most of his money selling drugs. He is in complete control of both their incomes, and starts making plans for the future.

Some days, when business for Christopher is slow, he hangs out with Geronimo. On one such evening, they are at Christopher's house, smoking weed and drinking when the doorbell rings. Christopher peeps through the curtains to see who it is, then bolts back. "Quick! Put it out! Get everything out of sight!" Christopher orders as he runs to the bathroom and returns with air freshener.

"Who is it, the police?" a worried Geronimo asks as he complies with his friend's orders.

"No, nothing like that, don't worry." He sprays the room, and hurriedly opens the only two windows of the apartment to circulate fresh air in. Finally, he opens the door.

"Hello Laura, come in."

Laura steps in. She seems worried and strained, taking some time to notice Geronimo sitting in the easy chair. "Oh, I'm sorry. I didn't know you had company." says Laura, apologetically and somewhat embarrassed.

"That's all right. Don't worry about it. Laura, this is my good friend, Geronimo."

"I'm very pleased to meet you Geronimo." says a smiling Laura, pretending to overcome her upset.

"It's very nice meeting you ma'am." replies Geronimo, rising to his feet and shaking her hand. Geronimo senses that he should leave them to be alone. "I better be going."

"Oh no, don't leave. Sit down." Christopher insists.

"I have to report to my union office early tomorrow morning. I should be getting ready." Geronimo bids them farewell.

After he leaves, the worried look returns to Laura's face. "I haven't heard from you lately. I've tried calling, but you don't ever seem to be home. I decided to leave you alone and not bother you anymore . . ." her voice tails off and she drops her head as if wanting to cry. ". . . but now something has happened, and I just don't know. . . I'm so confused."

"Well why don't you just tell me about it then." says Christopher as he seats her on the sofa.

"Christopher . . . I'm pregnant!"

Christopher turns to stone as the words sink in. Part of him does not believe what he is hearing. "But do you know for sure?"

"I'm sure."

Thoughts race through his mind: "Damned! Just when things are starting to move for me, something like this has to happen." He feels crowded and uneasy—as if the walls are closing in on him. He feels unwanted forces attempting to thrust him into a deep level of involvement and attachment—into a relationship requiring commitment and responsibility. Such things are too far removed from his realm of existence. He wishes desperately for a way out, and responds by saying, "So, I guess we'll have to have it taken care of."

"You don't understand, abortion is not an option for me!"

"But why not? People do it all the time."

Laura reads him clearly now—more clearly than ever before. She sees him not as the nice young man in the bank, but as an ugly person lacking any values, and devoid of a capacity for true love. She thinks to herself: "He told me I was special. He *promised* he'd look out for me." She feels broken and hurt, but her pride is still intact. She looks him in the eye and says, "I'm not 'people' . . . I'm Laura . . . and I have to leave now."

Christopher raises his hand to beckon her back. He tries to form words, but before he can she is out the door. He starts forward, but stops. To pursue the matter any further is to embrace an unwanted situation. Inaction seems the better solution.

8

THE QUEST

It isn't long before Christopher and Angela move into a nice two bedroom Mediterranean style apartment located on a hilltop. According to Geronimo, the area was once called Sugar Hill. In the forties and fifties it was home to many black entertainers, and other people of means. The construction of the Santa Monica Freeway effectively cut the area in two. The homes closest to the freeway became less desirable and cheaply built apartment buildings sprang up on narrow tracts of land bordering the freeway. There are still some well-kept mansions here and there. Signs of a past grandeur are evident as one strolls up and down the streets, but the malignant cancer of urban decay asserts itself daily. Little does Christopher know he is only a few blocks away from the site where the large rooming house with the attic apartment, now demolished, once stood—the place where his now forgotten Grandma Mary died—where his happy childhood ended, and his life changed forever.

Business is thriving. Christopher offers better nickel and dime bags of marijuana than anyone else—three fingers for ten dollars. Soon he moves up a notch, selling only pounds and kilos to select individuals. Three of his clients, Bird, Squirrel, and Brim buy his product on a regular basis. They, in turn, break the product down into smaller units to sell at a profit. Thieves and heroin addicts find their way to Christopher's door with stolen goods to sell: some of these goods he keeps, most he resells.

For Angela, life on the streets is precarious. She has to deal with the ever present threat of the police and an occasional arrest, requiring Christopher to bail her out of jail. Then there are the lunatics: the stranglers, the slashers, and the rapists to worry about. To reduce the threat of these kinds of problems, Christopher takes her off the streets and sets up an out call service. He runs advertisements in the local trade papers. The calls from prospective clients are first routed to an answering service, then to a private number. Things are slow going at first, there are the crank callers and those who are simply gun shy. Many look for free 'phone sex'—a phenomenon not generally recognized at this time.

Eventually, Angela manages to build an exclusive clientele. One of her regular clients is a doctor who lives in Bel-Air. He pays her handsomely to do nothing more than give him a 'golden shower'—even the simple act of urination can command a price in this singular profession. There is a certain prominent Beverly Hills attorney whose greatest thrill is to fondle Angela's feet. Another customer of note is a popular movie star of the late forties through early sixties. He likes to start things off with a bottle of scotch before indulging himself in oral and straight techniques.

Not all the time does she earn her money as easily, or predictably. There is one man who at the last minute insists on doing it 'Greek style', and Angela, not desiring her anal canal traumatized, refuses. This act of rejection causes her great difficulty with the irate would-be client. Another time, a butler greets her at the door and instructs her to enter a room, where a hundred dollars rests on a table—all she has to do is take the money and leave. Angela enters the dimly lit room, and spots a table on the far side. She walks toward the table, passing what turns out to be a coffin. A man dressed as a vampire rises from the coffin, frightening Angela half out of her wits. She barely manages enough self control to grab the money, and flees from the house, never to return again. Yes, life as a call girl certainly carries with it the potential for danger and unexpected outcomes, but even so, it is a far cry from the perils of the streets of Hollywood.

With things going so well financially, there is ample time for play. Christopher and Angela occasionally take weekend trips to such places as Las Vegas, San Francisco, or Baja California. Whenever possible, Geronimo joins them, and the three get along well together. At other times, they simply remain at home. They might stay in bed making love until well into the day, then spend the evening having drinks and dancing to romantic music. On one such evening as they are dancing to slow music, Angela breathes softly into her lover's ear, "Baby, I love you so much."

"I love you too . . . you know I do." Christopher tells her, but it is not likely he really means the words or feels as she does. There is no doubt he has some affection for her, but that affection is justified by her ability to bring him income. Even if he is capable of such feelings, he knows the first rule of the game is never to fall in love. It is better to simply make a woman feel loved, and then, only when she has earned it. Irregardless, they find some measure of happiness together, and each seems to provide the other with something
they need.

The doorbell rings. Christopher looks through the peephole, recognizing two men. One is short with buck teeth. The other is taller, and has a sharply pointed nose. He opens the door and greets them:

"My main men! Bird and Squirrel!" Christopher gives them each 'the handshake' and invites them in. "Have a sit down." The two seat themselves on the sofa. "So tell me, what's been happening?"

The sharp-nosed Bird, and the buck-toothed Squirrel go into a summary of the state of affairs on the streets; who went to jail recently, who was released, and the location of the next house party. Christopher listens with lukewarm interest, but tries to show some enthusiasm. Finally they run out of words, looking to each other for support, as they attempt to verbalize a matter much dearer to their hearts. Squirrel, the more verbal of the two begins:

"Man, we were down at the pool hall last night. I was playing against this old man, and was winning all his money . . . close to three hundred dollars. Then all of a sudden, he made a comeback. I lost everything I won from him, and went down for everything I had . . . about five hundred dollars. Bird here was making bets on the side, and lost all of his. Right now, between the two of us, we have almost enough for a pound."

"We were wondering if you could front us just a little, and we'll pay you as soon as we make it back." Bird adds.

Christopher thinks on the matter for a moment as he sits in his easy chair and Angela positions herself on the floor near him. "All I have right now is a kilo, and I really don't want to break it up . . ." he pauses, and the two unfortunate gamblers are visibly disappointed. ". . . but I'll tell you what. I'll front you for the kilo. Keep what you have in your pocket so you can eat, but stay away from the pool hall for a while. All right?"

"Hey man, you ain't got to tell us that." Squirrel assures him.

"Hell no, that's it for me!" adds Bird. The two men look at each other and display smiles of relief. Christopher goes to a back room and returns with a paper bag, placing it on the coffee table. Examining the contents briefly, Squirrel turns to his friend and displays an animated smile. The low-keyed Bird, with eyes perpetually at half mast, responds with not so much a smile as a rudimentary attempt at one, as though a true expression of happiness might cause him some pain or discomfort.

"Just give us two or three days, and we'll get your money to you." promises Squirrel.

Bird affirms with a nod of the head, and the two are off.

"That was very nice of you." Angela beams admiringly.

"I don't know if you can trust them or anyone else completely, but the fact is, it's good business to do what I did. They've always come through in the past, and they helped get us where we are today."

"That's true, but you know, I don't think anyone has turned over more kilos than Brim."

"You're absolutely right about that. Brim is a real businessman. He has style and ambition, and he certainly would never get himself into the same kind of fix as Bird and Squirrel." adds Christopher.

"You know what baby?" purrs Angela seductively as she places herself on Christopher's lap in the easy chair, stroking him on the neck, and blowing softly in his right ear, hitting all the right spots.

"What?" responds Christopher with a soft murmur, eyes half closed.

"It might be good for business if you showed Brim a little appreciation. I mean . . . maybe you should have him over socially sometimes . . . you know what I mean?"

"Maybe you're right . . . just a social thing . . . no business involved. I can invite Geronimo to come also. He's been working a lot, and I haven't seen him lately. You should invite your friend Camille, just to balance things out a bit."

"Yes, I guess I could . . . You don't think Camille might go for Brim, do you?"

"Oh, I didn't really think about that. Maybe, maybe not. What difference does it make? All we want to do is have a good time."

Christopher becomes hopelessly aroused by Angela's caressing fingers and soft, sultry voice. They make love on the living room floor. Afterwards, feeling famished, they drive to Hollywood and have dinner at a favorite soul food restaurant; one of their rendezvous points in Angela's street walking days.

They start making plans the following week for the get-together. Sunday seems the most compatible day, as Angela's friend Camille, a street walker, does not work on Sunday and neither does Geronimo. Brim is flexible and can arrange his schedule accordingly.

The day arrives and the first person to arrive is Camille. Angela takes Camille to the bedroom to show off her wardrobe. Christopher sits on the sofa in the living room listening to music while sipping a rum and cola. Geronimo arrives next. Christopher mixes him a rum and cola in place of his usual beer. As the two men nurse their drinks, Christopher peers through the front window.

"Who do you suppose lives in that big mansion across the street?" Christopher asks.

"I really don't know. I think it used to be owned by a church, and run as some kind of convent or rehabilitation center."

"I always wonder; people do live in it. I know, because I can sometimes see them passing by in the windows, but no one ever seems to come and go. It's a hell of a house . . . or estate I guess I should call it . . . wrought iron fence and brick walls all the way around . . . and the smaller house behind it . . . must be for guests, or maybe servants."

"I think that was once Hattie McDaniel's house."

"You mean 'Mammy' in *Gone With the Wind*?"

"Yep."

"Wow!"

"Oh yeah. All of them lived here, or came to visit people who did . . . Dorothy Dandridge, Nat 'King' Cole, Eddie 'Rochester' Anderson, you name it. Most of them were real friendly, especially 'Rochester'. They would wave when people saw them, and even strike up a conversation at times."

"Didn't Hattie McDaniel win an Academy Award?"

"She sure did. Some say they gave it to her because she wasn't allowed to attend the movie premier, which took place in Atlanta you understand."

"Do you think she deserved the award?"

"Personally, I think she did a beautiful job the way she took the role of a simple house servant and turned it into something special. She should have won anyway, but it makes me feel good to think people would do that to make a statement. Makes me feel like maybe there's hope."

"Hope huh? Look at what you've got now . . . guys like me carrying on the legacy of the Hill." Christopher gazes out the window, shaking his head. "They must be rolling in their graves."

"Why are you concerned about that house?" queries Geronimo.

"It seems so mysterious, and that makes me curious about it. Sometimes, when the curtains are open, I can see a big, round clock on the wall of what looks like the kitchen . . . If those walls could only speak . . . I can't help but wonder what it looks like in the rest of the house. It might sound like a crazy idea, but I'm thinking maybe one day I can buy it, or at least live in one like it."

Geronimo gives silent acknowledgment. Just then the doorbell rings. Christopher answers it, and in walks a man, dressed in a black leather coat, with black shirt, black slacks, black alligator shoes, black nylon socks, and a black, narrow brimmed hat on his head, with a black head band, and black feather to match. In fact, the man himself appears to be truly black in color. This man is black, on black, in black.

"Well, well, well, he made it. What's happening Brim?" says Christopher in greeting.

"Ain't nothing man . . . you got it all." Brim replies as the two shake hands.

"You know Geronimo, right?" Christopher asks Brim.

"Yeah, we met a couple of times." he answers, shaking Geronimo's hand.

Christopher leaves the room as Brim settles on the sofa. He is not a highly talkative person, rather introspective in nature. He strokes his left index finger down across his temple, seeming to contemplate some complex matter. The overall 'black' effect accentuates the depth of the unknown mystery.

Angela and Camille come to the living room and start entertaining. Angela leaves the room momentarily, returning with a beer, and hands it to Brim. Christopher soon returns with a tightly wrapped waxed paper bag filled to a diameter of about three finger's width.

"What do you have there?" Brim inquires, by now aroused from his transcendental state.

"This here is my private stock. It's Acapulco Gold."

"All right! 'po Gold, huh? I ain't had any of that shit in a while." Brim replies excitedly.

"Well you gonna have some today, my man." Christopher says. He then rolls a couple of joints, lights them, and passes them around. The music sounds better and better as the drug takes effect. So much so, that Christopher and Angela get up and start dancing, while the rest look on. After the dance, Christopher asks Brim, "Are you ready for another beer?"

"Sure, why not?"

Meanwhile, the rum is having its effect on Geronimo. His eyes become red and glazed. His lips draw tight. Angela notices and asks, "Geronimo, are you all right?" But he does not answer immediately. His mind is deep in the past. The euphoric effect of the spirits transform his memories into a highly stylized version, not nearly as colorful as the original. Suddenly he shouts, "That's right! I *am* Geronimo!" He vibrates his hand over his mouth making stereotypical Indian war sounds. "Raised on the reservation! Grandmother was a full-blooded Apache Indian . . . They call me Yellow Hand . . . that's right! Yellow Hand." He stands and takes the floor. "We would go through the woods and hunt." He assumes the posture of a hunter lurking in the bushes. "We would walk very quietly. Ssssh! Eyes don't miss a thing. There it is!" Pointing at some unseen object. He brings forth an imaginary arrow, and draws it back in an equally imaginary bow, takes careful aim and fells his prey. "Wop! Got it!" He lets out a loud yell then continues chattering incomprehensible things to himself.

"This brother has a serious problem." declares Brim, who has been quitely watching the episode.

"He gets like that when he's had too much to drink." Angela responds sympathetically.

"Well then, maybe he shouldn't drink so much." Brim replies.

"Maybe not, but he has a heart as good as gold. In fact, he'll probably still be my partner when everyone else is long gone." declares Christopher in defense of his friend.

Camille meanwhile sits quietly. Her eyes secretly follow Christopher around. He picks up on her interest and acknowledges her occasionally with a smile.

"Oh man, I almost forgot! Hey Chris, let me have a word with you." interjects Brim with great urgency. The two men go back to the kitchen where Brim continues, "I need a little favor from you man. I've got this new shit." pulling a foil wrapped package from his coat pocket, "It needs to go into the freezer, or else it'll go bad."

"What is it?" Christopher asks.

"They call it Infinity."

"Infinity huh? What's it like?"

"It's hard to describe . . . but this shit will take your ass for a spin. I'm just now coming down from two hits of it myself."

Christopher takes the package, turning it in his hand. "Two hits, huh? Mind if I try it?"

"Be my guest." Brim replies.

The two men sit at the kitchen table while Christopher opens the package. He is struck by the pungent aroma. "Smells like mint."

"They marinate mint leaves in the liquid chemical, then set it up to dry. Roll it small now, you don't need much."

Christopher rolls one, then places the package in the freezer. He lights the spare little 'pencil joint', and takes one deep drag, holds it in, then waits. In a matter of moments, a strange new feeling overcomes him. His mind seems to expand, and his awareness of things around him seems more acute.

"Well, do you feel anything yet?" queries Brim.

"Wow . . . this shit is something else! How much did you pay for it?"

"A hundred dollars for an ounce. I can break that down into maybe thirty seams, and sell them for ten dollars each. Pretty good, huh?"

"You got that right. Let's talk about this some more later."

When Christopher steps back into the living room, everything seems changed. The atmosphere is enhanced. The music seems slower and more rhythmic, with deeper, mellower bass tones, and brilliant trebles. Christopher's interest in Camille heightens, and the prospect of what may come fills him. She has dreamy eyes, and a generously fleshed face surrounding a cute button nose. Her naive smile suggests an innocence beneath a preferred persona of street wisdom. He asks her for a dance and she accepts. As they dance, he whispers to her, "Don't leave too soon."

Christopher has his next dance with Angela. When the dance is over, he takes her to the bedroom to have a word.

"You know baby, I've been thinking . . . it's time we expand. If Camille came in with us, it might be a good thing all the way around."

"I see." she responds slowly. "So tell me, has that big behind of hers gotten to you?"

"No. That's not it at all. You know you're the only woman I love. You're my number one . . . and always will be. Camille could make things easier for you by taking the jobs you don't want. We could make more money and move out of here into a really nice place. It's just another step to help get us where we want to go."

"I've gotten used to having you all to myself . . . but you say it's something we need to do . . . It's all part of the game I suppose, and I have to accept that. I see the way she looks at you. The only thing I ask is that you never hurt me."

"Baby, you know I could never hurt you. Now give me a kiss."

Christopher and Angela return to the living room. Camille and Brim have taken to the floor dancing. Geronimo is back to his normal self, smiling and tapping his foot to the music. Everyone has a good time, and by one o'clock in the morning, Brim and Geronimo ready themselves to leave. Camille accepts an invitation from Angela to stay the night. Angela retires to her bedroom, leaving Christopher and Camille alone in the living room.

"I've been wanting to talk to you for quite a while, but I've been holding out until just the right time." begins Christopher.

"Oh really?" she responds with mock surprise.

"Don't give me that. You know I have . . . and I know you've been waiting for me to make a move."

"Well, if you know that, then what took you so long?" asks Camille.

"Like I said, I was waiting for the right time . . . a time when I could do things for you . . . the kind of things a woman like you deserves."

"Is that right?" beams Camille, obviously pleased at his words, and smiling.

"You'd better believe that's right. Personally, I think you're too good to be working on the streets. You should be a high class call girl. That's not an easy thing to break off in to, but I'm going to make it possible . . . or should I say, *we're* going to make it possible."

"You and Angela have been together for a long time. Just where do I stand? How do I fit into all this?"

"You know how it is. You don't always meet just the right person straight up off the bat. Sometimes, it takes a try or two." Christopher now reaches into his shirt pocket. "Here, I have something I want you to try."

"What is it?"

"They call it Infinity. Don't worry, I just had some myself, it's okay." He lights the half smoked joint, and hands it to her. Camille takes a couple of short hits. "Take one good hit, and hold it in." Christopher advises. Moments pass, then he asks, "How do you feel?"

"I don't know . . . maybe a little bit scared."

"Scared? Of what?"

"I don't really know for sure. It's strange."

Christopher wants to get inside her head and know what makes her tick. He recalls from his group home days a certain therapist who believed in hypnotism as a means of getting to the root of problems and finding things out about the individual. On more than one occasion Christopher watched through a keyhole as the therapist worked with his subjects. It didn't seem that complicated.

"I'm going to find out what you're scared of." declares Christopher. "I want you to relax your body and concentrate on my voice." She does. "Now as you relax, you feel yourself becoming very sleepy. Your eyelids are becoming very heavy . . . relax . . . relax . . . relax. You are becoming very sleepy. Your eyelids are very, very heavy. You cannot keep your eyes open." As Christopher repeats these words, over and over, Camille's eyes slowly shut down, until finally they completely close. "As you fall into a deep sleep, you will hear nothing but my voice. You will do exactly what I say. Do you understand?"

"Yes." comes the reply.

"When I count to three and snap my fingers, you will wake up and remember nothing of what happened. Do you understand?

"Yes."

"Now I want you to tell me what scares you. Do you see anything?"

"No."

"Go back in time. Go back to high school. Do you see what scares you?"

"No."

"Go back further in time. Keep going until you see what scares you." Camille's face becomes distressed. "How old are you?".

"I don't know." she whispers.

"What do you see?" Tears begin to form in her eyes. "What do you see." he repeats.

"He's hurting me!"

"Hurting you how?"

"He's doing things to me."

"What kinds of things?" Christopher demands. Camille is now sobbing uncontrollably, and will not answer.

"Who is doing these things to you?" She still does not answer. "Who?" he demands again. Her breathing is now spasmodic.

"MY FATHER!" She wails, as the floodgates of her emotions open.

"I'm going to count to three, and snap my fingers. You will then wake up. You will forget everything that has happened. Do you understand?"

Still sobbing, she nods affirmatively.

"One, two, three!" At the snap of Christopher's fingers, she starts to settle down. She opens her eyes, looking puzzled.

"Baby, you must be very tired." He gives her a warm hug, and leads her into the second bedroom. "This is our room from now on. You've been through a hell of a lot, and you deserve better. Not your father or anyone else will ever hurt you again, so long as you are with me." Her expression suggests the helplessness of a person whose every defense has been penetrated, or a child looking to the parent for guidance.

He seats her on the bed, then takes her purse and goes through it. He pulls out a bottle of pills. "I don't want you taking too many of these. I'll keep them for now." He puts them in his pocket. Next he takes out her wallet. It contains well over a hundred dollars. "You don't have to worry about managing finances anymore . . . that's my job." The money also goes into his pocket. "Don't say a word." he warns. "It isn't necessary." he whispers. Now he alternates between kissing her body, and slowly removing her clothing until she is completely naked. She is totally submissive. He directs her into the bed, under the covers, then removes his clothing and joins her. Flesh presses against flesh. Obedience yields to dominance as Camille becomes a member of the 'family'.

Angela is not happy with the new arrangement at first, but knows that to resist could work against her. To deny her man what he wants and thinks is best, might cause her to lose favor with him. She learns to accept the new addition.

Camille, like Angela, knows how to project an image of refinement and sophistication. This makes her transition into the call girl business all the easier, and more lucrative. She manages to build an impressive clientele of her own.

Between the drug business and the call girl service, Christopher has more money than he can spend. Success however, does not come without a price, and time for play becomes harder to find. Christopher and his women hustle seven days a week.

One Sunday he decides enough is enough; they will all stay home and rest. Christopher spends most of the day stretched out on the sofa, as he considers different ways to streamline his operations. The women remain asleep in their beds. At around noontime the doorbell rings.

"Oh, god. Who can that be?" he wonders, and gets up to look through the peephole. A smile comes over his face as he opens the door. "Geronimo! My man 'mo. I haven't seen you for quite a while!"

"You're a hard man to catch up with these days." replies Geronimo, stepping into the apartment.

"Things have been pretty hectic. It's starting to get to me, so I decided to just cool it for a day . . . So tell me, what's been happening?" Christopher asks excitedly.

Geronimo puts his hands in the air and replies, "Man, you're what's happening. It sure ain't me."

"What's wrong?"

"I'm just tired of having to report to the union every day to be told there's no work, that's all." sighs a discouraged Geronimo as he seats himself in the easy chair. Christopher returns to the sofa.

"Can I lend you some money?" asks Christopher, picking up a pencil joint, lighting it, and taking a drag.

"No, that's okay . . . I have enough to last me for the time being." Geronimo sniffs the air. "That stuff smells kind of funny. What is it?"

Christopher holds the drag as long as he can before exhaling, then he speaks. "This is some kind of new mint shit. They call it Infinity. It just hit the streets a little while back. Want to try some?"

"I better not . . . I need to make a run later on, and there's no telling how it might affect me."

"I'm thinking about moving."

"To where?"

"Oh . . . maybe the Hollywood Hills."

"Damn! I guess things are pretty good for you."

"I have to figure out ways to save time. Right now, I go back and forth to Hollywood, two or three times a day. If I lived in Hollywood, I could probably get away with coming down here once every couple of days. So you see, it makes good business sense. Also, some of these neighbors around here are pretty nosy. They try to get in to your business. I need a place that gives me more privacy." Christopher pauses for a moment. "Say, I have an idea. Why don't you move out there with us?"

"Me? I can't afford anything like that."

"You could help me by driving the girls to their calls. You see, I like to be close by just in case anything was to go wrong, but I can't be everywhere at once. I would pay you, and you'd have a place to stay besides."

"Man, I don't know. That's not the kind of thing I've ever done."

"You've never said much about it before, but what I do kind of bothers you, doesn't it?"

"What you do is your thing. Who am I to judge?"

"You're right. You shouldn't judge . . . and neither should I. I didn't invent it . . . and I don't go down to the bus station searching for innocent little runaway girls to turn out on the streets. If anything, *I* was the one who got turned out. Prostitution, as they say, is the world's oldest profession . . . and why do you think that is so? Because it fulfills one of the most basic needs of man, and to deny it is to create problems no one needs."

Geronimo has a puzzled look on his face. "I'll explain." Christopher continues. "Let's take for example the poor, miserable son of a bitch who can't get it any other way, or can't find a woman to give it to him the way he really wants it, because the things he likes are too freaky. The ones who don't go out and pay for it simply retreat into their own private little world of fantasies and learn to somehow survive. A few however, will lose it completely, and go berserk. They are the ones who commit some of the horrible sex crimes we hear about. Our society, with all it's efforts, creates people of high morals and values, but without realizing it, they also create monsters of the worst kind."

Geronimo looks skeptical as Christopher continues. "If you don't believe me, then you should check out countries like West Germany where prostitution is tolerated. They don't have all the problems we have here."

Geronimo now considers what Christopher is saying. "You said it yourself back when I first met you . . ." Christopher reminds him. ". . . Los Angeles used to be more open, and now it's tight. This might sound strange to you, but the way I see it, I'm doing good in society by preventing some of these people from crossing the line, and becoming terrible sex criminals."

Christopher's mind is fueled by the effects of the Infinity, and his words are charged to an extent that nearly brings Geronimo around to his way of thinking. Christopher, sensing his near victory adds: "They make you feel they are doing you some big favor by giving you little tidbits of work here and there, when in reality, you are born with the right to earn a living. If one way does not work, then you owe it to yourself to try another. So what do you say? Are you with me?"

Geronimo nervously rocks backward and forward, rubbing his hands together, struggling towards an answer to the question. He then clasps his hands tightly, and responds by saying, "Yes! I'm with you."

9

THE MAGICAL ERA

"I have a big surprise for all of you!" Christopher tells Angela, Camille, and Geronimo, as they sit in a restaurant having breakfast one Sunday morning. The three eye each other curiously, wondering what the surprise might be. "Don't worry, you'll find out soon enough."

After breakfast, Christopher drives them to Hollywood. They travel west on Sunset Boulevard for some time before turning north on a road winding up into the hills. Eventually, they turn off onto another road that leads them to a driveway. The driveway, carved into the hillside, descends abruptly to a level, tree shaded area. Beyond the trees is a beautiful, modern style home.

"Well, here it is! Our new home!" announces Christopher, smiling proudly. The others simply sit momentarily with their mouths open.

"It's absolutely gorgeous!" exclaims Camille.

"We must be doing even better than I thought we were." adds Angela.

"The owner gave me a pretty good deal on the rent. He's going to be living in Europe for the next three years at least, and just wants someone here to take care of things . . . Come on, lets go inside so I can show you around." urges Christopher.

The entry opens to a large living room. The hall to the right leads to a recreation room, dining room, and gourmet kitchen. The left hall leads to four bedrooms and a den. The completely furnished house has a built in stereo system, and televisions built into a wall in each of the bedrooms and recreation room. There are three sliding glass doors located along the far side of the house: one in the living room, one in the recreation room, and one in the master bedroom. The sliding doors all open up to a patio beautifully adorned with trellises supporting lush grapevines, flowering shrubs, and fruit trees. Beyond the patio beckons a swimming pool and hot tub. This urban paradise, situated high on a steep hillside boasts a beautiful view of Los Angeles as its backdrop.

Geronimo walks through the house as if in a daze before returning to the living room and confessing: "Man, oh man. I never thought that in my life, I would live in a place like this."

"You deserve to live in a place like this, Geronimo. In fact, we all do—especially my babies here." Christopher says as he puts his arms around his women, giving them each a kiss on the cheek. Camille and Angela are beaming, each secure in the belief they are the favorite.

Christopher hires professionals to handle the unwelcome tasks of packing and moving. They settle into their new home the following weekend.

Life is less hectic now. Angela and Camille are considerably closer to the majority of their clients, reducing the time traveled. Geronimo's assistance comes as a great relief for Christopher who now finds himself with more free time on his hands. The patio becomes his office, allowing him to enjoy the panoramic view as he conducts business by telephone.

After dark, Christopher spends hours gazing at the night sky. The heavenly bodies fill him with wonder, and the wonder stimulates his curiosity. He contemplates the possibilities of what might lie in the far reaches of the universe.

When he is under the effects of the Infinity, he feels closer to the stars, seeming almost able to touch them, and his curiosity soars. So much so, that he buys a high power extra-terrestrial telescope, complete with a motorized clock drive to track the slow movement of stars across the sky.

"What is the distance from the Earth to the other heavenly bodies? How big is the Universe? Are there other worlds out there with life? If so, are there any with intelligent beings like ourselves?" These and other questions he asks himself. He takes advantage of his considerable leisure time by reading books on astronomy, hoping to find the answers. As he reads, he is enthralled by the idea of great clouds of hydrogen gas collapsing under the force of gravity to form stars, and fascinated that a few of these stars might collapse further to form 'black holes'—regions of space where nothing—not even light can escape.

His mind burns for knowledge, and the more he reads, the more things he realizes he does not know. He soon discovers that in order to gain a thorough understanding of astronomy, he must study physics and chemistry, but to understand these, he must have a knowledge of mathematics. Christopher begins a systematic study first of algebra, then geometry, trigonometry, and finally calculus. He learns to differentiate and integrate complex equations with amazing speed and accuracy. As he progresses through the levels of mathematics, he finds it an easy matter to grasp the other sciences.

Through all of this he acquires a fuller understanding of the workings of the heavenly bodies, but the questions that concern him most are still unanswered. For instance, assuming the 'Big Bang' theory is correct, science is at a loss to give, or even attempt to provide, an explanation for the origin of the so-called 'singularity', or 'super proton' that is thought to have existed at the time the universe was first born.

Frustrated over the futility of finding an answer to this ultimate question, Christopher turns to another subject that arouses his interest during his study of chemistry—the origin of life. He finds the biologists able to provide fairly satisfactory explanations. They write about a primordial soup composed of water and certain basic elements. Radiation stimulates the soup to form increasingly more complex organic compounds. The biological trail of knowledge leads to more frustration and futility in the end, however, for it does not explain the concept of mind—the ability to think, reason, and possess a sense of being. He turns to the study of psychology in hopes of further enlightenment, reading many of the works of the great pioneers in the field.

As fascinating as these pursuits are to Christopher, he nevertheless must tear himself away to tend to the more practical business matters at hand. He must maintain the flow of drugs from his suppliers, to his agents—Bird, Squirrel, Brim, and others in Los Angeles. He must also monitor the activities of the out call service.

A man who calls himself Mr. Panama keeps calling for Angela. He claims to be a professional wrestler. This man has called on more than one occasion to make an appointment, only to call later and cancel, claiming he has a busy and unpredictable schedule. He manages to hold the interest of everyone with his incredible offers of money. Christopher becomes increasingly annoyed and finally listens in on a conversation between Angela and Mr. Panama in hope of interpreting the motives behind the rough, gravelly voice of the so-called wrestler. After the conversation, Christopher thinks on the matter, and advises Angela:

"Something's not quite right about this guy. All this talk about money is just bullshit. Forget about him. If he calls again, let me talk to him."

Soon after, on a clear summer night, Angela and Geronimo lounge around the pool enjoying pleasant conversation and starry skies when a call comes in from the answering service.

"Hi baby, this is Mr. Panama."

"Oh." replies an agitated Angela dryly.

"Look baby, I'm sorry about hangin' you up the last time. I had some business to take care of down at the Olympic Auditorium. I'll be competing there in a couple of weeks . . . Well anyway, I got some free time this evening, and I want you to come over."

"I'm sorry. I'm not interested, and please don't call again."

"Oh come on baby! Don't be mad at me. Things are gonna work out this time. I promise . . . Look, name your price . . . I'll tell you what . . . We'll make it two thousand! How's that? Straight business baby!"

Angela thinks to herself, "Two thousand dollars! If this guy is on the level, that would be the most money I've ever made on a single date." She tells him, "Look, I can be there in an hour, but I want all the money up front. If things don't work out, this will be the last time, and I don't want you calling anymore. Do you understand?"

"No problem baby. You know the address . . . the same one I gave you before."

Angela hangs up the telephone, turns to Geronimo and asks, "Did Chris say when he was coming back?"

"No he didn't. All he said was that he was going out on the desert where the view of the sky is better. Once he gets tied up with that telescope and them books, there ain't no tellin' . . . You know how he gets these days." remarks Geronimo.

"Chris is a very intelligent person. I guess he just has a natural curiosity about things. He spends a little too much time with it maybe . . . but I think it's just a phase he's going through. He'll get tired of that old telescope and all those books any time now. Let's not worry about that. For now, I need you to take me somewhere."

"Where to?"

"Not very far from here, in Beverly Hills."

Geronimo drives Angela to the location, only a few miles away. He first surveys the location. It is a sprawling single story newer house in a hilly area. He parks around the corner out of sight as he usually does so as not to alarm or upset the client. Angela gets out of the car and walks to the house.

Geronimo drives away after a few minutes, not desiring to draw the attention of the neighbors. After nearly two hours have passed, he comes back for her. She does not return at the agreed upon time. "The trick is probably just going into overtime." Geronimo concludes.

Another hour passes, then two. Geronimo becomes worried. He drives past the house, but there are no lights. "Shit! What the hell is going on? This has never happened before." he insists. "She must have left early." he reasons, and finds a pay phone to call home.

"Hello Chris. Is Angela there?"

"No man, I thought she was with you."

"She was! I took her out on this call, and she never returned!"

"Who did you take her to see?" queries Christopher.

"She said his name is Mr. Panama."

The hairs on the top of Christopher's head bristle, and a chill goes down his spine when he hears the name. "Tell me where you're at, I'll meet you." he insists.

Christopher picks Geronimo up at the telephone booth, together they drive back to Mr. Panama's house. Still, they see no lights from inside the house.

"Maybe we should just go to the police." suggests Geronimo.

"And tell them what? A whore is missing? They could care less. The fact that they hate me doesn't help matters either. We'll just wait it out for a while. Somebody has got to come or go from this house sooner or later."

After nearly another hour has passed, a car turns into the driveway of the house. What appears in the dark to be a man, gets out of the car.

"She's not with him! I'm gonna go over and confront that son of a bitch." Christopher threatens.

"Wait a minute! We can't just start stirring up things around here. The neighbors would have the police here in no time . . . and where would that leave us?"

"We have to do something!"

"I think the only thing for us to do right now, as hard as it might seem, is to go home. Maybe she'll show up. If not, we'll have to try to come up with some kind of a plan."

"Shit! I told her to leave this guy alone. How the hell could you let her come here?"

"Man, I didn't know! I thought it was just another thing!"

Christopher, angry and frustrated, starts his car and drives reluctantly back home. What little remains of the night does not pass easily. On the following day, a news report relates to a dead body found alongside a freeway off ramp earlier in the morning. Christopher's worst fears become a reality. The body is Angela's. Christopher goes into a rage, vowing to avenge her death.

Christopher drives by Mr. Panama's house several times each day. Two days later he sees three people in front of the house, two men and a woman. The woman and one of the men seem to be a couple. The woman talks to the second man as if he is a child: "Now Richard, we don't want you going anywhere while we're away. Do you understand?"

"Oh no! I'm not going anywhere. Where would I go?" responds the man. Christopher tenses as he recognizes the rough, gravelly voice—the same voice he had heard on the telephone days earlier. This man, however, looks nothing like a wrestler. He is rather short, and maybe of medium build at best, but that does not surprise Christopher, who feels certain he has found his man. The man has a dark beard, and a wild gleam in his eye—the kind of gleam one generally associates with madness.

That night, Christopher lies in bed with Camille, devising his plan for revenge. He confides to Camille, "I saw the son of a bitch who got Angela. We have to do something to make sure he never does it again, because the next person could be you."

"What are we going to do?"

"I want you to call him, and draw him out. Convince him to meet you, then take him to a place in the mountains. I'll tell you the exact location. After that, I'll handle it. I'll arm you with a gun in case he tries anything along the way."

Camille follows Christopher's instructions. She meets Mr. Panama, and takes him to a place in the Santa Monica Mountains. When they arrive, Christopher is not far behind. He has been following them. He approaches them and signals Camille to leave.

"Hello Mr. Panama." Christopher says coldly.

Mr. Panama's eyes widen as he says, "What is this?"

"You remember Linda don't you?" asks Christopher referring to Angela's street name.

"I don't know what you're talking about."

"She came over to your house a little while back. The next time anyone saw her, she was lying dead near a freeway."

"Come on! You're not talking about that filthy whore, are you? Give me a break . . . I mean after all, who cares about them?"

"I do." Christopher answers. He then pulls out a .38 caliber revolver.

"Oh come on. You gotta be kidding me!" Mr. Panama replies desperately. When he realizes Christopher is dead serious, his voice trembles, and his legs become wobbly as he falls to his knees begging for his life.

Christopher feels a touch of pity as he watches this pathetic piece of biological waste sobbing uncontrollably, and he recalls the cold, lifeless, mutilated body of the woman he had shared his life with for so many years. Pity is quickly replaced by vehemence, and Christopher fires a shot. Mr. Panama falls back into a grave that is already dug for him. He lies in the hole, clutching his wounded chest, and breathing heavily. Christopher aims carefully at his head and fires again. Mr. Panama is now motionless.

A cold sweat comes over Christopher. His throat locks tight, and he feels an eruption building within his stomach. He turns away and vomits on the ground, sick at the sight of a man with a gaping hole in the middle of his face. He gathers his composure enough to fill the grave, then goes back to his car where Camille is waiting, and returns home.

Meanwhile, Angela's remains are being prepared for burial. The following Saturday, she lies in state in a funeral chapel, on Sunday she is buried. There is a simple graveside service. The only people in attendance are Camille, Geronimo, and Christopher. A week later they return to the grave and find flowers placed there by some unknown person.

Everyone has a difficult time dealing with Angela's death. Camille is saddened, but she is also pleased at the prospect of being Christopher's only woman. Christopher takes it the hardest, spending days just sitting around the house thinking about Angela, and missing her greatly. The image of Mr. Panama sprawled out at the bottom of a makeshift mountain grave comes into his mind often. Killing was something he had never done, and hopes he will never do again.

With Angela gone, the level of income for the household has diminished. Christopher has not the desire to go out and find a replacement. Instead, he makes Camille work harder than ever. In time, she begins to show the physical signs of fatigue. Many of the clients find her less desirable than before. Business goes downhill. Christopher becomes angry and irritable over the turn in fortune. To compensate for the dwindling income, he turns Camille back out on the streets. She manages to bring in decent income for a while, but as in any business, there are peaks, and there are valleys.

One afternoon, Christopher is home alone. He sits in the living room, sipping a rum and cola, listening to music, and reflecting on his life. The loss of Angela has aroused feelings that seem strangely familiar. The sight of her in the casket—even the sight of Mr. Panama's dead body with blood on his face suggests things he has known before. While he is deep in his thoughts the front door opens. It is Geronimo and Camille. Geronimo goes to his room to rest. Camille seems exhausted also. She comes over to the sofa and sits down. Reaching into her bosom she pulls out some money and hands it to Christopher. Christopher unfolds the money to count it, finding it far short of his expectations. His disappointment soon turns to anger.

"This is bullshit."

"What?" asks Camille.

"I said this is bullshit!" more loudly than before. "How the fuck am I supposed to pay the rent with this? What the fuck do you think this is anyway—a god damned welfare agency?"

"But it's close to election time. Things tighten up."

"I should tighten my foot up your ass is what I should do! Look." Christopher shouts as he reaches over to pick up a pile of envelopes from the coffee table. "This is the fucking gas bill. This is the fucking electric bill. This is the fucking telephone bill. The fucking rent is due on the fucking first!"

"But . . ."

"But my ass! You stay your ass out there on the streets all night and half the next day just to bring me a lousy forty dollars?"

"But I'll make it up to you."

"Oh, you god damned right! You gonna make it up! I want your ass up and out of here . . . Now!"

"But I'm tired." pleads Camille, nearly in tears.

"I said out!" He takes her by the arm and pushes her out of the door. Just then, Geronimo comes in from his room: "Hey man, what's all the noise about?"

"Oh, it ain't nothing but a thing. I just had to put my foot down is all. I'm afraid Camille might be sandbagging . . . trying to run some game down on me . . . that's all."

"Well, you know it's getting close to elections."

"Yeah, I know, but I can't let the bitch use that as an excuse."

Geronimo sits down in a chair, runs his hand down his face, and contemplates the situation. "Man, what's happening to us? We used to laugh and always have a good time. Now we seem to have nothing but problems. You're always mad or upset about something. I know Angela is part of the reason for you feeling the way you do, but she's gone, and we can't do anything about that . . . and you shouldn't take things out on Camille either. We just have to go on. Sometimes I wonder if this is the right game for you. Maybe it's time you got out of it."

"Get out of it? And what do I replace it with?"

"I don't know . . . maybe just stick to selling weed, the way you used to. But what I do know is, how you feel inside is important . . . that much I know."

"Oh you do?"

"Yes I do."

"And how's that?" asks Christopher.

"I once told you when I first came to California, I lived in Oakland for a while."

"Yes?"

"But I never told you what I did while I was there."

"No, you didn't."

"I had a hard time finding a job, but finally I got one in an amusement park. They had a game there . . . where a guy would stand on a platform over a big tank of water. Alongside the tank was a bull's eye. People would pay a dime for three balls to try and hit the target. If they hit it, the platform would collapse, and the guy standing on it would fall into the water. The name of the game was 'Drown the Nigger'. I don't have to tell you who the nigger was."

"Damn! It sounds like things were pretty rough."

"Man, you better believe it was rough. I would stand there eight, sometimes twelve hours a day. They would throw and miss, throw and miss, then buy more balls. I'd watch their faces and see the hate in their eyes. Sometimes I'd get hit with the baseballs . . .

accidents. Every now and then someone would hit the bull's eye . . . I sure did hate going down into that water."

"That's a hell of a story, but I don't know what it has to do with this."

"The point is, I earned a living, but I didn't feel too good about myself. Things weren't right with me until I got away from it. It could be that neither one of us feels too good about ourselves right now . . . maybe it's time to get out."

"You know . . . sometimes when Camille is asleep, she has these dreams. She seems to be spitting something bad tasting out of her mouth. At other times she whimpers like a whipped puppy."

"What does she dream about?"

"She won't say, and it's starting to bother me," Christopher answers—then almost speaking to himself: ". . . but I have some ideas." Now changing the subject: "There was a time when I wanted to be respectable. I would have felt good about that. I tried, but it just didn't work out the way I planned."

"I remember a girl who came by your house once at about the same time you hooked up with Angela. She sure seemed like a nice girl . . . seemed to have a lot of class. What was her name?"

"That would be Laura."

"What ever happened to her?" asks Geronimo.

Christopher pauses, reluctant to speak, then forces out the answer. "I heard she went to Portland, Oregon and had a baby . . . a baby girl . . . my baby." And with that, Christopher turns his face away, feeling the weight of time building upon his shoulders. Geronimo, seeing the effect memory has on him, leaves him to his thoughts—thoughts that range from Laura, the woman he almost loved, to Angela, the woman he learned to accept in the absence of love. He struggles to come to terms with the cold, hard finality of life ended. Life to Christopher now seems a crazy game that plays to no worthwhile end. The final act is accompanied by the empty reward of death.

Christopher finds himself longing for meaning in his life. He has not taken the drug Infinity lately. It has enhanced his perception before, perhaps it can do so again. He goes to the kitchen, takes some from the freezer, rolls it into a cigarette, then returns to the living room to smoke it. A feeling of increased awareness comes over him. He becomes mindful not only of his own consciousness, but of a mass or collective consciousness—the combined consciousness of other individuals, both living and dead. He senses Angela is somewhere within this mass consciousness.

Christopher's consciousness moves outward, and with the voice of his mind calls to her. Suddenly, Angela seems very close at hand. He is able to smell the scent of her body, experience her emotions, and comprehend her thoughts. He feels the fingers of her delicate hands running through his hair, as they did in days past. She speaks to him in the way of the angels, a way that transcends language. She assures him she is at peace, and he is not to worry or be concerned. Her presence then floats away, above and beyond, back into the collective.

Christopher starts having these sessions daily. Sometimes Angela comes to him, and sometimes not. When she doesn't, he starts looking inward to his own subconscious. On the journey into his soul, he inadvertently takes with him mental images from the material world of the things that affect him most: Angela lying in her casket, and Mr. Panama with his face blown open. The two images seem to merge together, then separate, then re-combinate in different ways until Christopher sees faint, new images emerge. They are like something you can almost put your finger on, but not quite. When he tries harder to see the images, they fade away.

During his next session, Christopher attempts to form the images again, but with little success. He decides to forget the idea for a while, and just let his mind roam on whatever it might. When he does this, he finds himself standing before two coffins. There is a man in the coffin on the left, and a woman in the coffin on the right. Christopher is smaller than all the other people around him. Someone seems to be holding his hand. He turns to the left and looks up to see who it is. "Grandma!" he cries to himself.

Christopher is lost in his vision. The barrier to his subconscious is now ruptured. The memories rush forth into the conscious realm like a tidal wave: the Sundays at church, the ice cream and sherbet, the happy times with his playmates; yes, it is all there, and more.

He now realizes there was once someone who loved him as a child, and someone he loved in return. He finds this revelation comforting, but his recollections soon turn to the fateful day, and the sight of his grandmother lying on her deathbed, with the dried blood from her nose. Tears now stream from Christopher's eyes. His nerves strained by the sudden onslaught of repressed emotional experience. His breaths are actually heaves, and muscles throughout his body twitch uncontrollably. When the effects of the drug wear off, he surrenders to sleep.

Christopher awakens and his surroundings seem different. The entire world has greater depth and detail. Simple everyday objects that before appeared dull are now more radiant. Even the ordinary act of taking a shower becomes a source of visual wonder, as the rays of sunlight streaming in through the window play with the splashing droplets of water.

He now spends much of his time in deep meditation, recalling as many of the details of his early life as he possibly can. He has a faint recollection of the beautiful ballad sung by the ill fated balladeer. He recalls many of the stories Mary used to tell him. Realizing many of these stories come from the Bible, Christopher reasons that one way to know her better, might be to read the Bible. He obtains a Bible, and on the first page he reads, "In the beginning . . . God said, Let there be light: and there was light."

Christopher thinks to himself: "How simple and straightforward. The words were simply spoken, and it was so." This thought rearouses his interest in creation theory. He feels that perhaps by virtue of its simplicity there may be some element of truth in the statement. The possibility occurs to him that archaic ideologies might hold the key to an understanding of things modern science is at a loss to explain. He studies not only the Holy Bible, but also the Holy Quran, and Kabbalistic writings. He delves into Buddhism, and some of the religions of Africa. The Hindu practice of Yoga introduces him to the fine art of achieving various levels of consciousness.

Christopher traces each of these religions back to their roots. He finds eventually that they all lead to the practice of Magic, in one form or another. These early magicians were oftentimes either quacks or misguided, but a few gifted ones were apparently able to gain some remarkable insights during a time when science and technology, as we know it, did not exist. Christopher reasons there is probably more than one way of knowing. On that basis, he decides to pursue the study of the Magical Arts.

Great changes are taking place in Christopher's being. He is going, for better or for worse, through a transformation—a metamorphosis of sorts. His mental processes are slowly, but steadily accelerating due to the effect the Infinity has on the electro-chemical activity in his brain. He is becoming physically stronger, with seemingly boundless energy. Another interesting aspect of the change is that he is maturing emotionally. His capacity for love, an emotion so very long suppressed in his subconscious, is beginning to flower. His new found feelings naturally embrace those closest to him: Geronimo and Camille. As the basic, raw emotion of love matures, he experiences its finer, subtler shade, compassion, prompting him to call a meeting in the living room.

"The two of you probably noticed how I never talk about my past. I didn't think there was anything to talk about . . . but now I remember things . . . I know I had a grandmother. Her name was Mary, and she loved me very much . . . I want the both of you to know that I love you." He pauses to look around the room. "Living in this house is crazy. We're not making the money we used to. I don't really care where I live. It's not the most important thing. I'm thinking maybe we should move back to Sugar Hill, back to where we came from. How do the two of you feel about that?"

Camille raises herself slightly in her seat. With arms half folded, and the fingers of one hand placed thoughtfully under her chin, she gazes at Christopher in silent acknowledgment, then answers, "That would be fine with me."

A smile seems to hide somewhere beneath the surface of Geronimo's face, as he adds, "I've been wanting to suggest something like that for a while now, but I didn't know how you would take it. You've been kind of distant for quite a while, and more so lately."

"I understand what you're saying. I just want you to understand it has nothing to do with either one of you. I'm working on things. Just try to bear with me for a while." asks Christopher. Camille and Geronimo agree to his request.

Later in the evening, Christopher asks Camille to go for a walk with him. Camille has done more than her share of walking on the streets, and does not consider this a desirable form of relaxation, but agrees anyway. They start out walking down the main road by the house, then cut off onto a road leading higher up into the hills.

"I'm getting a little tired." Camille complains.

"We won't go much farther." Christopher assures her. They come to a clearing that offers them an even better view of the city than the one they have from the house. It is near twilight. The night-lights are just beginning to appear. "We might as well enjoy it while we're still here." he says as he puts his arms around her and kisses her. "I know I've been hard on you at times—too hard, and I just want to say I'm sorry."

"Sometimes I thought you were taking Angela's death out on me . . . Sometimes I think you wish it happened to me instead." Camille is now beginning to cry.

"If I ever made you feel that way, it's because I was crazy. I promise I'll never make you feel that way again." He hugs her and rocks her gently. "I have a request to make of you." She tilts her head and waits for him to continue. "I want you off the streets . . . I want you to quit the business."

"You do?" she inquires, almost not believing him.

"Yes. I figure that after the move, I can make enough money selling the 'herb yielding seed', and we'll see what else goes from there."

"Wait a minute, selling the what?"

"Weed. The 'herb yielding seed' comes from something I read. Don't worry about it."

"Chris, I have an idea."

"What's your idea, sweetheart?"

"Why don't we go back down to the house, take a hot, relaxing bath, have some dinner, then make passionate love?"

"I have a better idea."

"What's your idea, sweetheart?"

"Let's skip the dinner."

*   *   *

Within a month they return to the Hill. The ongoing urban decay has changed the face of things a bit during the three years away. Camille and Christopher find an apartment, smaller than the first, in the same building they lived in before. Geronimo rents a room nearby.

Christopher continues his drug dealings with Bird, Squirrel, and Brim. Camille manages to land a job as a receptionist in an insurance company. Every chance Christopher gets, he goes out collecting books on occult science. He knows both Camille and Geronimo have fears regarding such matters, so he tries to keep all things pertaining to his new pursuit out of their sight.

The idea of reading little known and understood archaic writings fascinates Christopher. He enters the world of magic as practiced around the world from as far back as the time when human beings dwelt in caves. Included in his readings are books on the Ceremonial Magic practiced in the middle ages that speak of such fantastical things as the infernal evocation of demons. The goal of the ceremonial magician, he discovers, is to exert his power over these demons, and force them to do his will, whatever that might be, typically to gain information regarding the location of buried treasure. The execution of these rituals, or 'grimoires' as they were known, oftentimes demand difficult if not impossible conditions be met. The would-be successful magician might be required to obtain the virgin wax of bees that never made fruit, the gall of a black cat, the blood of an owl, the hand of a criminal, human fat, or some part of a mummy. To make matters worse, many of these grimoires, written under false pretenses, claim authorship by such notables as King Solomon.

Christopher desires to gain knowledge of and conversation with his grandmother Mary. He comes across a book more tolerable than the rest. It is the Sacred Magic of Abra-Melin the Mage, and in this book is a procedure for making a corpse rise from the grave. It is a complex system requiring months of preparation, great expense, and a very special location for the performance of the ritual. Christopher tries the Sacred Magic in greatly modified form.

After a week of preparation, Christopher is ready to perform the ritual. He goes to the living room in the late evening hours as Camille sleeps in the bedroom. In the middle of the floor he forms a circle of protection with a piece of string. The circle is about six feet in diameter. He lights a single candle and places it within the circle, then turns off the lights. He sits on the floor within the circle, lights some incense and watches as the smoke curls into the air, filling the room. He has smoked a small amount of the Infinity, and begins to experience its effect. Christopher places a 'magic square' he has drawn on a piece of paper and consecrated previously, on the floor before the candle and begins to meditate.

After a while he hears an unearthly sound similar to the tinkling of bells. Then the sound dies away. It is soon apparent no more will happen this evening. He had tried reaching Mary before in the way he had reached Angela, but failed. His hope was that some form of magical ritual would help, but it did not. He supposes the reason for his difficulties might be because Mary is too long dead.

Strange things begin to happen around the house, intermittently, over the next few days. Small objects of value, such as jewelry and money mysteriously change location during the night. A watch left in the bathroom at night might be found in the kitchen the next morning. Money left on the bedroom dresser might appear in the living room. On more than one occasion the inside door latches of the apartment come undone with no apparent explanation. At the same time each day a common mouse appears, who sits in the corner of whatever room Christopher might be in, and simply stares at him. If Christopher approaches the mouse, the mouse does not even flinch. These occurrences are enough to convince Christopher his little ritual did accomplish something, but he does not quite know what.

Christopher continues his occult studies. In addition, he reads ancient history, and becomes acquainted with the Sumerian Epic of Gilgamish, part of which evolved into the later Book of Genesis. In this story, Gilgamish appeals to the god Nergal to restore life to his friend, Ea-bani. In the Holy Bible, 1 Samuel 28, he finds the story of how Saul appealed to Behalath-Ob, the Witch of Endor, to raise the prophet Samuel from the dead. Then he comes across a passage in another book that changes his outlook. The writer advises that magicians should make their rituals personal to them—even make up their own rituals if they feel so inclined—the most important considerations are to have a clear concept of what you are doing and why you are doing it.

It dawns on Christopher that creativity might be a helpful and important element in achieving success. The earliest human beings certainly had no written language, and therefore no documents to follow, yet their faculties for the kind of nonlinear thinking that seems to be required were probably superior to their more recent counterparts. There is also something to be said for tradition and the beliefs entire civilizations had, and in some cases, still have. Just as individuals can be greatly affected by what they believe, so the collective consciousness might also be affected by what it believes. Perhaps the best approach is a healthy respect for the old traditions, balanced with a generous amount of creativity. Armed with this bit of insight, Christopher sets out to formulate his own composite ritual.

Now inspired, Christopher declares: "I will incorporate the Obeah Stick, High John the Conqueror Root, and Graveyard Dust from southern Voodoo practices, since that is close to my grandmother's roots. I will time the performance of the ritual during an acceptable phase of the moon, in accord with the Cult of Diana. To these combined traditions I will add my own personal creative elements, and the result will be the Rite of Resurrection!"

In preparation for the Rite of Resurrection, Christopher changes his diet. He eats nothing but fresh fruits and vegetables, rice, and scaled fish. He drinks only distilled water and consumes no drugs or alcohol. He spends his time meditating and assembling the tools he will need. His pride and joy is a crystal tipped copper wand he himself makes from copper pipe and a choice specimen of quartz crystal he searched diligently to find. From the County Hall of Records he obtains a copy of Mary's death certificate. He has nothing that belonged to Mary to include in his ritual, this is perhaps the closest possible substitute for a personal possession he can hope to obtain. The next feat is to locate the grave, if there is a grave. As it turns out, he has no problems locating it. He calls the nearest cemetery, and the caretaker informs him that a Mary Campbell was buried there in 1961.

Christopher visits the cemetery. It is a peaceful place—an old place. Many of the graves and mausoleums have been there for over a hundred years. The cemetery is also an urban sanctuary for birds and squirrels that scamper up and down the mature oak and pine trees. He locates Mary's grave in the low lying 'poor man's' part of the cemetery. Here, there are no elaborate gravestones or mauseleums, only a single tree with branches hanging over her plot as if part of some master plan intended especially for her. As Christopher stands over the grave, he is moved by the thought that his grandmother's remains are only a few feet below the surface of the ground upon which he stands.

He notices one peculiar thing. Everywhere, there is beautiful green grass . . . everywhere that is, except on Mary's grave. Here, the grass does not grow. There is only bare, sparse ground. "Graveyard dust." Christopher whispers. He searches his pockets and brings out a piece of paper. He reaches down, and scoops a handful of the graveyard dust onto the paper, then folds it up, and returns it to his pocket.

The elements for the performance of the Rite of Resurrection are now nearly all in place. He has only to wait for the proper time. On the first night of the waxing moon, Christopher returns to the cemetery close to midnight, climbing over a brick wall with a knapsack tied to his back. He approaches the grave. The mood is quite different now than in the daytime—so still, so silent. Christopher stands at the foot of the grave. He looks up towards the sky. The faint glow of the moon illuminates the sky just enough to highlight the nearly leafless tree branches that hang overhead, creating a jagged and intricate pattern. The stars twinkle, but not as brightly as from the Hollywood Hills. The whole effect recreates a feeling of awe and wonder, penetrating deep into his soul.

Christopher kneels down, opens the knapsack, and first draws out a lantern, then a bottle containing oil for it. The oil is a special mixture of kerosene, castor oil, and olive oil. To this basic mixture he has added the graveyard dust, and High John The Conqueror root. He pours the mixture into the lamp, drops a small magnet into the mixture, then lights the lamp. Next, he lights a piece of charcoal, and places it in a brazier near the lamp. When the charcoal glows red, he adds pure resins of frankincense and myrrh. He takes Mary's death certificate, rolls it up tightly, then turns it upside down to symbolize the opposite of death. This he sticks into a hole in the ground. There is one last element to complete the mood. He turns on a portable tape player, and the beautiful ballad that Mary so loved, gently breaks the near total silence, enchanting the nocturnal air.

In his right hand Christopher grasps the Obeah stick, in his left he holds the crystal wand. He now rises to his feet. The wand he points up towards the moon, and the stick he directs down to the grave. As the music plays, he meditates. He is gathering up his energy and power of concentration. By the time the ballad ends, he starts focusing every fiber of his being towards the execution of the task at hand. Words begin to pour from his mouth:

"Gilgamish . . . Gilgamish of Sumer . . . Gilgamish of Sennaar . . . Gilgamish of Shiner . . . Gilgamish, come to me. Gilgamish, I await you . . . I appeal to you for aid and guidance." Christopher now utters sounds that to him are meaningful, perhaps even sacred. They are vowel sounds, the first sounds humankind had ever made, uttered in a way that reach towards the past, deep into man's collective consciousness. Much time passes. His chanting becomes softer. Christopher thinks he hears something. He opens his eyes, but sees nothing. The sound becomes more audible, more definite. It is similar to the tinkling sounds he has heard before, but more musical, like a surreal,
flutelike melody. He feels something penetrating through him from above, like little points of energy that make his nerves tingle. He has tapped into a force he perceives as Gilgamish. Now he makes his appeal.

"Gilgamish! I petition you. Lead me to Nergal, the giver of life." Christopher's emotional energy builds. He returns this energy to the cosmos by resuming the utterance of the sacred vowels, only now with more intensity than before. Suddenly, there is a deep sound, similar to a gong or bass drum. The sound is overwhelming by virtue of its size or scope, rather than its intensity. Christopher continues his appeal.

"Nergal, giver of life, lord of death. Do for me as you once did for Gilgamish. Restore the life of the one that lies in the ground before me, as you once restored Ea-bani, or grant me the power you once granted to Behalath-Ob." Christopher starts chanting the sacred vowels more frantically now than ever. He is acting as an amplifier of energies that might prove too much for him to handle, but it is too late to turn back—he has come too far for that! Suddenly, he feels a surge of energy different from the one before. Whereas the first energy comes down from his head, along the surface of his skin, this second burst comes up through the core of his legs. The surge feels strangely cold. His legs become weak. He feels the ground shake beneath him, as he falls down to his knees, but continues his efforts to maintain contact with every ounce of strength he has left.

The ground before him erupts violently. Christopher sees a crack form in the ground over the grave. The crack widens, and as it does, it emits a force that throws him backwards several feet. Something rises up from the ground and materializes. It is Mary—crystal clear—as if yesterday! She wears a familiar print dress and an apron. She is suspended over the opening in the ground, but the bottom most part of her body seems to fade out, as if not completely materialized. Christopher realizes he is not holding his crystal wand, or his Obeah stick. "They must have been knocked away." he thinks.

Christopher becomes a little boy with tears in his eyes. "Grandma! Are you okay?" he asks. She does not answer. He becomes a man again and now asks, "What is it like on the other side?" A look that can be described as fear bordering on horror comes over Mary's face for an instant, then she turns away. It is hard for Christopher to know whether he asked something that is forbidden to ask, or if the answer is so terrible she simply chooses not to say. She turns to Christopher again, but a look of panic comes over her, then her body breaks up into tiny particles. The particles reform into the shapes of three skeletons. The skeletons run off in three different directions.

Christopher passes out from exhaustion. When he awakens, he finds the crack in the ground has disappeared. The lantern is still in its proper place, but the flame is extinguished. He checks the lamp, finding there is still oil remaining. "Maybe the spirits put the lamp out." he thinks to himself. He gathers up his tools, places them in the knapsack, and heads home before the rising of the sun, thankful he managed through the whole thing undetected.

When Christopher gets home, Camille is in bed, but she is not asleep. "So where have you been?" she asks.

"At the cemetery."

"The cemetery?"

"Yes, the cemetery."

"And you really expect me to believe that?"

"I guess it is hard to believe, but it's the truth. I'll tell you all about it later. Right now I'm tired. I just want to get some rest." By now, Christopher has taken off his clothing, and gets in bed. "Come on, give me a hug." he says as he snuggles up close to her.

"What a night!" Christopher declares as he rolls out of bed the next morning. It is Sunday, so Camille is not working. She is in the kitchen preparing breakfast, and after washing up, Christopher joins her.

"Good morning baby." he murmurs, embracing her while she works over the stove.

"So, how's the cemetery man doing this morning?" inquires Camille dryly.

"What am I going to have to do to make you believe me?" Asks Christopher. Camille says nothing. "The food smells good. You know what I'd like for dinner? I'd like a nice juicy steak." he adds.

"What's the matter? Getting tired of fish?"

"I just miss having red meat. Suddenly I find myself craving it."

Later in the morning, Geronimo drops in to check on his friend. Even though Christopher has made an effort to keep things out of their sight, Geronimo and Camille both realize he has been dabbling in things which they would rather not have to deal with. They usually seem content pretending not to know. As the three of them sit in the living room talking over the background of a radio playing, a news bulletin interrupts the normal broadcasting.

"Listen to this!" urges Christopher.

". . . I repeat. We have several reports from motorists of a woman appearing, and suddenly disappearing, repeatedly, on the Santa Monica Freeway . . ." comes the announcement.

"That must be my grandmother!" exclaims Christopher.

"Your grandmother?" queries a doubtful Camille.

"Yes, my grandmother. You see, I went to the cemetery last night, and called her back from the dead."

"You did what?" demands Camille.

"That's right! I raised her up from the dead!"

Geronimo is chilled to his bones, as if recalling some dreadful experience from the past. "You shouldn't do that! Now you've got her wandering around in some kind of limbo. You should leave the dead alone. Let her rest in peace!" he begs.

"But she is not resting in peace." discloses Christopher.

"And how do you know that?" quizzes Camille.

"Because no grass grows on her grave, and because of the way she looked when I saw her. That's all I can tell you right now." Christopher, seeing that Camille and Geronimo are shaken adds, "There are things out there we don't understand. Our fear and disbelief keeps us from gaining an understanding, just as fear and disbelief almost prevented Columbus from sailing across the Atlantic Ocean. I'll help her find her peace. Don't worry, everything will be all right." Christopher assures them as he turns toward a corner of the room. Camille and Geronimo take notice, then Camille shrieks, "A mouse!"

"Don't worry, that's my friend. He comes to visit me every day about this time." Camille and Geronimo look at each other, and then at the mouse, who sits undeterred, staring at Christopher. "I think my friend is leaving, I won't be seeing him again." The mouse then turns and walks away.

That evening, the three of them enjoy a dinner of thick, juicy steaks. After the meal Geronimo goes home. Christopher, not fully recovered from the rigors of the Rite of Resurrection, feels tired and goes to bed early.

Later, Camille comes to the bedroom to join him. Christopher's body is sprawled gracefully across the bed. He awakens from his half sleep, startled by her presence. He raises his upper body with the coordination and grace of a magnificent animal. His posture is not human, more like that of a cat. He sees Camille, then hisses and snarls at her viciously. Camille is terrified and runs from the room. Christopher rests his body back down on the bed, hovering between a waking and sleeping state. Later, he becomes himself and apologizes, but Camille worries nevertheless, and Christopher wonders why he reacted the way he did.

The answer to Christopher's question comes to him by the following morning. He declares to Camille, "It is the red, half raw meat I ate last night that caused me to regress to such a primitive animal nature. From now on, I will eat no flesh. I will eat only the fresh fruits and vegetables that grow on the face of the earth. I will drink only water purified through the process of distillation. Anything less might prove detrimental, due to the high state of sensitivity my body is now in to all external forces." Camille does not know what to make of Christopher's new attitude, but convinces herself maybe everything will work out if he does not eat the meat.

That night as Christopher lies in bed trying to fall asleep he hears voices. The voices are high pitched, similar to an audio recording played at high speed. Three voices speak in unison. The voices say, "Come play with us." Christopher turns to the left and sees three beings. They appear as human forms consisting of fuzzy, red light, hanging in midair alongside the bed, holding hands. Their faces have sharp features: long, narrow, slanted eyes, pointed noses, and wide, deeply cut mouths. The being in the middle is the tallest, maybe six inches in height, and the one on the right is the shortest.

"Who are you?" Christopher asks. The beings answer, but their name is an abstract concept, and therefore unpronounceable.

Christopher's astral body leaves the bed and follows them. The beings take him to the middle of the Los Angeles Coliseum, where they rise up into the air, maybe a thousand feet above the field, and return to the ground. With the next ascension the beings take him farther. They go through storm clouds across the Atlantic Ocean. Christopher can sense a cold wind and swirling rain around him, but does not feel the effects. They hover over a place that might be somewhere in Scandinavia, Germany, or Switzerland. There are hills, blanketed by thick forests, dotted by villages. Christopher can see railroad tracks winding through the hilly countryside, and a train slowly making its way uphill. He comes close to one of the villages, and spots a church just off the main boulevard. The modest houses are well-kept with green lawns in the front, and most with tidy vegetable gardens in the rear. Christopher feels a desire to stay here. It seems a place he has once been, but has never known.

The beings urge him onward, until Christopher finds himself standing in a window two or three stories up from the ground. Looking out of the window he sees a busy boulevard below and a gasoline station across the street. In the gas station he sees attendants in uniforms pumping gas into cars of an old style, yet appearing new. He turns around, and in the corner of the room he sees an old lady sitting in a rocking chair. It is Mary. She raises her arms and beckons him to come. He comes to her, falls down on his knees, and rests his head on her bosom. She says to him, "There are seven keys that affect your life. The first two keys were before your time. The third key, you have already found. The next three keys, we will provide—they will be made available to you when needed most. The seventh key you will discover, but it may be too late."

Christopher listens to the words, then raises his head to ask a question. Mary raises a hand cautioning him to be silent, and as she does, he experiences a feeling of great pain and suffering. In the next instant, Christopher is back in his apartment, returning to bed. The next morning Camille comments:

"I had trouble sleeping after you got back in bed last night."

"But I never got up. I dreamt I went on a journey, came back and got in bed."

"Maybe you did have a dream, but you were also sleepwalking. I'm certain I saw you get in bed."

Christopher chooses not to argue the point. His concerns are of the new world that has opened up to him. His contact with Mary seems to suggest a goal to be reached. That, and the desire for the answers to the ultimate questions of existence never leave his mind. Day by day he becomes more obsessed, spending hours at a time in a darkened room, engaging in what might be called contemplative mysticism. He is convinced the dead either will not or can not give him the answers he seeks. He concludes that in order to find the answers he must go beyond the realm of the dead, perhaps even beyond the realm of human consciousness.

Frequently, during these mystical sessions, Christopher becomes drowsy, slipping into a state of consciousness somewhere between the sleeping and waking states. While in this trance state he is able to leave his body. At first, the time span of the trance is short, lasting only a moment or two. He discovers by simply not trying so hard, he is able to maintain the trance for a much longer period of time. He uses this talent to travel many times the speed of light through deep space. Stars rush in and out of view as he penetrates deeper into the universe. He wonders if he will ever reach an end, but the trance always breaks before that happens. Traveling too fast tends to kill the trance, and end the journey. The trick he learns, is to maintain a certain ideal speed. With practice, Christopher is able to master this hypnogogic technique of astral travel.

While on one of these journeys a certain star attracts him with its reddish color. Christopher moves close to the star, then feels himself being drawn to a planet in a nearby solar system. He comes down to rest on a bench in a garden. The garden is luxuriantly landscaped with shade trees, shrubbery, and lush, ivy-type plants.

In the middle of the garden is a red brick, single story building. As it appears, it could be a small school, library, or temple. The trees and green shrubbery shield it from the relentless rays of the sun. The ivy type plants climb the front of the building and the left wall. There are no flowers, no birds, and no butterflies—just red brick contrasting nicely against the green growth. There is the soft, gurgling sound of water, as in a nearby brook or stream.

Beyond the garden is a vast, flat, barren desert with nothing but pure white sand for as far as the eye can see. The air is very still. This world seems to have a perpetual lack of wind. "I wonder what's inside the building?" he asks himself. In the next instant, however, he loses his trance and is back in his body.

Later at night, while in bed after Camille is asleep, Christopher tries to repeat his journey to the mysterious planet. The red star proves to be rather elusive. It is not until a second attempt early the next morning that he finds his way to the star.

Once again he is in the garden. Everything is exactly as before. He moves toward the building. There are three steps leading to an entry level, and beyond that, an open doorway. He passes through the doorway and peers into a dimly lit room. Several feet away stands a human figure in a hooded robe with his back turned. The person is standing before what appears to be a control panel with buttons on it. Beyond the panel is a clear, egg shaped vessel, about four feet wide by five feet high, the smaller end being at the top. The robed figure begins pressing some of the buttons. Christopher notices there are seven rows and seven columns of buttons, and that the order of the buttons pressed suggest the shape of a pentagram. The vessel starts filling with an opaque liquid, then the top end of the vessel opens.

The robed figure turns around, but before Christopher can see the face—the garden, and everything in it disappears. Nothing but the desert, the sky, and the reddish sun surrounds him. A feeling of terrible loneliness overcomes him. He is anxious about leaving this place for fear of being exiled here for eternity. He returns to his bed, then wakes up completely. Camille, who is also awake tells Christopher: "A funny thing just happened as I was waking up. I thought I saw you getting into the bed, but when I looked down, you were already there."

Christopher is now more completely drawn than ever into the world of the unknown. He wants more, and he doesn't intend to wait very long to get it. He reasons, "The drug Infinity might be a way to speed things up." He knows while it is a potentially dangerous drug, it is also a powerful psychic catalyst that allows one to reach levels which might not be achieved otherwise. Whereas before, the use of Infinity was sporadic, trailing off into nonuse, it now becomes a part of the daily regimen.

The Infinity combined with Christopher's improved abilities of control and concentration prove to be a powerful combination. He begins to see the planets as particles, and the revolution of each planet as a frequency of vibration, each a musical note on a higher order. At the solar level, he sees cycles of sunspot activity and magnetic reversals, all lending a unique signature to the melody of human events. But there are higher orders of harmonics still. The universe becomes an orchestral symphony, strangely beautiful and more complex than any human composition ever conceived. He sits in the middle of his bed, yet light years away, proclaiming: "I can hover and float among the stars for as long as I care. My God! It's fantastic! I feel tiny, pinpoint shots of energy throughout my body. I can even touch the heavenly bodies! My awareness is truly multidimensional. I can travel in all directions at the same time—take in the big picture—the ever grander scheme of things. "

Day after day, his conscious awareness expands. He perceives increasingly greater concepts as he moves to higher frames of reference. He reaches some kind of barrier and has trouble passing, but when he does, he sees matter and energy coming into existence from apparently nothing. He sees gas clouds forming, then collapsing to form stars and galaxies—and from that, a very special blue-white light emerges—It is the light of consciousness. It appears first as tiny, luminescent balls scattered throughout the universe. Fine threads of blue-white light radiate from each ball, connecting with other balls. The balls grow, then multiply, then grow again. Christopher is passing through the fourth dimension of time, and as he does, he sees all the moments of material existence converge into a single identity, existing as one grand event! He now knows the purpose of material existence is to create consciousness, and the goal of conscious evolution is to fill the Infinite Void with its presence.

Certainly, one would think he has gone as far as anyone should expect to go, or would want to go, but no, this is not enough for Christopher. He feels he should go as far as he possibly can— as far as his abilities will allow. He continues the Infinity sessions. He had gone farther than he ever imagined, yet he was going farther still, and beginning to lose touch with his earthly existence. He is totally absorbed in the Rite of Progression.

He slams into another barrier, but the energy loop he has created with the cosmos keeps building, and building, until finally the barrier ruptures. What happens next is beyond words to describe. It is a situation far beyond the point where all the known laws of physics break down, becoming useless. It is a psychic explosion. The experience is like having a huge skyscraper slammed into your face, crammed up your nose, then explode. His mind is now beyond the point of overload. His energy is totally depleted. He has collapsed on the bed, in a daze, struggling to put it all back together.

This is the state Camille finds Christopher in when she comes home from work that evening. She now knows something is terribly wrong. Christopher drifts in and out of reality unpredictably. At times he is able to hold an almost normal conversation, but at other times he is completely unaware of his immediate surroundings, preferring instead to drift out into the cosmos. Camille calls on Geronimo for help. The two of them spend hours talking to Christopher, trying to keep him grounded.

It should be pointed out that Christopher evoked demons unintentionally through the Rite of Resurrection, and that they never left completely. They are Mary's demons, and they, together with her pain and suffering, become Christopher's. They now take advantage of his weakened state. The demons do everything they can to tear him apart. At night, they torment him relentlessly. All he can do is pace through the house frantically, while the blood vessel on his left temple throbs violently, like the throat of a bullfrog. He is lucky if he gets an hour's sleep, and even then, the sleep is shallow. This tearing and eating away at his nerves goes on for weeks. The constant mental anguish makes him paranoid, and therefore fearful. He senses mortal danger lurking at a distance. The evil forces beyond that he has awakened are devising a new and sinister plot against him.

A solution comes to Christopher as a memory early the next morning. Struggling to hold himself together, shivering from a drop in body temperature, he packs some things in a bag, and drives out to the country. He buys the most flawless male goat he can find that is less than a year old. He takes it to the desert, and finds a remote place on higher ground than the surrounding area. Here, it is peaceful and serene. The big blue sky extends down to touch the pale mountains of the distant horizon. He spreads a white cloth on the ground as a makeshift altar, and on the altar he places the goat. He holds the goat down with one hand, and in the other he holds a dagger high up in the air. As he recites the sacred vowels, a stiff, nearly constant wind seems to carry them off to a far away place. He brings the dagger down, and glides it across the animal's throat. At that moment Christopher feels a surge of energy come up through him. He drains some of the blood into a jar, then skins and guts the goat, and roasts it over a fire with plenty of spices. When the meat is cooked, he gorges himself, burns the remains of the goat, and heads for home.

On the way home he buys a small shrub from a nursery. His next stop is a hardware store, where he buys lumber, nails, a saw, and a hammer. When he gets home, he immediately goes to the kitchen table, and begins sawing the wood into shorter lengths. Camille comes to the kitchen.

"What are you doing?" she asks.

"I have to board the windows." he answers without looking up, or missing a beat.

"Why?"

"How can you ask me something like that? Don't you have any idea what's going on here?" an exasperated Christopher shouts.

"No. Tell me."

"They're after me! My life is in danger! There's going to be a convergence, and if I don't do something . . . I won't live to see tomorrow! Look, I don't have time to explain any more to you. Please! Just leave me alone and let me finish!" he implores.

Camille is frightened and confused. She calls Geronimo, who comes over immediately. Christopher ignores them both as he races against the approach of nightfall. After he has nailed a board across each window in the house, he splits a piece of leftover wood lengthwise, and drives a nail through the two pieces to form a cross. Then he rushes outside with the shrub and lamb's blood. Using the shrub as a brush, he dips it into the blood, and strikes marks on the tops and sides of the doors, and windows. When this is done, he hurries back into the house. Amidst the pleas of Camille and Geronimo, he strings cloves of garlic together with a needle and thread. This he ties around his neck.

Now it is time to settle in and simply wait for the dangers to pass, but that is easier said than done. As he sits on the sofa clutching the wooden cross, Camille and Geronimo pace the room nervously, trying to figure out how best to handle the situation. Christopher shouts, "No! I will not drink alcohol!" A look of amazement bordering on horror comes over Camille's face as she turns to Geronimo and exclaims, "He's reading my thoughts! I was just thinking maybe a stiff drink would help settle him down." Now they must be careful what they think.

Then the sound of a police helicopter draws near. "They're after me!" Christopher shouts as his head jerks nervously towards the ceiling. "Go away! Leave me alone!" he pleads to the unseen enemy.

Frustrated, Camille approaches him. "Stop it! Just stop it!" she shouts. "There's nothing out there for you to worry about."

Christopher sees anger in her eyes and bolts back, raising the cross towards her. "Stay away from me! Get back! You have the devil in you!" he cries as he huddles in a corner of the sofa.

Camille is struck by the fear and repulsion Christopher displays towards her. She immediately changes her attitude. "Oh baby, don't worry. I understand. We'll get through this." she reassures him.

Christopher pays little attention to her, checking to make sure the string of garlic is still around his neck. He settles down briefly, only to have a discomforting vision pass before his eyes as Camille and Geronimo listen.

"I see disaster and devastation . . . Planes falling from the sky, the sky aglow as if on fire . . . Sharp, intense hues bursting forth. . . reds, yellows, blues. Explosions! Popping, biting, stabbing sounds . . . No where to go! No where to hide!" Much time passes before he settles down, and a look of contentment comes over him. "Peace. Harmony. A transition. Everything will be all right."

The night is long and wears terribly on the nerves of Camille and Geronimo, but it does pass, leaving them to only hope that the worst is behind.

Now that the Rite of Passover has been performed the demons are held at bay. Christopher is in a super conscious mode most of the time. As the days wear on he shows no sign of improvement. He has lost weight and his face is sunken. He cannot complete the signing of his name to a check without forgetting what he is doing.

The ordeal has become unbearable for Camille and Geronimo. They can not sleep for worry, and know not what to expect next. Their greatest fear is that he might be too far gone to ever come back. Desperate measures will have to be taken.

10

A TOUCH OF MADNESS

One week after the Rite of Passover, Camille and Geronimo tell Christopher they would like to take him out for a drive. Christopher agrees, but he is so incoherent that he repeatedly forgets to complete the simple task of putting on his clothes. Instead, his mind drifts far away, and he wanders through the house aimlessly. After constant reminders, he is at last ready to leave.

As luck would have it, Geronimo has problems starting the car. The starter motor turns, but the engine will not fire. He tries over and over, but to no avail. Finally, Christopher, whose faculties temporarily return, offers to help. Camille and Geronimo look at each other in a way as if to ask 'What do we have to lose?', and accept the offer. As Christopher sits in the front passenger seat, a fire builds in his eyes. He points the tips of his fingers towards the engine and tells Geronimo to try again. As Geronimo holds the key to engage the starting system, Christopher's hands begin to vibrate. In a few seconds, the car starts.

After a long drive into the country, they pass through some gates, and enter a large complex. They take Christopher to the rear door of a building, where a lady greets him. Once inside, the lady invites him to stay for a couple of days, but Christopher tells her he can not stay. She insists, and Christopher becomes a bit irritated. Upon seeing his irritation the lady summons a man. The man seems very friendly and smiles as he introduces himself and shakes Christopher's hand. Soon, the man invites Christopher to stay. Again, Christopher declines the invitation, explaining he has other things he needs to do. The man excuses himself, leaving Camille, Geronimo, and Christopher seated in chairs along a hallway.

Christopher sees some people walking down the hallway. The people look peculiar. "Something is not quite right about them." he thinks to himself. He turns to Camille and discloses, "This is an insane asylum." Camille and Geronimo look at each other, speechless. Just then, the man returns with a second man in a white jacket. The two men invite everyone into a room. The man in the white jacket tells Christopher, "I think you should stay for a while." By now, Christopher is becoming impatient with these people. Add to that the obnoxious grin that was almost a smirk on the face of the man in the white jacket, and it is enough to trigger his already sensitive emotions into a state of anger. He takes a couple of steps towards the man, and yells at the top of his voice, "I DON'T WANT TO STAY!" Christopher sees fear build up in the eyes of the obnoxious man through the thick lenses of his horn rimmed glasses. He backs off, having no intentions of trying to hurt him, but the man's pride has already been compromised by Christopher's manipulation and he gives a signal to the lady for more help.

Christopher's mind is now alert. His senses are sharper than they have ever been. He hears something come from above—a humming sound. The sound gets louder and louder. He tries to look up towards the direction of the sound, but before he can, it fills his head, overwhelming him, then he faints. Camille and Geronimo grab hold of him before he can fall to the ground. After several seconds, he opens his eyes and stands upright under his own power, then, in a voice of supernatural proportions—a voice so powerful that the walls of the room shake, he proclaims:

"I AM TRIKRISATON: THE REALIZATION OF GOD THE FORCE, GOD THE BEING, AND GOD THE CONSCIOUSNESS! THE REUNION OF THE FAMILY OF OLODUMARE, LORD OF THE POSSIBILITIES—B'ESU'S AND S'ATON THE OBATALA!"

Everyone is stunned, both inside and out of the room. Geronimo regains his composure sufficiently enough to plead: "You are Christopher! Your name is Christopher!"

The voice answers more softly: "I AM HE, AND I AM MORE! I AM THE CHILD OF HADIT AND NUIT—I AM THE OVERMAN—THE FIRST MAN, AND THE LAST MAN!"

By now, two burly guards in uniforms are on the scene. The guards attempt to grab Christopher's arms, but he throws them off. The guards try again. In earlier days, Christopher might have been impossible for them to overcome, but the deficient diet of fresh fruits and vegetables for over three months, save for the single meal of goat's meat during the Rite of Passover, has left his body physically weakened. The guards get the better of him and carry him off as he rants and raves in an unknown tongue. Camille cries hysterically while Geronimo tries his best to comfort her.

The guards drag Christopher off to a ward and strap him in a bed. The straps are bound to his ankles and wrists. They are made of thick canvas and are impossible to break. He is in a room all alone so as not to excite the other patients with his constant struggling and indiscernible outcries. He feels humiliated, defeated, and doubtful of all the things he has come to know of life. Sometime during the night he ceases to resist. His mind shuts down to the outside world. He becomes completely unaware of things around him—cataleptic, the psychiatrists call it.

Christopher had dared to look upon the face of God, and the price he pays is insanity. He had tried to impose his will on the Universal Mind, and now the Universal Mind has imposed its will on him. The two minds have mated. Conception has taken place. Christopher might now become one of those rare beings that walk the face of the earth only once or twice in an age. His mind is now a psychic fetus that might either abort, or grow to maturity. The final outcome is uncertain. Only time can tell.

For the next three weeks, the attendants wash, bathe, and spoon feed him. After that time, he ever so slowly becomes aware of his surroundings. He hears sounds, but can not interpret their meaning. For him, there is no appreciable difference between the sound of a human voice, and a spoon rattling in a cup. He sees light, but is unable to differentiate the light into patterns. When he finally does start seeing patterns, he can not at first identify them as people, places, or things. Usually, he just sits and stares blankly into space, responding only minimally to external stimuli.

By the fifth week he is able to perform basic tasks of eating and drinking. The doctors order him moved from his private room to the common sleeping area with the other patients. Most of the patients are also withdrawn, but not nearly as much as Christopher. Two of them are much livelier than the rest. These two take a special interest in Christopher, that is, when they are not arguing with each other. They watch him with great curiosity, and exchange comments, but Christopher is not cognizant enough to actually notice or care.

By the ninth week, Christopher's rate of recovery rapidly increases. He interprets the world around him, but prefers not interacting with it. Instead, he walks around aimlessly in a world of thought, attempting to assimilate his ideas and come to terms with reality on all its levels. At times, the enormity of his thoughts overwhelms him. The pain and anguish of his recollections become too much to bear, but he manages to hold himself together till the thirteenth week.

Christopher is now fully returned to reality, but he is quiet, withdrawn, and melancholy, spending much of his time staring out through the barred window in the lounge. He tries to block from his mind the nearly constant bickering between the two livelier patients, whose names—or at least the nicknames they have given to each other, are Cowboy and Soul Man.

Cowboy is white, from Oklahoma, wears cowboy boots, and hates black people. He believes North America is the original Garden of Eden that the superior white man has come to reclaim. Soul Man is black, from Georgia, always throwing up a clenched fist as the sign of black power, and hates white people. He feels Islam is the black man's only true religion, and that the black man is destined to have his own separate nation in America. The two men probably have more in common than they have differences. They would like nothing better than to be away from each other, yet they are inextricably bound to each other within these limited confines by their mutual hate and disgust, in the absence of more desirable bedfellows.

Most of the patients, when not in psychotherapy or knocked out on tranquilizers, spend their time watching television or shooting pool. Christopher prefers to go outside for walks through the garden areas, where he takes in the sun and fresh air, enjoys the trees and flowers, and studies the birds and insects. He occasionally sees a squirrel scampering up an oak tree. This reminds him of the cemetery where his grandmother is buried, and where he performed the Rite of Resurrection.

After one of these walks, Christopher returns to the ward by way of the recreation room. He passes Cowboy and Soul Man, who are playing a game of pool. Soul Man, in jest, invites Christopher to shoot a few balls. Christopher has come to know these two by hearing their conversations. He doesn't want to get involved with them, feeling such an association would be tedious at best.

Christopher says nothing, but raises his hand and nods a polite no. Soul Man says, "What's the matter, you don't like us or something? You can play Cowboy here. He'll be easy on you."

Christopher doesn't want to, but he agrees, figuring if he has to live with these two, he might as well be on good terms with them.

"All right then. You rack." Christopher tells Cowboy.

"Well, look here! We got us a heavy mother fucker. He talks and everything!" exclaims Soul Man as Cowboy racks the balls.

Christopher drops three balls on the break. He begins to feel the blood course through his veins as he takes more shots and the balls drop one after the other. He is playing as well as, or better than, he had ever played back in the old days on the streets. It feels good. Playing gives him more human interaction than he has had in a while. He works rapidly down to the last ball, and calls a bank shot in the side. "Well, thanks for the game." Christopher says after making the shot. He places the cue stick on the table and walks off, leaving Cowboy and Soul Man standing stupidly in place.

Christopher goes to the lounge and is delighted to find one of those rare moments when the television is free. Flicking through the channels, he finds a documentary. "That looks interesting." he thinks to himself as he settles in a comfortable chair. It isn't long before his solitude is broken. Cowboy and Soul Man, apparently tired of playing pool, come busting through the doors engaged in one of their stimulating conversations:

". . . What the hell are you talking about? Everyone knows the black man is superior to the white man. That's why you try so hard to keep us down." remarks Soul Man.

"I see this place hasn't helped you any. You're still crazy as hell if you think that. You're the inferior ones. We're the ones in charge. Remember?" argues Cowboy.

"Hey look! There's the pool shark over there. He's watchin' some kind of educational television. You see? I told you he was a heavy mother fucker. Let's ask him." suggests Soul Man, walking towards Christopher.

"You can forget that!" Cowboy replies as he follows.

"What's the matter? You mad because he kicked your ass on the pool table?" teases Soul Man, laughing heartily.

"Hell no. It could just as easy be your ass he kicked. I'm not gonna let you go and ask one of your own brothers. You know damn well he's gonna take your side."

"Man, what the hell you talkin' about? This ain't no brother. At least, he ain't no true brother. Hell, he probably has more white blood in him than anything else. So what does that make him?"

"Still makes him colored as far as I'm concerned."

"Who the hell are you callin' colored? I'm a Black Man! You got it?" shouts Soul Man angrily.

"Here we go . . . now you listen. There was a time when you wanted to be called colored . . . not black, because that would have been an insult . . . but colored. Then you decided that bein' called colored wasn't right. You wanted to be Negro. Then you said 'No! I'm not a Negro! I'm an Afro-American! But if you want to call me black, well shucks, that's okay too!'. I tell you . . . it's enough to make a person's head spin
. . . Only God knows what you'll want to be called next!"

"What the hell difference it makes to you what we call ourselves, and what business is it of yours anyway?" asks Soul Man.

"Now look here Bubba, as far as I'm concerned, you can call yourself anything you want . . . Negro, colored, black, Afro-American, an alien from outer space, or the man on the moon. Personally, I don't give a damn! Just make up your mind what it is you want to be called, and then stick to it so that I don't have to be remembering to call you something different every few years, or make the mistake of callin' you the wrong thing. You got a problem with that?"

Soul Man is silent for a moment, then says, "Stop tryin' to change the subject. You know what I'm sayin' is true." Then he turns to Christopher. "Come on man. What are you gonna say about all of this? You know I'm right."

"I done already told you. He don't count." maintains Cowboy, then reconsiders, telling Christopher, "Oh well, go on and talk. Let's see if you got any sense at all."

Christopher is by now angry. He humored them with a game of pool. Now these two characters come and invade his solitude. In a fit of rage he flies up from his chair and shouts, "FUCK THE BOTH OF YOU! I could give a damn about your petty, little differences that the two of you perceive as somehow being great, and sacred, and holy. You . . ." referring to Soul Man, ". . . would have me believe that I am not as good as you because I am not so dark. And you . . ." pointing now to Cowboy, ". . . would have me believe I am not as good as you, because I am not of the 'pure race'. I say the hell with both of you. I am a human being with just as much right to breath the air, and drink the water of the earth as the two of you . . . and if either of you don't like it, then that's just too god damned bad."

"But . . ." begins Soul Man.

"But my ass!" interrupts Christopher. "You talk a lot of shit, but deep down inside you are afraid. You hide in your little ghetto world, and there with your comrades, you convince yourself you are better than everyone else. Sooner or later you have to come out into the greater world . . . the world run by whites . . . and then you realize how little you really matter."

Cowboy sees the broken look on Soul Man's face and is delighted. Christopher then turns to Cowboy, "What you hate most about blackness is not in the people you see around you." Christopher steps forward within inches of Cowboy, stares him straight in the eye, and tells him, "What you hate most is the black blood that you know flows through your veins." Cowboy swallows hard, and his face turns green. "Other people are fooled, but I can look in your face and see it. I can look into your eyes, down to the depths of your soul and see the hate you carry over that fact. What you fail to realize is that you are hating part of yourself, and self hate is self destructive." Christopher now withdraws from Cowboy and continues: "I have caught hell from the both of you because of all the bullshit you try to dish out. I don't owe either one of you a damned thing. There is no special honor or privilege in being black, nor is there some ultimate and absolute glory in being white. I don't care whether you think I am more black than white, or more white than black. The answer to that is your problem, not mine. The two of you can take your 'white supremacy', and your 'black separatism', roll it all up nice and tight, and stick it up your asses." Having said his piece, Christopher leaves the lounge, passing the attendant at the door, who had come to check on the commotion.

Soul Man gets a light for his cigarette from the attendant, then returns to Cowboy. The two are quiet for a while. After several drags on his cigarette, Soul Man turns to Cowboy and says, "I told you . . . that's a heavy mother fucker!"

"Yep, you sure did . . . talks and everything." sighs a defeated Cowboy.

Meanwhile, Christopher goes to lie on his bed. The thought of being confined with the likes of "those two idiots" incenses him. He tries to block them from his thoughts. A short time later Cowboy and Soul Man come in through the doors of the sleeping area. Upon seeing Christopher stretched out on his bed, the two men look at each other, then turn around and walk the other way.

The attendant comes later to inform Christopher he has visitors. He goes down to the visitor's area where Camille and Geronimo await him, smiling, and happy to hear that he has returned to reality. Christopher's sees the two and something clicks in his head. Anger overcomes him. "You two have a lot of nerve coming here, pretending to be my friends when all along you've lied, tricked, and practiced deception. Now look at me. Locked up . . . caged like an animal . . . and all because of the two of you. Get out! Get out and never come back! I hope I never see either of you again."

"Now come on Chris. You don't mean that." voices Geronimo.

"Don't you miss me baby? asks Camille.

"OUT! I SAID OUT! OUT! OUT! OUT!"

Camille and Geronimo leave feeling hurt. They return several times thereafter, but Christopher's attitude toward them never changes. They come less and less frequently as time goes by, until finally not at all. The psychiatrist is concerned about his patient's reclusiveness. He tries to get him to open up and talk about his feelings, but Christopher prefers having as little contact with other people as possible. He is deeply affected by experiences he feels others can not even begin to imagine.

One night after the lights are out, the attendant comes through making one of his normal rounds. In the dim light, he notices the faint outline of a person sitting upright in bed. The attendant approaches, and shines his flashlight. A look of horror comes over his face. The person appears to have tiny beads of blood all over his body.

Christopher is rushed to the medical ward, where the baffled doctors verify the excretion is indeed blood, but can find nothing medically wrong. The nurses wash the blood away, but it returns. They sponge bathe his body repeatedly until finally, the blood does not return. They keep Christopher in the infirmary for two days of observation after which time they return him to the psychiatric ward. He lies on his bed, staring at the ceiling until evening, when an impulse prompts him get up and wander around.

It is the time of evening when most of the patients can be found in the lounge. Christopher walks in and finds two of them sitting and staring blankly at the television screen while two others pace the floor nervously. He sees an old man sitting near a wall chewing the sleeve of his pajama shirt, and staring at the ground with a terribly worried look on his face. Christopher takes a seat near the old man.

Cowboy and Soul Man sit nearby having an argument. Cowboy has just said something Soul Man doesn't like. Soul Man responds by saying, "You'd better be careful what you say. You might be going there with the rest of us. Especially now that the dirty little secret's out . . . the skeleton . . . or spook I should say, in your family's closet." Soul Man laughs heartily as he turns toward

Christopher in acknowledgment of his previous insight, then continues: "Just tell me this my brother. What hot, black stud was humpin' your great granny anyway?"

This is too much for Cowboy to take. Finished with words, he lunges at Soul Man and the two end up on the floor scrapping. The attendant runs across the large room to break up the fight. Before he reaches them, Cowboy shrieks in terror, "Oh my God!"

Soul Man, startled by this sudden change in behavior, turns toward the west end of the room to locate the thing that frightens Cowboy. What he sees horrifies him as well. "Shit! It's happening again!" cries out Soul Man. The attendant looks toward the west end of the room, but sees nothing.

Gazing across the room, Christopher indeed sees something. It is like a swarm of millions of fireflies, each emitting a red light. The swarm is about eight feet high and a few feet wide. Cowboy and Soul Man are both so afraid they are unable to speak or move. They recognize it well, as an unknown thing that has haunted them in the past. Christopher rises from his chair and approaches the strange phenomenon, stopping just short of it. He raises his hands to chest level, faces his palms toward the light, and then steps into it. A feeling of ecstasy overwhelms him. He can sense from it no intellect, and no ego or personal identity. His impressions are entirely of the realms of mood and emotion. Cowboy and Soul Man are less afraid now. Instead, wonder and amazement fill them as they sit on the floor like little school children. Five minutes pass, before the light disappears, and Christopher returns to his chair. Cowboy and Soul Man can not comprehend what has taken place, Christopher ignores them entirely.

Up until now, Christopher has suffered from uncontrollable swings in emotion—feeling very joyful and omnipotent at some times, then anxious, depressed, and persecuted at others. According to the psychiatrists, he suffers from acute hysteria and psychosis. After his encounter with the unknown entity, he has gained confidence that all is not delusion. He is calmer and in better control of his emotions. It becomes clear that the mastery of emotional control is the foundation of mind control. This realization allows him to control his swings of mood and mind. He develops the ability to, at will, grovel in the garbage of the individual subconscious, or soar to the incredible heights of the collective superconscious, where he gains enlightenment through conversation with the depository of humankind's most sublime knowledge.

Common sense also seems a by-product of Christopher's most recent changes. He wants to get out of the hospital, but in order to do that, he has to start talking to the psychiatrists, which means attending the therapy sessions.

At the first session the psychiatrist gives Christopher a series of tests. He calls off six numbers and asks Christopher to repeat them. He calls of another six numbers and asks Christopher to repeat them in reverse order. Everything that the psychiatrist asks of Christopher, he does flawlessly. The psychiatrist then goes down a list of routine questions:

"What is your age?"

"Twenty-nine."

"Have you ever been involved in a homosexual relationship?"

"No."

"Have you ever attempted suicide?"

"No."

"Have you ever thought about doing it?"

"No."

"Do you know why you are here?"

"Maybe I reached too high. I perceived infinity, and that caused my brain to go into overload." answers Christopher.

"You are here because of the use of drugs that affect your thinking."

"The effect on one's thinking can be a positive one."

"Any substance that makes you high can do damage to your brain cells."

"Any drug you prescribe has side effects . . . sometimes very damaging side effects, but you prescribe them anyway. You simply take care to monitor the dosages given so the benefits outweigh the disadvantages."

"There are no benefits to living in a world of delusion and fantasy."

"How can you be so sure it is all delusion and fantasy?"

"Because it is a departure from reality."

"It can lead you into other realities that I have found to exist."

"How can you be so sure?"

"How can you be so sure the book sitting on that table over there is real?"

"We can both see the book. There is agreement between us that it is there."

"If we both saw a ghost standing in this room, would that make it a part of reality?"

"No, of course not, but two people can experience the same delusion or fantasy."

"Well then, can we extend that idea by saying all or nearly all people can experience the same delusions."

"Theoretically, I would have to say yes."

"How then, can you distinguish between mass delusion and what you regard as reality? If you suddenly became blind, would you and everything in this room become my delusion simply because you lacked the eyes to see?"

The Psychiatrist pauses to think, gently tapping his pen on the table before responding, "I don't know the answers to all of your questions, but I have some friends who might. Would you mind if I invited them to our next session?"

"I suppose not."

After the session, Christopher takes a walk through the garden areas. He passes through the recreation room where Cowboy and Soul Man are engaged in a game of pool. "Hello." Christopher says in passing. The two of them do a double take.

Christopher has not said a single word to them since his big outburst. Before the two men can return the greeting, Christopher is through the door. There is a stretch of grass, and at the far edge of the grass is his favorite shade tree. He finds a comfortable spot under the tree and meditates. He ponders the life he has lived in a world of thieves, prostitutes, and dope pushers. A world in which he has been an active member, where attitudes tend to remain base and superficial, where no one contemplates matters more deeply than necessary to stay beyond the clutches of the authorities, or to avoid being shot by an enemy. "Such an existence is considered evil," he reasons. "But even there, some good can be found. Angela was no evil person, neither is Geronimo, or Camille for that matter. Bird and Squirrel have never tried to hurt anyone. They've only tried to earn a living for themselves within the confines of the world they know. Have we made mistakes? Probably. And that is our major crime. I've learned something from each one of them. I've learned that perceptions of good and evil are fleeting. Morals and values are what we choose them to be."

After about ten minutes he hears footsteps coming toward him. It is Cowboy and Soul Man. They stop a few feet short of Christopher and stand there, hesitating to say what is on their minds. Christopher voices it for them.

"You are both curious about the light we saw. Aren't you?"—Cowboy and Soul Man say nothing, but the answer is in their eyes, "Have a seat." offers Christopher. The two men rest on the grass as he continues: "Each one of us radiates the light of consciousness. All of our little lights add up to create one big light. This big light is the collective consciousness of humankind. Much activity goes on within the collective. The little lights play with each other on a very fine, but far reaching, level of existence called the subquantum level. On this level, they combine and mutate in different ways. Through all this playing of the lights, sometimes an entity, like the one we saw is created."

"You make it sound like something that's really there." says Cowboy.

"It's real . . . not in the way that we are, but in a way that is hard to understand, becoming more real as time passes, by growing and maturing. Each generation that lives and dies leaves behind a contribution to the collective. As humankind evolves, so evolves the collective, and everything that arises from it."

"Why can't anyone else see these things? asks Soul Man.

"Because our senses are more acute, and span beyond the range of normal human senses . . . traits commonly found in hysterics. We also have a strong intuitive sense working with our other senses of sight, sound, and what have you. We pick up on things other people can't . . . and I should warn you . . . the worst thing you can do is fear these things you see. Some of them actually feed on your fear. They are usually built up from the remains of wicked souls, and they will return time and again. So the key is to control your fear. There is nothing wrong with being afraid at the right time. Fear, after all, is one of the three primary emotions. The other two being love and hate. All other emotions are varying combinations of the three. Keep them in balance."

The three patients spend the remainder of the afternoon under the shade tree, talking about these matters in greater detail, and learning to become friends.

The psychiatrist makes good on his promise. Soon, he brings in three people from an interdenominational society of which he is a member. When Christopher goes to the therapy room he is introduced to three people. The first person is a Buddhist monk; the second, a Catholic priest; the third person, a physicist. These people are not here solely for Christopher's benefit: to answer the questions the psychiatrist was unable to. The psychiatrist has taken a special interest in this case. Christopher's ideas and special brand of logic intrigues him. The stigmata-like phenomenon of spontaneous, unexplainable bleeding might carry with it certain religious connotations. He hopes with the aid of these people, he will be better able to deal with other similar cases in the future. The psychiatrist directs his opening words to Christopher:

"I have briefed our consultants on the last session. Particularly your question about the nature of reality; specifically, how mass hallucinations differ from what we commonly regard as reality. Then he turns to the consultants, "Would any of you like to comment on that?"

"I'd like to say one thing." Begins the priest. "We should be concerned with only one reality besides our own, and that is the reality of God and heaven. Even then, we can never know God completely, and only after we have passed on can we truly know heaven. These are the only realities we need concern ourselves with, even if others were to exist. There are enough problems in this world. To worry about such things is fruitless, and has no purpose."

"I disagree. I believe man is destined to know all the realities he can possibly come to know." argues Christopher.

"Why?" asks the psychiatrist.

"For the same reason man has journeyed to the moon. It is our instinctual birthright. Heightened awareness, after all, is mainly what separates man from the other animals. If we choose to remain in our narrow band of perceived reality, eventually we will stagnate, and stagnation is the surest way to extinction."

"What are your religious beliefs, if I may ask?" inquires the priest.

"That would be difficult to define. Let's just say I believe in the Father, the Son, and the Holy Ghost. I also believe in the concept of a Christ and a Satan. I also believe that each person should embrace his own Christ and his own Satan and keep them in balance."

"Are you saying you believe evil is necessary or desirable?" the priest asks in a manner conveying both concern and disgust.

"I'm saying that to shun Satan is to cause him to go out to find a place somewhere else in society—and that creates an imbalance. Harmony is achieved when the opposites are equal. Concepts of good and evil are simply value judgments that vary from society to society, and from time to time. The Universal Christ is not totally good, nor is the Universal Satan totally evil. If that was not the case, and there really was such a thing as heaven and hell, then we would have to come up with a different heaven and a different hell for everyone."

"In your way of thinking what is the main difference between Christ and Satan?" asks the Priest.

"The ideal Universal Christ, by whatever name you wish to give Him, is totally constructive. The ideal Universal Satan is totally destructive. Both are implicit in a world where life leads to death, day rolls to night, and spring turns to autumn. We consider it evil to have more than one wife in our society, but the way the Muslims see it, if the woman is a widow with children who might otherwise starve, then the polygamous marriage is constructive. To execute a mass murderer might be socially acceptable, but it is a destructive act. The act of executing him, however, ensures he does not kill more people, making it a less destructive act than the worst alternative."

"The taking of a life is a sin, and those who would do such a thing will have to pay." warns the priest.

"That is a moral matter, taking us back to concepts of good and evil for which there is no universal agreement. I can not accept that all who execute murderers are doomed, any more than I can accept that all the billions of otherwise decent people who have not accepted Jesus Christ as their lord and savior are likewise doomed."

"Earlier you said that awareness is the main difference between man and animal. I gather your increased awareness has given you some special insight or knowledge. Would you care to go into more detail?" asks the psychiatrist.

"There are levels of existence farther removed from us than we are from the atom. If one can transcend to these levels, he can know things about the universe not presently within the realm of human knowledge."

"I don't doubt there are a lot of things that we don't know, but there are a few things we do know. We can look into space over hundreds of thousands of light years. We can determine the composition of stars. We can convert matter into energy, and create subatomic particles . . . Maybe all of what I'm saying doesn't make much sense to you, but the point I'm trying to make is this. A lot of research by the greatest minds, armed with state of the art scientific equipment has brought us to our present state of knowledge. It is not possible that you, through some mysterious means could hope for more! I don't think you really know what you're saying." expounds the physicist.

"I agree. Things have come a long way. You can calculate the mass of an electron, and the distance to far away stars. You have taken the atom, and broken it down into subparts. Not only have you discovered the existence of quarks and antiquarks, but you can classify them as having different 'colors' and 'flavors', and 'spins'. You have gone beyond relativity with quantum theory . . . but there is one thing you can not do. You can not explain the creation of the universe. Oh, you have a Big Bang theory all right . . . but then there is the question of the singularity that the whole theory relies on . . . and you are at a loss to explain its origin. Why? Because all of your laws of physics depend upon the existence of matter and energy. To go beyond that threshold, into the realm of preexistence, you need a science that can function in the absence of matter and energy. The science of transcending conscious levels can provide answers to questions about phenomena that predate the material universe."

"So what *is* the origin of the universe?" queries the physicist sardonically.

"To explain that I will first have to describe the force that exists in the absence of matter and energy. It is the Force of Infinite Possibilities—based on the principle that given an infinite number of opportunities for an event to occur, then the given event will inevitably occur." The physicist looks puzzled, so Christopher offers an interpretation. "Suppose we have a six sided die. Let's say we want to throw the number two. How many times do we have to throw the die to come up with the number two?"

"That would be difficult to answer." replies the physicist.

"Maybe six times? asks Christopher.

"Maybe. Maybe more, maybe less."

"Now let's imagine a hypothetical die with an infinite number of sides. How many throws would it now take to come up with the number two?"

"That would be impossible to say. Maybe never."

"Let's say the die was thrown an infinite number of times. Would the number come up then?"

"Perhaps equations could be worked up where the infinities cancel out . . . I suppose it's possible."

"Well, the infinite void of space is similar to the hypothetical die with an infinite number of sides. There are an infinite number of potential 'positive one-negative one' pairs in the Infinite Void. For any given potential pair, one of two things can happen: The potential pair can remain neutral, or it can divide into a particle/antiparticle pair. Overwhelmingly, the potential pairs will remain neutral, but there are an infinite number of them, and at least one possibility that the alternative will occur. The nature of infinite space is like throwing our special die over and over, throughout eternity, waiting for our number to come up. The difference is all the throws are made simultaneously. This is due to the fact that time does not exist in the Infinite Void, because the Infinite Void is changeless, and time is nothing more than the duration of change.

So, imagine if you will that in the beginning there was the Infinite Void, possessed of the three undefined characteristics: infinite length, infinite depth, and infinite width . . . at once, infinitely dimensioned, yet dimensionless. These three undefined characteristics are the Ultimate Trinity.

The Infinite Void is a highly unstable state. It implies infinite nothingness . . . but infinite nothingness has an opposite, and that opposite is infinite somethingness. Somethingness and nothingness seek to balance each other out. The Force of Infinite Possibilities approaches infinity under conditions of infinite nothingness. The Force thus applied generates the word, vibration, or cyclic dislocation that separates neutral space into particle/anti-particle pairs. Particles predominate in the positive time frame, and anti particles predominate in the negative time frame. The pairs do not annihilate because they exist in time sequences that move in reverse order relative to each other. They are like two would be lovers, perfect mates, who never meet because they are born centuries apart . . . wandering aimlessly, but at times evolving to higher forms in their search to regain perfection. The origin, or zero point of time and anti-time is the center of the black hole. The black hole exists by virtue of 'the other great force'.

Nothingness can be thought of as increasing the possibility of particles being driven into existence, giving rise to somethingness. For the sake of symmetry, if for no other reason, somethingness must have a force associated with it that complements the Force of Infinite Possibilities, and that force is 'the other great force' . . . the Force of Gravity, which arises by virtue of the existence of particles. Gravity attempts to squeeze particles out of existence. Fewer particles mean more nothingness, which causes more particles to be driven into existence. I am referring to only two gravities—the quantum variety, and the larger scale one we know from everyday experience in the same sense, but infinitely many others exist.

To put it another way, the two great forces each possess an infinite potential. As one force grows stronger, the other force grows stronger still. The potential difference between somethingness and nothingness increases without bound. The struggle for dominance between the two great forces continues throughout eternity, and the increased potential difference is what drives an infinite number of universes into existence, to infinitely higher orders of complexity. The potential difference I speak of here is not much different from the concept of voltage. In general, you need higher voltages to operate bigger machines. As seen from our vantage point, this same struggle for dominance manifests as a universal oscillation. This oscillation is the basis of the quantum effect, and is also the spirit that drives particles to evolve into matter/energy, matter/energy to evolve into biological life, and biological life to evolve into consciousness. All that we are, is the result of a periodic oscillation about the point of absolute zero."

"Many of your ideas sound similar to those found in theoretical physics, but not everyone is in agreement. How can you be sure these oscillations will continue throughout eternity? Don't you think there's some possibility they might just stop by way of some dynamic you haven't considered?" the physicist asks, intrigued, but reluctant to show it.

"Some people have come up with concepts such as 'pure duration', and 'slumber' in an attempt to qualify nonexistence, but as I said before, the Infinite Void is changeless and therefore timeless, this means that no time span can be assigned to it. No distinction can be made between one second, and a hundred billion years. 'Pure duration' either exists, or it doesn't. The life span of 'pure duration' is therefore either infinite, or not at all. Those are the only two possibilities. We have to accept the conclusion we exist, if so, then we are not in a state of 'pure duration'. It can then be said there was never a time when the material universe did not exist. Even if annihilation occurs, no time passes before it springs back into existence. The material universe has always existed, and always will. If one universe exists, then the others exist as well, because they are a natural progression or regression of each other—in other words, they are all interdependent. Notions of 'pure duration' and 'slumber' can be relegated to an imaginary non-time epoch of non-existence."

The Buddhist monk has been silent up to this point, but listening very intently. Of the group, he is the one with enough freedom of thought to easily grasp what Christopher is saying. The priest is inwardly struggling with these ideas within the confines of the dogma of his faith. The physicist is like a fish out of water, trying to deal with concepts which can not be assigned numbers. The monk now takes his turn:

"You speak of a beginning and an end, then you say the universe has always existed. Can both be true?"

"We are finite beings living on the outer edge of a three dimensional reference frame, proceeding steadily along a time line. The passage of time can be thought of as a phenomenon of our limited perception. From our standpoint, beginnings and endings are absolutes. If we were to move ourselves to the outer edge of the fourth dimension, things would look much different. Our perception broadens. The entire process would start appearing before us in one grand sweep. If we were to reach a vantage point in the fifth dimension, all the moments of eternity would become one. The beginning and the end are simply two of those moments. They also would merge into the one, and no distinction could then be made between them. The universe could then be said to have no beginning and no end. I will also say that just as there are an infinite number of universes, there are also an infinite number of vantage points, and from each of them things would look much different. In a sense, all that is or will ever be exists simultaneously on some level, but we should never expect to reach it, and that is why we will forever experience the passage of time on some scale, no matter what level of order we ascend to."

"You spoke of consciousness evolving from life. That is simple enough to understand, but what can we expect of consciousness on the next level of order?" asks the monk.

"The ultimate goal of consciousness is to fill the Infinite Void with its presence. Consciousness eventually becomes an omnipotent, omniscient being . . . in effect, God, and therefore lonely. Loneliness causes God to reach out into the Infinite Void and dream a new reality into existence. I should also say this: I speak of the Infinite Void as if it is a thing, but in fact, it is not. It is non-existence like 'pure duration', and therefore does not truly exist for us. It exists implicitly at the base of this great system of things. It is the cause of all that is. The cause manifests as reality, and the very presence of reality nullifies the Infinite Void as an explicit state of existence. Looking at it from our three dimensional, time dependent frame, it can be thought of as the moment between annihilation and re-creation."

"In Asia we have ancient thought systems that deal with many of the same issues you do." adds the monk.

"I am a great admirer of ancient Chinese thought. The principle of the Yin and Yang is so pure and simple, yet sublime that its significance tends to escape the modern mind . . . The Yang sends its seed forth and plants it into the womb of the Yin. The copulation of the Yin and the Yang produces life from which springs enlightenment. Enlightenment flowers to Godhead and becomes one, therefore lonely."

"Lonely enough to create a new world?" asks the monk.

"Yes, I believe so."

Then the physicist jumps in, "Look, you tell the priest you believe in the Father, the Son, and so and so. You give me some high sounding brand of pseudo scientific theory. Now you tell the monk about the Yin and Yang. No offense, but you tell every one what they want to hear. You should decide exactly what it is you stand for, and then stick to it."

The priest agrees adding, "You should strive to be more consistent in your beliefs. You might even consider accepting Jesus Christ as your lord and savior. He will then show you the way, and eliminate all confusion."

The Buddhist monk says nothing. He simply gazes at Christopher with a slight smile on his face. Christopher looks at the others in despair, then says, "But I have told you all essentially the same thing!" The priest and the physicist along with the psychiatrist appear confused. Christopher continues, "The Yang is identical to the Father, and the Force of Infinite Possibilities. The Yin is the Force of Gravity. The seed that the Yang sends forth is the matter/energy that arises from neutrality. The seed finds a home in the womb of the Yin, in other words, attracted by the gravitational force. The copulation between the Yin and the Yang, the Possibilities and Gravity, or the androgynous Father leads to the birth of the Son, or the material universe. The enlightenment or consciousness that evolves and flowers to Godhead is the Holy Ghost."

"Well, all right, maybe there are parallels . . . but as a physicist I have to say that other than a theoretical statement on probability, you haven't provided anything that couldn't be dreamed up, nothing a scientist can work with."

"Fine then. I will give you something you can work with . . . something involving numbers that can be entered into a calculator. I will say this: If humankind survives long enough for the free energy flux density of the brain to reach two raised to the twenty second power ergs per gram-second, then human consciousness will pass into the next great stage of cosmological evolution."

"And how did you arrive at that?"

"I examined scientific data on the free energy flux densities of all the major evolutionary structures: the universe, the Milky Way Galaxy, the sun, Earth's climasphere, Earth's biosphere, the human body, and finally the human brain. I took these numbers and expressed them each as the number two raised to the nearest power. The numbers I derived in this way do not correspond precisely with the scientific approximations. There are two reasons for this: one, the scientific calculations are only approximations, and two, the changes that occur, especially in the more complex systems are cyclical, which means that the numbers fluctuate over time. What I found is, starting with the sun, the exponents increase in alternating steps of five and three. I call it the five-three exponential progression of evolution.

When the human brain first emerged, it had a free energy flux density of two raised to the seventeenth power ergs per gram-second, and is steadily increasing. It has the highest value of anything known to us. The sun is only two raised to the first power, or simply two. What this means . . ." Directing his next statement to the monk and priest. ". . . is if the human mind had the mass of the sun, and fluxed all of its energy in the form of visible light, it would shine at least sixty-five thousand times brighter! If the pattern is carried out to the next step, we can see that the next great change occurs when a system reaches two to the twenty second. Using the same analogy as before, with the sun, we can say the new system would shine over two million times brighter than our own sun! Humankind has the chance of becoming truly a god. Manifestations now regarded as delusion and fantasy would evolve into an undisputed reality in their own right. It would then be clear that reality, as we now know it, is the ripened fruit of imagination."

"You are saying humans might not reach that level? asks the monk.

"That is correct. There are no guarantees that humans or the descendants of humans will ever become the bearer of this highly exalted torch. To a great extent, it is up to us. If we remain stubbornly stagnated in our beliefs in the names of faith and conviction, then the chances are slim, if at all. If, on the other hand, we strive to embrace total existence and come to know it on all possible levels, then we greatly increase our level of awareness, and the chances are good. Language has been defined as the ability to communicate about communicating. I submit to you that higher consciousness is the ability to be conscious of consciousness. In this respect, we are much closer to the beginning than the end."

"Well okay, you've given me some numbers, but how can you be so sure the pattern is really a pattern and not just a coincidence?"

"It is the business of transcendental magicians, mystics, and the like to consider the possibilities, unfettered by preconceived notions . . . to explore the boundaries of science and beyond. You are the scientist. It is your job to separate truth from falsehood and to present the truth in a form that all can except. In this way we push the boundaries of science toward a more ultimate truth."

The panel of experts came with the intention of helping Christopher to understand the nature of his problems. Instead, they find themselves pitted against a system of ideas they did not expect, even drawn in at times to Christopher's philosophy. They are now tired and weary. The physicist sits with his hand on his chin, lost in a world of thought. The psychiatrist is in a daze, grappling with his own standard of reality, constantly having to remind himself he is dealing with a patient and not some guest speaker. Only the Buddhist monk appears relaxed and resolved. Sensing the discussions are nearing an end he tells Christopher, "I am honored to have been given the opportunity to hear you speak. What you say gives one much to think about. I hope one day our paths will cross again."

"Well, I think that just about does it. You're welcome to stay longer, or leave as you wish." the psychiatrist tells Christopher.

"I'll leave you to discuss this among yourselves." Christopher rises from his chair, smiles to everyone, and leaves the therapy room. His first stop is the lounge. The old man sits in a chair against the wall, chewing his sleeve as always. Cowboy is watching television. Christopher takes a seat near the television.

"You were in there a long time." observes Cowboy.

"They had a lot to say." replies Christopher.

"Are you cured yet?"

"Probably not." The two men then laugh.

"Oh hell! The television's acting up again."

"Here, let me try something." Christopher says as he directs the finger tips of his right hand toward the television set. The screen instantly stops rolling.

"I'll be damned! How did you do that?"

"It's energy from the body. Everyone has it . . ." Christopher now takes notice of the television broadcast. A famous singer was killed—shot in the head by a close family member. This news affects Christopher in more ways than one. Not only was the singer one of his favorite entertainers, also, he knows the drugs he sold often ended up in the hands of this unfortunate and troubled, but highly talented person. He can only hope his enterprise did not contribute to the singer's early demise. The thought of a gunshot wound to the head evokes images of Mr. Panama lying in his grave, and a deeply troubled look comes over Christopher's face.

"What's the matter? Did you know this guy?" asks Cowboy, observing Christopher's distress.

"No. Not really . . . I'm going to take a walk outside. Would you like to come?"

"Might as well. I don't have anything else to do."

When they get outside they find Soul Man lingering around the rose bushes.

"Hey man, what are you looking at?" Cowboy inquires of Soul Man.

"I'm just watching these bees. It's something else how they all work together, and know exactly what to do."

"Instinct is an amazing thing." remarks Cowboy.

"What do you suppose instinct really is?" queries Soul Man.

"I don't really know." admits Cowboy. They turn to Christopher.

"Do you remember when we talked about collective consciousness?" asks Christopher. The two men acknowledge they do. "The collective conscious is an extension of our long term memories. It holds the long term memories of the entire group. If everyone in the group learns how to do a particular task extremely well, then that task tends to become imprinted in the group's collective conscious more deeply than a task that is not. Over many generations of relearning the task, the collective conscious evolves to exert increasingly more control over the nervous systems of the individuals in the group. The net effect is that the task becomes easier to learn over time by succeeding generations. If the group performs the task for a long enough period of time, they reach a point where no learning is necessary. In other words, it becomes instinct. We see it today in children who instinctively step over cracks in the sidewalk. They are responding to lessons learned long ago not to step on anything resembling a snake. These bees are controlled almost totally by their collective conscious. It looks as if they're born knowing what to do, and in a way they are, but really it's their collective conscious."

"Maybe they just pass it down from one generation to the next through their genes." suggests Soul Man.

"They can't." answers Christopher.

"Why not?"

"Because the worker bees don't breed."

The three say nothing for several moments. They just watch the bees busily working. Christopher continues, "I think that we should learn to accept being crazy."

"You mean stay in this place for the rest of our lives?" asks Cowboy doubtingly.

"No. What I mean is this: If we have the visions, we should keep them to ourselves, and not let any one else know. We can be crazy by their standards, but they don't have to know we're crazy. Do you guys follow what I'm saying?"

"Yeah, we follow what you're saying, but sometimes the visions catch me by surprise, and I feel like I'm going to lose it." confesses Soul Man.

"I'll guide both of you through the world that others can't see. The more familiar you become with it, the less you will fear it. I will show you ways of keeping your sensitive energies in balance. If you find yourself drifting too far away, you need to know how to return to your base . . . be it Jesus Christ, or the Merciful Allah, or whatever. I will show you how to keep harm from coming to yourselves."

"You just said something about being able to find our base. I'm just curious. What's your base?" asks Cowboy.

"I follow my own path. I call it the path of Trikrisaton. It represents me and my connection to the cosmos."

Cowboy and Soul Man do not attempt to judge or ask questions. They simply accept the offer.

"It's best done in a quiet place, where we won't be disturbed, but that might be a problem . . . well, we'll figure something out."

"I know how to get into the attic. Would that work?" offers Soul Man.

"Yes. I believe it would. We can try to meet there tonight." suggests Christopher.

That night, when all are asleep, the three men creep to a small room that no one ever uses. In the far corner of the room is a three square foot removable panel in the ceiling. With the aid of a chair to stand on, Soul Man removes the panel and climbs up through the opening. He then helps Cowboy and Christopher. The inside of the attic is totally dark and smells of old dust. It still holds some of the heat of the day, but it will do for their purposes. They take positions on the floor facing each other.

Here, night after night, the mad philosophers meet. The attendant knows something is going on, but sensing it harmless and maybe even beneficial, chooses to look the other way. Christopher teaches them the quintessence of transcendental magic. He shows them how to move through the levels of consciousness horizontally and vertically, then out into the vast ocean of the quantum field with its many wonders. He explains the elusive, ambivalent nature of the quantum field and how they might utilize it to gain insight and knowledge. He gives them the methods and procedures they might use to reach these goals by performance of the Four Rites:

The Rite of Passover—to ward off overwhelmingly destructive forces. If ever needed, it should be performed at the height of psychological turmoil, and then only if you feel compelled to do so with all your heart and soul.

The Rite of Progression—the path to the light by way of the outer self. Consciousness is directed to the far reaches of existence. Here, the dimension of time can be transcended. The great hazard of performing this rite is that one can transcend the quantum realm and become lost in the Infinite Void.

The Rite of Resurrection—a means of summoning the dead. In this rite, the operator communicates with the part of a person's consciousness that survives within the collective after death. It is advised not to disturb the dead unless absolutely necessary.

The Rite of Regression—the path to the light by way of the inner self. This rite can take one back to the womb, or even further through the ancestral line, to the beginning of time. If carried out to the extreme, it will lead one into the Infinite Void, and for that reason can be dangerous.

Christopher cautions them not to accept everything he says as the final word. He makes them understand there is still much he does not know. He advises them to take only that which seems reasonable, then find their own answers to the rest. He helps them realize humans are the most potent force in this region of the Universe, and it is our destiny to inherit the power of godlike conscious ability to bring about change, evolving into beings that exist independently of matter yet bound to the whole as all things ultimately are.

The day comes when Christopher is called in for his last therapy session. It is a one-on-one meeting with the psychiatrist.

"It has been decided you will soon be released—probably in a couple of days." begins the psychiatrist.

"So, do you think I am cured?"

"I'm not altogether sure. I believe you still experience what you call manifestations from other levels of reality, and even welcome them with no apparent desire for wanting them to go away. However, you seem to keep it all under control. You have not shown yourself to be a danger to society."

"I can't help it if I see and hear the world differently."

"You know, you're a very intelligent person, and you present some very interesting arguments, but the fact is, this a very competitive world we live in. In order to be successful in it, you have got to tune into it totally, which means tune the other worlds out. We could not function as a society if everyone lived in your unseen world."

"I agree, society could not function if everyone suddenly shifted to a different reality, but the fact is, there are some people who touch on other realities and come back with something to offer humanity—artists, philosophers, and prophets for example."

"Do you see yourself as one of these people?"

"I see myself as maybe being born at the wrong time."

"If you can find an occupation that allows you to profit from these tendencies, then I might say fine. For the vast majority of people however, that is not the case. It is better to center one's self within the established norm."

"Now you see, that is precisely the problem. You, along with the psychologists try to establish these norms and then cram everyone into them. Growth and development is not about permanent norms. It is about anomalies, mutations, and ever changing norms. If that were not the case we would not even be here. If Ezekiel was alive today, he would be in a straight jacket. If Jesus Christ himself appeared, you would straight jacket him, or else declare him a mass hallucination. You claim to want to know your gods, but your fear prevents it. You should realize that the best way of knowing is by becoming."

"The subconscious is a very dangerous thing and tampering with it can be disastrous."

"Tampering with the collective subconscious can bring about even more disastrous results. We have seen it with Hitler in World War II. If humankind is not careful, if it does not confront and reconcile itself with deeply hidden savage subconscious tendencies, then a mass psychosis of cataclysmic proportions will emerge. People will then realize that World War II was a mere prelude to the worst that can happen. The advanced human of the future must have the ability to perceive all levels of consciousness safely, and to transcend them freely. You should be able to distinguish between the truly diseased and those with heightened perceptions. The first group requires a cure. The second group needs to learn how to overcome their fears and develop a means of inner control."

"Those are your speculations. I can not know for sure whether they are right or wrong, but I do wish you the best of luck." says the psychiatrist, ending the session.

The day of Christopher's release arrives. He and his two friends, Cowboy, and Soul Man take one last walk down the garden path. It is both a happy and sad occasion, marking the end of a very special period in their lives. Cowboy is the most emotional as he makes a confession: "All my life I've been around people who taught me to hate blacks . . . as far back as I can remember. I got it from my parents, my friends, everybody. I don't know if I'll every change completely. It's hard to get rid of ideas that have been with you from day one . . . but I do know one thing. I don't hate you guys."

"You're all right Cowboy." affirms Soul Man.

Christopher takes his turn: "I appreciate what you are saying, and I respect you for being able to admit it. I guess we all just do the best we can with what we are given to work with. Just promise me one thing."

"What's that?"

"Promise me you won't pass the hate on to your children."

"That much I *can* promise you."

"When we're all out of here we should start some kind of organization." suggests Soul Man.

"I like that idea, but we'd better not." replies Christopher. "If we ever became noticed, they would see us as a cult, and cults are viewed as a threat to the government. They would do whatever they could to destroy us. It might be better if we all strive to help others on an individual basis. If you run into someone with the gift of 'the sight' as we have it, and if that person seems to be losing his mind or is frightened over things he does not understand, then help him, teach him, and encourage him to do the same for someone else."

Christopher reaches into a pocket and pulls out three folded sheets of paper, each with an identical drawing on it. He hands one of the drawings to each of his friends, and keeps one for himself. "I want you guys to keep this and never lose it. In this drawing is contained the symbology for all the concepts and ideas we discussed. I call this the Seal of Trikrisaton, but you may call it whatever you wish. If you ever feel the urge, just stop what you are doing and take a look at it. In time, with study, you will come to know what all of the symbols mean. One day, we will all look at the seal at the same time. We'll know, because we'll feel the connection." Christopher then embraces each of the two men in a display of true brotherly love and affection, says his last good-bye and departs.

On his way out he sees the old man sitting in a wheelchair chewing the sleeve of his shirt. Christopher goes to the old man. He gazes at him momentarily, then takes his left index finger and places the tip of it at the top of the old man's head. He runs his finger down to an area just below the center of the old man's forehead before pulling it away. The old man stops chewing, and drops his hand into his lap. Christopher smiles at the old man, then continues out through the gates.

11

THE VIRTUE OF SELF-PITY

Christopher passes through the main gate and out to the road where he waits for a bus. As he waits, he thinks about Camille and Geronimo. He feels badly about the way he treated them. He had tried calling them after he came back to his senses, but the telephone was disconnected. "Maybe she just got the number changed. It will be good to see them again." he thinks to himself.

It is a four and one half hour ride back to his neighborhood, with three bus changes. When he arrives, he finds his old apartment occupied by strangers. Camille has moved. "She must have found a better apartment somewhere nearby." he reasons. "I'll go over and see Geronimo. I have a lot of things to tell him anyway." Christopher walks about a mile to his friend's house, but finds he also has moved. Now he is becoming worried. "There's got to be someone who can tell me where they are! I'll go to Brim's house. Brim will know." Christopher arrives at Brim's house. He knocks on the door. The door opens. He feels relieved to find a familiar face.

"Hey Brim! What's happening?"

Brim stands silent for a moment, then a smile comes over his face, but it is not really a smile. It is more akin to the prelude of laughter. "Well, well! If it ain't the Wizard of South Central!" Brim says laughingly. "Man, I didn't think I'd ever see you again. I thought you had gone too far over the deep end."

"Maybe it seemed that way, but I'm back. Do you know where I can find Camille or Geronimo?"

"Last I heard, Geronimo got a construction job up in Palmdale or Lancaster. As for Camille . . . well, word has it a mean, dirty pimp got a hold of her and took her out of town, but I don't know where to."

"You mean she just disappeared?"

"Seems that way."

"How long ago?"

"I'd say about two or three months back. Well anyway, they asked me to hold on to your car for you. It's in the back. Come on, I'll show it to you." They go to the back of the house owned by Brim's grandmother. The car is parked outside the garage. It is dirty, but otherwise intact. "I take it out for a drive every now and then. It's a little hard to start, but it still runs. Here's the keys." Brim says as he takes them out of his pocket and hands them to Christopher. "Look man, I don't mean to rush you, but I have some business to take care of . . . you know how it is."

"Yeah, I know how it is." answers Christopher, knowing a put off when he hears one. "I want to thank you for holding on to my ride."

"Hey, no problem."

Christopher gets into his car, starts it, and drives away. He cruises up and down the streets, circling the same blocks many times, then decides to go down by the pool hall. On the corner he sees another familiar face. Bird is standing there holding a conversation with three other guys. Christopher stops his car. Bird recognizes the car, thinking at first that it is Brim. His head hangs to the right as he looks harder. He realizes it is not Brim, but Christopher. Bird turns to the other three guys, says something to them, and breaks out laughing. Everyone in the neighborhood thinks Christopher is crazy. No one takes him seriously.

Christopher drives away with absolutely nowhere to go, and only forty dollars in his pocket. Somehow, he ends up on the west bound Santa Monica Freeway. He drives until he reaches the beach, and there he parks. He removes his shoes, and takes a long walk along the shore. Here, it is peaceful and pleasant, allowing him to think things through a bit. He stops to kneel down, and scoop up a handful of wet sand. In the sand he finds a sand crab. "I might have to start eating these." he jokes to himself, returning the sand crab to its home. A few sea gulls circle over head, diving down into the water occasionally. Christopher wonders if he might not be better off as a sea gull or a sand crab.

His thoughts go to Camille. Her disappearance leaves him with a great sense of loss, an emptiness he did not anticipate. "How could she just disappear without saying anything?" he asks himself, but knows it is he who is at fault. "I've got to make some money . . . I'll find a job . . . that's it . . . tomorrow I'll start early. I'll search really hard and accept the first offer that comes along. Tonight I'll sleep in the car. One night won't kill me."

Christopher stays at the beach until well after the sun has set. He has a hamburger for dinner, then searches for a suitable place to park for the night, finding a street in the industrial area of Culver City that will serve his purpose. It is fairly quiet and secluded, but not so much so that his presence should attract attention. It is a difficult night—the car seats are uncomfortable, there is not enough room to stretch out, and the weather is cold. Periodically, between naps, Christopher starts the engine to heat the car.

The night mercifully passes. By morning, his body aches from trying to sleep in all sorts of contorted positions. His eyes feel grainy and his mind is hazy, but he forces himself awake enough to start the car and drive away. He uses the men's room in a fast food restaurant to wash up, has a little breakfast, then buys a newspaper to begin his search for work. Sitting in his car in the parking lot of a convenience store, he peruses the employment ads. "Damn! Everybody wants experience . . . even for janitorial work. I worked in a bank once. Maybe I can try that." he thinks. "Here's a position for a teller. I can stretch the truth a little bit and tell them I did some telling before."

Christopher has a decent shirt in his knapsack, but no tie. He stops to buy a tie on his way to the bank. When he arrives at the bank a receptionist gives him an application to complete. He fills in his name, and freezes at the next line. He realizes he has no home address or phone number. Clearly this is a problem with no immediate solution. He returns the application to the receptionist, telling her he will have to return, then departs. The world has suddenly receded for Christopher. All the activities on the street— the noise, the cars and people passing by seem far away. Christopher feels he is in a separate world. The greater world goes on about its business without him, completely oblivious to his plight.

It is obvious he will be spending at least one more night in his car. In anticipation of another cold night, he buys a blanket at a thrift shop. That night, he is so tired the uncomfortable car seats do not matter. He at least stays warm and sleeps better than the night before.

Day after day, Christopher runs into brick walls. Life becomes a succession of failures. What was initially panic turns to self doubt, finally giving way to despair. He supplements his dwindling dollars with change earned from collecting bottles and cans, reaching a point where he has to choose between putting gas in the car, and eating. He chooses the latter. The car is ticketed for a parking violation. In time, a notice to tow the vehicle away is issued. Christopher walks to the gas station with an empty plastic jug and his last eighty-five cents to purchase some gas. He returns to the car with the gas, but receives another blow. The battery is dead.

The next morning, cold and hungry, he gathers enough cans and bottles to make a telephone call to a junk yard, telling them that he has a car to sell. He answers a man's questions, informing him the car runs but the battery is dead. The man tells him he considers the car not running, and he would be paid the standard fee. Christopher sells the car for a pittance at seventy-five dollars.

A bed and some hot food would be a great relief. Christopher knows where some of the cheapest rooms can be gotten in an area of downtown Los Angeles. The area encompasses the garment district, where in his heyday, Christopher would frequently go with his ladies to shop for fine clothing. He has a good meal before heading out on the cross town bus journey that ends at Main Street, downtown Los Angeles, otherwise known as Skid Row. He finds his way through the door of a flop house, walking across a creaking wooden floor to a caged reception desk. Inside the cage sits a clerk. The man seems more like a zombie and appears disgusted because his idle state is being interrupted. The hotel clerk reluctantly goes through the motions of renting out a room.

Christopher takes the keys, walks up a flight of stairs that also creak, then down a hallway to the third room on the right. The room is furnished with a table, chair, bed, and night stand. The bed consists of a thin mattress placed over a basic metal spring frame. The pillow is as flat as a pancake from years of use. A sickly smell lingers in the air, but the olfactory sense will soon adjust. Christopher collapses on the bed, barely getting his shoes off before drifting away to the relief that deep slumber provides.

Later that night Christopher awakens to the sound of voices outside the window. He stumbles to the window and opens it. Two men are arguing in the alley below him. One of the men tries to take something from the other. There is the sound of glass breaking. One of the men starts screaming obscenities, while the other man sounds to be closer to tears. Apparently they were fighting over a bottle of wine, and now they are both left to do without the highly prized beverage. Christopher closes the window, leaving the thirsty fellows to work out their differences in private. He turns on the light, and notices the room for the first time. The walls are badly cracked and peeling of old, mottled wallpaper. The colors they once were can only be guessed. Plaster is missing from part of the ceiling, and other sections appear ready to fall at any time. This is a dwelling that used to be, and should be no more.

Christopher drops into the chair, staring at the hole in the ceiling, the sound of the arguing becoming fainter as the two drunks move farther down the alley. His body slumps forward. His head hangs low. He buries his face in his hands, and asks, "Dear God, why am I here? Why am I left so all alone . . . so hopelessly trapped in this hellhole . . . this pitiful existence to wallow in so much misery? Bottles breaking . . . people screaming and shedding tears over a bottle of cheap wine. Is that to be my fate as well?

"Fate. Fate and destiny. Now those are interesting concepts to ponder. I suppose it would be reasonable to say that as an orphan the cards were already stacked up against me, but that is no excuse. I once heard of an infant who was found in a trash can, and later grew up to become a judge. Most of us are born with hearts of gold, but the harsh realities of the world can turn that heart into stone. I guess the judge was lucky."

Nature calls and Christopher must leave his room to seek out the toilet. He passes a room with the door opened. There are several older men inside sitting around a table. The sound of a small radio mixes in with their half-drunken talk and laughter. Christopher finds the bathroom at the far end of the hall. He is startled when he sees a man sitting on the floor of the bathroom with his back against the wall. His eyes, sunken and closed, oblivious to the world. His face pale, cheeks hollow, and lower lip hung to reveal gums of an unnatural color. The man sits on his right hand, while the other arm is soaked with blood. Near the bloody arm is a medicine dropper, razor blade, spoon, and matches.

Apparently, the man did not have a hypodermic needle to administer his drug. The cut in his vein is so large he can not stop bleeding. Already a cadaver, yet still breathing, barely, as if defying the inevitable fact of death. The sight makes Christopher sick to his stomach, but he manages to take some toilet tissue and use it to apply pressure to the wound long enough for the bleeding to stop. Then he wonders if he really did the man a favor.

As he returns to his room a voice calls out, "Hey Red!" Christopher stops at the open doorway. "Come on in and have a little taste with us." It is the first invitation of any kind anyone has extended to Christopher in recent times. He is not likely to turn down their offer. "Bring your chair so you can have somewhere to sit." another man says. He returns with his chair. The man who extended the invitation introduces himself as Tyree, a man whose mouth seems to curl upwards, while his nose and browridge curl downward; the upper and lower features struggling for a confrontation somewhere in the center, like soft clay that has been squeezed from top and bottom. He hands Christopher a disposable cup and invites him to pour himself a drink. At the center of the table is a half-full gallon bottle of cheap bourbon. Christopher introduces himself as he pours a drink.

Over the course of a couple of hours Christopher learns something of each man. Tyree is a sometime golf caddie from Arkansas. He has an animated personality and a tenor pitch that turns his thick, southern drawl into a colorful tapestry of expression. His greatest accomplishment in life is to have survived a pitchfork injury clear through his body. He bears the scars as proudly as a soldier wears his battle wounds. In Tyree's case, the battle was over a woman, and the bearer of the pitchfork was the woman's husband.

There is Alonzo—tall, thin, and erect—a retired railroad worker now in his seventies. He clings to Skid Row as a vested jewel from the past, recalling its heyday when the passenger trains stopped often. The area at that time had a vibrant night life of a caliber that attracted people from all walks of life.

Lumpky is perhaps the most mentally imbalanced of the group. When he is not rubbing his mustache or adjusting his glasses, he tries to impress the others with his command of the English language, articulating words with the assuredness of a scholar, but usually lacking much meaning as a complete thought. Every so often he gets into an argument with one of the others over some trivial matter. He becomes angry, reaching for the radio to use as a weapon. He never follows through with his threats, so the others pay him no mind. Lumpky's wife had died recently. Rumor has it he suffocated her with a pillow. Apparently, Lumpky had met a younger woman who needed a place to live, and Lumpky wanted his wife out of the way. It wasn't long, though, before the younger woman moved on, leaving Lumpky all alone to contemplate the sinister deed he vehemently denies.

There is a fourth man who is a different type again. His name is Archie. He has powerful-looking arms, and a pot belly. His voice is deep and soft, like an orchestral bass. Archie preaches on the street corners of downtown Los Angeles by day for donations. By night he drinks the donations away. He is like a child trapped in a massive exterior, and his emotions run accordingly. As he passes through the stages of drunkenness he laughs and teases the others, recites passages from the bible, then withdraws for a while only to start crying for no apparent reason, mumbling things no one can understand.

Christopher can not keep up with the drinking of the other men. He excuses himself after a couple of hours and thanks them. He returns to his room feeling lifted by the fact he has made contact with people who can accept him at face value, with no strings attached.

With the exception of going out for food, he spends the entire following day in his room. In the evening he pays his new found friends a visit. Only Archie is missing. An hour passes and everyone wonders where he is. Christopher offers to check Archie's room. He goes down the hall and knocks on the door several times. There is no answer. He turns the knob and the door opens. As he walks into the room, a terrible odor hits him. Looking across the room, he sees Archie sprawled out on the bed, naked, and maybe asleep or unconscious, but more likely in a drunken stupor. Archie must have lost control of his bodily functions. Feces are smeared on the floor leading up to the bed and on the sheets of the bed itself. The disgusting smell of his digestive waste is made more pungent by the huge intake of wine and liquor. Christopher closes the door and returns to the others telling them simply, "It looks as if Archie is out for the count."

Christopher offers to contribute some money to help pay for the liquor, but the men refuse to accept it. They are happy to have someone new around to listen to their tales. The men feel a need to pass their hard learned wisdom on, and Christopher, as the youngest, makes a befitting benefactor. They speak of their past victories and conquests, their dids, their didn'ts, their should haves, and wishes. Christopher imagines, "They probably started out with all the ambition, vitality, and vigor that life can offer. Somehow things just didn't work out. The world certainly does take its toll."

The gathering breaks up early this evening, even though it is Friday night. Tyree is heading out to the golf course early in the morning. Christopher, in the hope of finding work for himself asks if he can come. Tyree is more than happy to bring him along, and teach him the ropes.

That night, Christopher lies in bed, unable to sleep. He faintly hears a noise, a strange surreal noise not of this world. Not the tinkling sound of bells he had heard in the past, but the sound of marching feet. The cadence is menacing and ominous. He hears a chant along with the marching, an evil chant, the devil's chant. Christopher feels certain the evil eye is upon him. It surrounds him, encloses him, but does not invade him. In time, the sound fades away and he goes to sleep.

The caddie and his protégé leave at four o'clock the next morning. The golf course is quite a distance away in the San Fernando Valley. They want to arrive early so as to increase their chances of getting work. When they arrive, Tyree takes

Christopher into the caddie room where he maintains a locker. He pulls an extra pair of golf shoes from the locker, and hands them to Christopher. The shoes are a bit small, but they will have to do. They return outside, standing around with many other caddies, waiting to be called to service. Over the course of the day all the caddies are called—all that is, except Christopher, who watches as the caddies returning from the earlier games return to the course for the later games. The supervisor rejects him for lack of experience.

Christopher does not have enough money to pay for his room the following day. So that evening, he announces to Tyree and the others he will be leaving for a while. At checkout time on the following morning he throws his knapsack on his shoulder and walks down the battered wooden stairs for the last time, being careful not to run his hand along the time battered banister for fear of splinters. The lethargic clerk barely shows acknowledgment when Christopher hands him the keys through an opening in the crude looking cage.

From there, he disappears out onto the streets and walks around for hours. He sees a woman pushing a shopping-basket full of dirty plastic bags and old cardboard. "That woman must be crazy. She's hoarding sheer junk." he thinks, then he sees a working woman of the day stop to offer the crazy lady some money. The crazy lady refuses to accept it.

He continues wandering for hours more. The feeling that goes through him is similar to the way he felt when he first stepped off the bus on Main Street—the feeling of loneliness, having no one to talk to, no where to go, and now without a room or car, no where to hide. People all around him, but looking past him, through him, above him, or pretending so.

As night time comes the working people of the day go home and the homeless people appear in greater numbers. They are busy setting themselves up for the night. Seeking whatever partial shelter they can find, such as the enclave of a building or a shop canopy. Many of them arrange their makeshift beds on the sidewalk and line up for nearly the entire length of the block against drab, run down buildings, like sardines in a can. Christopher can now appreciate the value of plastic bags and cardboard. They are excellent for insulating one's body against the cold. He goes out in search of his own cardboard and plastic.

In the days that follow, he has no choice but to scavenge the dumpsters of restaurants for food. What money he can scrape together from washing the windshields of automobiles, and selling bottles and cans, he uses to buy the simulated sleep of drunken unconsciousness. This becomes the daily cycle. He is now dreadfully tired of the bullshit of life, even losing his desire to keep clean.

Christopher survives the first winter, but desperately hopes he will not have to go through a second. His heart aches and his spirit weeps. Days turn into years, and hope turns into defeat. The hard life and heavy drinking take their toll. He feels himself becoming weaker and weaker as his health declines. He suffers memory blackouts sometimes for days on end. At times, he partially returns to his senses, and finds his skin dry, scaly, and hanging loose on his body, a consequence of the terrible, progressive effects of alcohol abuse. His kidneys are pained, and his urine possesses a dark, brownish cast—the sign of liver destruction.

The alternative to being drunk however, is to feel the full intensity of the pain—a deep, gripping pain that reaches down through the throat, past the stomach to the guts—a relentless, wrenching sensation that causes the breath to become erratic or difficult . . . then, wanting again and again to cry tears that will not come—feeling the pain that will not go away—living the life that will not end.

Money is more difficult to come by at some times than at others. Such is the case near the end of a cold winter several years down the line when Christopher is thirty-eight years old. Finding himself unable to maintain his alcohol intake, he becomes frantic, but has no other choice than to face the reality he wants so desperately to avoid.

Day after grueling day, Christopher roams the streets, feeling lost and desperate. The effects of alcohol withdrawal have him in a nervous frenzy. Against his most fervent desires, the dense fog slowly lifts from his mind to reveal a fuzzy, impressionistic representation of his blighted surroundings—like an experimental Monet painting gone awry. The fog continues to lift. His vision becomes blurry, then sharpens to reveal a decadent Rembrandt. He gazes deeply into the sullen faces that have begun to line the streets just before nightfall. The external images on the streets coalesce with the inner images of his mind, like a collage, creating within him moods and thoughts that emerge as a soliloquy, faintly mumbled through broken, parched lips before a ghostly audience.

"As I walk up and down these dismal streets, I see faces of disappointment, hopelessness, and despair . . . faces I have seen all my life, but have never known . . . only here, tending to the extreme. Faces I have seen, but failed to understand. Faces deeply lined, if not wrinkled . . . the corners of the mouths curved downward in homage to dreams lost . . . with brows tightly knitted above eyes drawn tightly that can no longer cry . . . shed tears.

"As I walk along, I contemplate: how sad is this fate that crushes the human spirit, and how reckless a life one lives can be. I continue further and turn down a street. There, I come upon a window. I gaze through the window and into a room where I see another face of disappointment, hopelessness, and despair . . . a face deeply lined, if not wrinkled . . . mouth curved downwards, and brows tightly knitted above eyes drawn tightly. I gaze a little longer until I notice that beyond the window, there is a mirror . . . then I realize to my horror, the face is a reflection of me."

The revelation leaves Christopher with much to think about—He needs seclusion, but has trouble finding it. Darkness falls, and still he searches for a suitable place to spend the night. He ends up settling far short of his hopes, taking instead a spot under a long row of canopies near the flower district among many other people.

As Christopher lies in a cocoon of plastic and cardboard he vows to pull himself together—to cut down on his drinking and feel the brunt of his existence, if that is the way it has to be. His body has lost much of its sensitivity to the harsh environment, but is physically weakened nevertheless. His liver and kidneys are damaged, but can recover. He mostly has to deal with his emotional state. Feelings and thoughts drowned out by the years of drinking begin to well up within him. Turmoil becomes his nocturnal companion. Night after night, he has trouble sleeping. The sounds of the evil chant and marching feet return from years past. It is, at times, so real to him he is surprised to find no one there. He can even sense the direction of its movement.

One night, unable to take it any longer, he decides to follow the sounds. They prove difficult to follow, passing diagonally across streets and through buildings. For all his efforts, he is unable to keep up with the movement and reaches a point of exhaustion. He collapses against a building to catch his breath before returning to his sleeping place. Just then, he hears the screams of a man not far away. Christopher continues on for less than half a block, then turns right at the corner to find a man hunched down in the middle of a deserted street, crying out as if he is in great pain, or being tortured. The man is desperately trying to protect his whole face and body with his arms from some unseen force. "The poor man must be a stark raving lunatic!" Christopher concludes, but as he draws closer, he is not so sure. "Wait a minute . . . Something is there!" He can see faint images fade in and out of view. They are of soldiers—many of them. They surround the man on all sides. Several assault him with bayonets while others try to pull him away. Christopher approaches the man, and as he does the soldiers disappear, leaving the poor victim on the ground whimpering like an abused animal. "They are gone now. You don't have to worry." Christopher assures him.

The man, thinking Christopher an agent of the enemy, fears him at first. It soon becomes obvious Christopher means him no harm. He raises his head and asks, "You saw them?"

"Yes. I saw them."

"They want to take me and skin me alive! That's what they want to do!"

"Do you think they will return tonight?"

"No. They never come more than once a night."

"Maybe we can figure out a way to keep them away for good."

"Why would you want to help me?"

"Because you need it . . . and because, in a way, they are my demons as well. Try to get some sleep. I'll meet you here in the morning if you like." Christopher says, then walks away.

"By the way . . . my name is Nick. What's yours?"

"I'm Chris."

"I'll see you in the morning, Chris."

The following morning Christopher returns to the scene of the previous night's hostility to find his new acquaintance already waiting. Nick appears to be in his sixties. He is short in stature with a receding hair line and dark hair that falls back on his head. The two men decide to go to the north end of Skid Row to a little park frequented by the homeless.

They reach the park and are fortunate to find some of the people who sleep there have begun to scatter, so it is not overly crowded. They find seats on a bench. Nick seems to want to tell Christopher about himself, so Christopher listens.

"I was born in Hungary. As young boy, I spent time in a Nazi concentration camp. My parents died there. They were used as subjects in medical experiments too horrible to describe. After the war, I was brought to the United States to live with relatives in New York. They were good people, but very strict. As I grew up, I thought more and more about becoming a Rabbi, but it was already decided I would become a doctor."

"I should have guessed." Christopher says with a laugh.

Nick joins in the laughter, then continues, "I stayed in college for four years, but never made it to medical school, my heart just wasn't in it. Instead, I got a teaching job in a high school, got married, had children, then later on a divorce. After that, I moved to Los Angeles, hoping for a better life, but somewhere along the way, I just lost control.

My relatives . . . that is . . . my aunt and uncle meant well, but I don't think they ever realized how deeply the holocaust affected me, and I was never one to complain much. I suppose I held a lot inside. I thought becoming a Rabbi might help me in a way that a medical career could not."

"And the Nazi soldiers . . . How long have they been haunting you?"

"For years . . . at first, just every now and then, but lately it's been every night. It's driving me crazy! Why do you suppose it is that some people hate Jews so?"

"I've thought about that quite a bit. It seems to me the Hebrews, more than anyone else, accumulated the wisdom of ages past. In doing so, they intermarried with the darker people of Africa. There was a time when Europeans held Hebrew philosophy and teaching in high regard, but as Europe continued to rise, and Africa decline, the European grew to despise the Jew for being tainted, and for holding such an esteemed position in the world . . . a position that reflects in your scriptures as 'God's chosen people' . . . the same scriptures the Europeans adopted. Your descendants were the transferors of knowledge from the old regime to the new, and once that purpose was served, you became a sore reminder of the past. Regardless of what they say to the contrary, the same tenacity and intelligence that served you so well then, survives to this day, making you a credit to the human race . . . but of course, you don't need me to tell you that. You, as an individual, are a bit of an oddity though. We don't find too many homeless Jews around here."

"Some of us fall through the cracks from time to time, not many, but a few . . . You know, you say things that might offend some people, but you say them with such honesty and lack of sarcasm, and in such a superficial way. A person can easily see that your thoughts and concerns go much deeper. You don't seem to hate anyone."

"No. I don't hate anyone. Do you?"

"I don't believe so . . . not even the Nazi's. At this point, I just wish they would stay out of my thoughts."

"To me, they were people with misplaced souls, misguided into thinking they could get away with the kinds of things conquerors got away with a long time ago. They were remnants of an archaic and ruthless past. You, on the other hand, are in the present . . . the here and now. You have the power to control these phantoms that haunt you. They have already been defeated, but refuse to die out completely, preferring instead to attack the weak and recruit the gullible. It is only your fear that prevents you from realizing it."

"I believe you're right. Maybe the solution does rest within me. I used to blame my problems on the Nazis, on my relatives, on this, on that . . . but now I see much of it was within my ability to control. I simply was not assertive enough to pursue my aspirations. All I had to do was take one foot and put it in front of the other, but I chose not to. This is not a bad country to live in after all. Almost anyone can find a niche for themselves if they work at it."

"Yes . . . and I guess this is ours."

"You know what I mean." adds Nick.

"Yes I do. I know exactly what you mean. It all has a lot to do with the choices we make."

"Let me ask you something. Do you ever feel like it's too late to change things?"

"Yes."

"Did you feel like that, say five years ago?"

"Definitely."

"Did you feel the same way five years before that?"

"I probably did to some degree."

"Do you ever say to yourself now that you should have made a change earlier?"

"Of course."

"My point is that we almost always tend to feel it's too late, when in fact, the best time to begin making change is in the here and now. Like the old saying goes . . . it's never too late. I'm trying to look at the present as if it is the beginning and do whatever it takes to improve my life—I will once I rid myself of these 'phantoms' as you call them."

"You know Nick? I'm glad I met you. You've helped me a lot."

Nick and Christopher become great friends. Each man has a definite something to offer the other. The pairing of the two might seem odd at first, but if one thinks about it, their lives have been similar in many ways. They each had a traumatic childhood. They were each raised by people other than their parents. Each of them aspired to goals early in life they never achieved, and both have shown an interest in things spiritual. Nick turns out to be a good substitute for the alcohol that has subdued Christopher's life force for so long. Christopher in turn helps Nick to deal with the evil phantoms of his past by telling him some of his own experiences, and by sleeping not too far away from him at night.

Nick receives left over food from a local delicatessen that is considerably better than the usual fair. He shares this food with his friend most evenings as they engage in stimulating conversation. Christopher, in a show of appreciation, gathers bits of wire, chain, and broken jewelry from the dumpsters of the many costume jewelry shops in the area. With these fragments, he fashions a gift, and presents it to Nick.

"I have something for you." Christopher says as he pulls a chain from his pocket. At the end of the chain dangles a strangely beautiful Star of David. "I thought this might help you to get in touch with your past . . . to bring back positive memories of things forgotten. It might even help you to overcome the phantoms once and for all."

"Thank you. Thank you very much." Nick says over and over as he accepts the gift with a genuine display of gratitude. It has been a long time since he has received a gift from anyone.

"Are you familiar at all with the teachings of the Cabala?"

"No, I'm afraid not. I never got as far as I would like in my spiritual studies . . . but maybe that's something I should think about doing."

"Maybe so. There's a lot of wisdom in it and other teachings that could help you. It's never too late. You said so yourself."

Christopher and Nick start spending much time at the downtown library. As homeless people, they are made to feel less than welcome there, but as citizens, they have the same right to be there as anyone else. The time spent is well worth it for both of them. It reopens their minds to the world they have been isolated from for so long. When not in the library, they usually discuss the books they have read, or strategies on how to escape the vicious cycle of homelessness. Nick looses his fear of the phantoms and they cease tormenting him, even when Christopher is not nearby.

The friendship tragically ends, however. One evening, Christopher seeks Nick out at his usual roosting place behind stacks of wooden pallets at the rear of a garment building. He is shocked when he finds his friend on the ground in the alley, cold and lifeless, with a pool of blood surrounding his head. Christopher plunges into despair, and asks himself, "Why would anyone want to do this? For what reason? It seems everyone who has ever meant anything to me manages to drop out of sight one way or the other."

Rumors travel quickly on the streets. Christopher soon learns the identity of Nick's assailant. It turns out to be a man Christopher knows from his first days on Skid Row. The name echoes in his head as a past warning of disaster to come. The man's name is Lumpky—the one from the flop house whom everyone said killed his own wife. Apparently, Lumpky has once again gone beyond the point of making idle threats with makeshift tools of destruction.

Christopher is determined to find out the circumstances surrounding Nick's death. It is an easy matter to track down Lumpky. He finds him holed up, off to the side of a urine stenched alley everyone else avoids, clutching a 'long dog' inside a brown paper bag. Christopher has seen him on the streets off and on over the years, but the two would never acknowledge each other—each man perhaps avoiding the specter of his own diminished state of affairs. At the moment, Lumpky is well on his way to heavy intoxication. He is hardly responsive as Christopher approaches him.

"Why did you kill Nick?" Christopher demands.

Lumpky slowly raises his head and asks, "What are you talking about?"

"I asked you why you killed my friend."

"Your friend?"

"Yes, my friend."

Lumpky begins to come out of his stupor. Anger builds in his eyes. Then he spits out words with the type of delirious conviction found only among drunks: "You might think he's your friend, but he's not really. These Jews don't give a damn about anyone else . . . only themselves! Even the bible says it . . . Deuteronomy 14:21 . . . If they find a dead animal somewhere, it's okay to sell it to a heathen, but not to another Jew . . . Think about it! My father worked for a Jew for over twenty years, at a low wage with hardly any raises—then my father got sick. The Jew was nice for a day or two, then all he wanted to know was when my father would be able to come back to work. It wasn't long before the Jew replaced my father with someone else, right after that my father died. We never heard from that Jew again. You're worried about one damned Jew. I say the hell with all of them!"

"You're one sick son-of-a-bitch. Nick didn't own a thing. He lived right here on these streets with the rest of us, and he hated no one. Now you blame him for something somebody he didn't even know did to your father God knows how many years ago?

You know something? I've killed one man in my life, and I swore I would never do it again, but now I'm not so sure."

At that moment, Christopher wants to snatch the wine bottle from Lumpky's hand, smash it over his head, then slash his throat with the bottleneck. He knows that life—and death, for that matter, are different out here on these streets. The County routinely scoops up bodies and carts them off to the morgue with no questions asked. There they are tagged as John or Mary Does for a period of time, then cremated . . . but no, that will not be the case here. Christopher does not want to fall deeper into the cycle of ugliness and destruction. He will not become the judge and the executioner, even though the world would be a better place without Lumpky. Besides, it would be out of character with the goals he and Nick had aspired to. Instead, he forces himself to turn and walk away, figuring at the rate Lumpky is going, he will meet his fate soon enough.

Once again, Christopher is alone, without a friend in the world. He feels broken and downtrodden. What little enthusiasm for life he has managed to muster seems to be slipping away from him. The following days are slow and painful. He comes dangerously close many times to pursuing the refuge of the bottle, but each time he does, he thinks of his friend Nick who never touched a drop in spite of his troubles. The thought inspires him to hold on, but just barely, for he has little to hold on to, save for memories.

While violence is not exactly unheard of on these streets, it definitely seems to be on the rise. Christopher is out scavenging for food behind a restaurant one night when he hears a disturbance, and the cries of a woman in distress. He runs down the alley to find a man holding a woman from behind while another man is in the act of raping her.

Suddenly, an uncontrollable rage comes over Christopher. Without even thinking, he charges towards the man committing the rape, pulls him off, kicks him in the groin, and slams his fist into the man's face. The accessory to the vile offense has already taken flight, and the rapist hobbles off as best he can. Christopher is livid, screaming at the top of his lungs, "You son's of bitches! This could be someone's mother. Don't you understand that?" The woman crouches on the ground, whimpering in a way that reminds him of his first encounter with Nick. Christopher starts toward her to lend a helping hand, but she lurches away. He tells her, "Don't worry, I won't hurt you. It just seems like you could use some help."

The woman settles down and starts talking. Her name is Rose. It turns out she is a mother. Her daughter is somewhere in the child welfare system. She obviously has a great deal of love for her child, but the severity of her addictions is just too great. It becomes apparent to Christopher that this is one of the most painful dilemmas a person can face—one that can only be understood by the addict, with little sympathy coming from others. Christopher advises her to, "stay out in the open as much as possible. That is much safer, especially for a woman." Rose thanks him for the advice, and for coming to her rescue. She seems to want him to stay, but he prefers to move on, perhaps afraid of losing another friend.

Sleep does not come for Christopher that night. Instead, he just lies there thinking about the ever present problem of escaping Skid Row. Before the break of daylight, Christopher rises, unable to take trying to lie still any longer. He feels he must do something, anything—but what? Suddenly, he recalls Nick once saying that early on in life, all he had to do was take one foot and put it in front of the other, but he chose not to do it. "Can it really be as simple as that?" Christopher wonders. "Maybe so. Maybe sometimes you just have to plant yourself squarely on the ground, and start putting one foot in front of the other, irregardless of the forces that seem to be working against you." Christopher does just that. He gathers up his meager belongings into a plastic bag and walks away. Only now, he does not walk in the circles of the past that determine the boundaries of Skid Row, but rather a straight line out of Skid Row, and unbeknownst to him, into a past of a different sort.

Christopher walks for several miles. The skyscrapers of downtown give way to smaller commercial buildings, and residential areas in the low, hilly areas to the north. He follows a road at the foot of the hills in a westerly direction. The sun has already risen when he comes across a very beautiful sight. To Christopher, it is like a sea of tranquillity in the midst of chaos. It is a lake surrounded by trees and grass. There is a dock where boats are kept. At the far end of the lake is a bridge leading to a small island that seems to serve as a bird sanctuary.

He wanders into the park and sits on the grass. The effect is like a lulling, hypnotic spell. Things seem strangely familiar, but Christopher knows he has never been here before—or has he? "It is such a relief to be away from Skid Row, and in such serene surroundings." He sighs.

As the sun continues to rise, filling the little lakeside hamlet with its life giving rays, he watches people engaging in the simple, normal, very human things he never paid much attention to before: People fishing, or taking their morning exercise—at noontime, a mother picnicking with her children under the cool shade of a tree—a little girl, breaking away from the protective grasp of her father's hand, running playfully towards pigeons as they flutter away—then in the evening, lovers carelessly strolling in a tender embrace—and now he, the homeless one, feeling a great sense of loss over things he never had.

Christopher spends the entire day there undisturbed by the police or anyone else, as the homeless sometimes are. By late evening, the clouds have gathered in the sky, and the rains come. The rain is heavy, and sudden. "Oh shit!" Christopher says to himself. "Now I've got to find somewhere to go and wait it out. I'm so tired of having to seek shelter every time the rain falls, or the wind blows too hard." he sighs, then looks around to see what might be available.

Across the street from the park he sees water gushing down from the busted rain gutter of a building. He looks to his left, towards the downtown skyline, and is reminded of Skid Row. He looks again at the pure, clean rain water streaming down to the ground in a steady flow. The thought of returning to Skid Row disheartens him. Instead, he crosses the street and stands under the water. He stands there for a long time, allowing the water to hit him in the face and all parts of his body. Finally, the rains subside, and the flow reduces to a trickle.

Christopher now realizes how wet and cold he is, but at least he is clean—a condition he has not known for a long time. Shaking and shivering, he stumbles down the street, looking for a way to get dry. He comes across a small, neighborhood market. The shop keeper asks if there is anything he would like to buy. Christopher glances around the store. His eyes settle on a collection of milk cartons behind a glass refrigerator door. "Milk!" He says to himself. "The basic nourishment. The first food of life." He has a couple of dollars in his pocket and uses it to buy the milk. He also gets a book of matches from the shopkeeper.

He continues his search, and eventually comes upon a building that appears abandoned. Behind the building he finds a spot offering some shelter from the wind and rain that might return. Near the rear of the building grow several large eucalyptus trees. From these trees, Christopher gathers the driest strips of bark, branches, and leaves he can find, and uses them to build a fire. Soon, the fire is intense enough to provide the much needed warmth to his shaking body—warmth made more pleasant by the smell of the aromatic eucalyptus oil. He gathers some more wood and sits beside the fire, feeding it occasionally. He closes his eyes and thinks not of the past, and not of the future, but simply of the here and now—of the welcome sensation of heat on his face and hands. He opens the carton of milk and drinks—and as the milk flows down his throat, pleasant sensations radiate outwards as his body eagerly accepts the much needed nourishment.

Christopher takes a long, deep sigh as he passes his hands over the fire. He looks up to the sky and gazes at the heavenly bodies. He wonders where Jupiter might be—for Jupiter represents strength and healing. He recalls his friendship with Cowboy and Soul Man, and wonders how they are doing. Then he remembers something. Reaching into his pocket, he pulls out what remains of a wallet. From the wallet he takes out a folded piece of paper. He unfolds the paper, and studies it. It is the Seal of Trikrisaton.

He stares deeply into the flame, and as he does his mind wanders back in time. He thinks of Angela, Camille, and Geronimo, the thought of them brings a smile to his face. He thinks of Squirrel, Bird, and Brim. He now realizes they were an integral part of his life, yet when they were around, they were merely business associates. He feels a great warmth at the thought of having them around now. He recalls the foster homes, the feelings of isolation and alienation, the taunting and teasing for being different. Mary passes into his thoughts and he feels comforted by the memory of her loving kindness. His thoughts drift again to the cruel callous conditions of Skid Row. Images play before his eyes like some terrible slide show, the junkie lying half dead in the bathroom of the flophouse, Archie sprawled in his own waste, Nick in a pool of blood, and Rose being brutally raped. The sheer range of experience becomes unbearable.

Christopher now does something he has always tried to avoid. He indulges in self-pity, and as he does, his emotions build. His chest heaves. Tears flow from his eyes. He collapses sideways to the ground. His body at the mercy of uncontrollable spasms causing him to contract into a fetal position. He is now stripped of all superficial ego, and his soul is exposed in its rawest, primordial state. The austerity of homelessness has prepared him for the Rite of Regression.

Smoldering embers in the heart of the fire burst into flames that leap about wildly. In his mind's eye, the flames grow into a raging fire. He passes through the inferno, and emerges on the other side, where all is peaceful and tranquil. Through space and time, an image slowly forms, like a ship coming to port on a foggy sea. Looking upwards, he sees a beautiful woman with long, flowing blond hair and deep blue eyes. She holds him, rocks him, caresses him. Christopher feels safe and secure. She speaks words difficult to understand. He comprehends only part of a sentence: ". . . call Stanley Du Bois in New Orleans." Instantly, Christopher comes out of the trance, repeating the words over and over to himself. He takes a small rock and scratches the words into the wall next to him, then passes off to sleep.

12

I WILL TO ASPIRE

Christopher awakens the next morning feeling more rested than he has for a long time. He recalls having a dream, and knows there is something he needs to remember, but he can't quite put his finger on it. He remembers the wall, abruptly turns toward it, and is relieved to find the crudely written words—these he burn into his memory. Christopher is excited. He knows he has reached something from deep in his past. As he recalls the details of the dream there is no doubt in his mind the woman who held him is his mother.

Later, he finds a pencil and paper, and dials long distance information in New Orleans for the telephone number of Stanley Du Bois. The directory assistance operator gives him three different numbers, apparently for three people with the same name. He calls the first number and gets no answer. Then he tries the second number. This time a woman answers.

"Hello. May I speak to Stanley Du Bois?" asks Christopher.

"I'm afraid he has recently passed away." The woman, still grief stricken, replies.

"I'm sorry ma'am, but if I may ask . . . Does the name Mary Campbell mean anything to you?"

"No. I'm afraid it doesn't."

"I apologize for disturbing you. Thank you very much for your time." replies Christopher, fearful that his best hope for finding his family, or at least discovering anything about them, might be gone forever. On the other hand, he still has two telephone numbers, including the 'no answer', but not enough money to make the calls. So he takes to the streets to make money in the ways most familiar to him—collecting cans and bottles, and washing the windshields of automobiles. When he has enough money, he calls the first number again. Still there is no answer. He closes his eyes to say a silent prayer, before dialing the third number. The line is busy. "Well at least someone is there." Christopher utters under his breath, waiting approximately ten minutes before trying again. He is reluctant to try any sooner than that, knowing the pay phones occasionally do not return the change. This time the line rings.

"Hello." comes a man's voice.

"Yes, hello . . . Is this Stanley Du Bois?"

"Yes it is."

"Sir, my name is Christopher. Does that, or the name Mary Campbell mean anything to you?"

There is a long pause before he replies, "Yes. Yes it does. You say your name is Christopher?"

"Yes sir. That's correct."

"May I ask what your relationship is to Mary?"

"She was my grandmother."

"Grandmother?" Du Bois says doubtfully. "What ever became of her?"

"She died when I was very young."

"Where did you grow up?"

"In Los Angeles, where I am now."

There is a long pause. "So that's why I could never find you . . . We need to talk. Is it possible that you can come here?" asks Du Bois with a tinge of desperation.

"Yes. I can come, but not right away. I will contact you later and let you know exactly when."

"Please do without fail. It is very important. Give me your telephone number so I can stay in touch with you."

"I can't. I don't have a telephone right now, but don't worry. I'll call you back. I promise."

"Very well then. I will be looking forward to hearing from you."

Christopher hangs up the phone feeling excited and motivated. Hope has returned and fills him with optimism. He is not sure what to expect in New Orleans, but he feels the appropriate way to find out is not through a telephone conversation.

Over the course of the days and weeks that follow, Christopher saves every penny he can. His new found enthusiasm lands him a job at a construction site cleaning up debris. He earns less than minimum wage, paid by the day, under the table. Part of his earnings he uses to rent a private mail box and to enlist an answering service to take calls for him. A fellow he befriends on the job helps him by taking him in his jalopy to get a driver's license.

Now, with a mock home address and telephone number, together with the driver's license, he lands a job as a taxi driver. He beat's out the other applicants, because of his spotless driving record—a consequence of not having driven an automobile for several years. Hustling as a cabby for twelve hours a day, seven days a week, allows him to accumulate more money than he has seen in a long time. He rents himself a room, and eats good, hot food every day. He even buys a modest automobile. The difference that having a goal or purpose in one's life can make is truly amazing!

Three months after Christopher's first contact with Stanley Du Bois he feels ready to make the journey. He takes a leave of absence from his job, and buys a bus ticket to New Orleans. The long ride is relaxing. The vast stretches of desert are peaceful and serene. He spends much of his time sleeping. As he approaches his destination, a nervousness overcomes him. Filled with anticipation, Christopher wonders what this fateful meeting might unfold.

The bus arrives in New Orleans. Christopher now has to make his way across town to the French Quarter. Arriving later than expected, he is fearful Du Bois might not be home. At last he finds the house. It is a well kept home on a street not heavily trafficked by tourists. He knocks on the door three times before it opens. Beyond the doorway stands a tall man in his seventies, with shaggy, gray hair, dark eyes, and a slight slump in his posture. There is at first, a hint of sadness in the old man's eyes that seem to brighten as he looks into the face of his visitor.

"Hello, I'm Christopher."

"I figured as much. I'm Stanley Du Bois. Please come right in."

Christopher makes himself comfortable in an easy chair while Du Bois prepares coffee and cakes for the two of them. "It has been a long time since I've lived in a real home." he reflects to himself as he looks around the room. It is cluttered with stacks of books and papers on tables not originally intended for that purpose, and even on the floor. Du Bois obviously ran out of shelf space years ago. The furniture is mostly antique, a little dusty and in need of polishing, but even so, the house has a warm, cozy feel to it.

Soon, Du Bois returns with the refreshments. He is a remarkably agile man for his age, easily negotiating a silver tray to the coffee table. Du Bois takes a seat on the sofa. Christopher picks up a spoon, and begins to prepare his coffee.

"Did Mary ever mention me to you?" asks Du Bois.

"Not that I can remember."

"How on earth then did you find me?"

"I had a dream. In it, I was a baby. My mother was holding me. She seemed troubled. She mentioned your name."

"That's fascinating! You know, you resemble your mother quite a bit."

"Do you know my mother? Is she here?"

"I knew your mother . . . I'm afraid she died when you were a baby."

"And my father? What of him?"

Du Bois does not quite know where or how to start. Instead he takes Christopher into his study. In a corner of the study is a table. Du Bois lifts a black cloth from the table to reveal the Clay Tablet of Aten. From a wooden box sitting on a shelf near the table he draws the luminous sphere, and hands it to Christopher. Then, Du Bois tells him the whole story: How he first came across the tablet—the involvement of Peter and Marilyn Mallinger—and the terrible fire that nearly took the lives of Mary and Christopher as well.

"So you see, Mary was not really your Grandmother." adds Du Bois.

"She was a grandmother to me, and more. That's all that really matters."

"Of course, I understand."

Christopher stands in silence, holding the two halves of the sphere in his hands. He would have been satisfied with the simple knowledge that his mother was a bright, beautiful woman who loved him dearly. He would have been content to know he was not simply abandoned and left to be raised by a grandparent. The knowledge of his father's identity, though, adds a whole new dimension to the situation. Christopher clasps the two halves of the sphere together in his hands, and raises his clasped hands to his chest. He tries desperately to resist a surge of emotion that overwhelms him nevertheless. Still fighting to resist, a tear forces its way through his tightly closed eyes. Du Bois is also affected, but stands helpless to lend any immediate aid or comfort.

"All my life . . ." Christopher begins. ". . . I told myself it doesn't matter. To hell with it I'd say . . . but it does matter . . . it does."

"Of course it matters. It's who you are."

"It's just too much to take in at one time . . . It's too much. Do my mother or Mary have any relatives still around that I can talk to?"

"Yes . . . as a matter of fact . . . Mary had a niece. I used to keep in touch with her when I was looking for you. I haven't seen her for some time. I can give you her address if you'd like."

"Yes, I would like that."

"Very well then, let's go back to the den and sit down for a while." Du Bois offers.

Christopher pulls himself together, then places the sphere back in the wooden box, and returns with Du Bois to the den.

Du Bois pours the two of them more coffee as he continues: "After the fire I heard a rumor that Mary went to Chicago. I tried to find the two of you there. Now, I understand why it was so impossible." There is a silence before he continues. "I deeply regret I remained uninvolved after you were born. I don't expect you to understand, but it was a different time. There was a lot of hate all around and I simply was not up to the task. I'm glad to see that in my lifetime things are beginning to change."

"I wouldn't worry much about the past. We can't change it. All we can do is go from here."

"Thank you. I appreciate that." Du Bois feeling somewhat relieved goes on to say, "The origin of that sphere is perhaps one of the most perplexing mysteries one can imagine, yet, you and I are the only ones who know of its existence. I knew you must be out there somewhere, and I didn't know if you wanted your life sensationalized, or if anyone would even believe such a story for that matter . . . so I kept it to myself all these years. It has been a heavy burden to bear. It's almost a miracle you were ever born. The chances of that happening are, I would think, enormously against it . . . and yet, here you are."

"It does seem that way when you first think about it, but I believe the mere presence of man in the world reduces randomness or chance occurrences."

"I can see how that might be true with respect to the control that man exerts on his environment through the development of technology, but this is another matter still."

"It seems to me the same forces that drive instinct and the evolution of consciousness can, on a subtler level, affect the thoughts and actions of individuals. We are sometimes caught up in loops that are not much different from the currents of history people talk about. In this way determinism increases."

"Very interesting. Have you been to college, if I may ask?"

"No. I used to read a lot. What I am now realizing is I've always had an odd feeling of not really belonging here. That has caused me to question everything around me and to seek answers elsewhere. The search has taken me from books, into the world of the intangibles, and the other side of life . . . Of course, I don't expect you to take all of what I say seriously."

"I am an old man, as you can see, and in my long life, I have discovered one thing for sure. The more I learn, the more I realize there is that I don't know. In the pursuit of higher knowledge, I have found that my destination is not much different from my starting point. The same fairies I might have believed in as a child seem, in some ways, to start making sense again. I don't know, maybe it's just a symptom of old age, but I have my doubts. You are not so old, and you say you've seen the other side of life. What exactly do you see?" probes Du Bois with the seriousness one might expect of a man nearing the end of his life.

"I see a realm that can provide a form of immortality for those capable of surviving the ordeal of death. To survive requires a highly developed sense of being, a complete abandonment of fear, and an attitude of total control. In this way, a good part of your personality—your very consciousness, can remain a distinct part of the whole, rather than merely a diffused quantity of raw energy randomly scattered throughout the realm." Du Bois is silent as he sits on the sofa, hands folded in his lap. His mind seems a million miles away as he contemplates the mystery of death.

Christopher, feeling his visit is nearing its end says, "I'm very grateful to you for your help, and for the hospitality you've shown me."

"You are more than welcome to stay here as long as you like. I don't mean that as an idle invitation. I want to help you in any way I can."

"You're very kind to offer, but I wouldn't want to impose on you, and I really should be getting along."

"Please . . . if not for yourself, then do it to help ease the conscience of an old man . . . Besides, there are still many things I would like to show you."

"If you're sure you don't mind, I will be happy to stay for a while."

"Excellent! Well, let's see here . . . Are you hungry by any chance?"

"The cakes seem to have hit the spot for now."

"There's food in the refrigerator so feel free to help yourself. It's been a long day. You must be getting tired. I'll show you to your room. Oh, and by the way . . . here's an extra key to the house. Should you choose, you can take a walk through the Quarter. I might be asleep when you return, so just let yourself in. We can talk more tomorrow."

Christopher is surprised that a man who has known him for less than a day trusts him with a key to his home. He takes the key and says, "Thank you. You're right . . . I am a little tired. Maybe I'll take a shower and lie down for a while."

Christopher takes his shower and tries to get some rest, but his mind will not slow down enough for sleep to come. After a half hour or so, he decides to go out for the walk. He strolls for about three blocks admiring the French architecture until he comes across a voodoo shop and enters. He is mesmerized by the massive display of occult paraphernalia: dolls, books, amulets, and talismans on row after row of shelves that nearly reach the ceiling. The familiar smell of frankincense and myrrh fills the air.

Most of the people in the shop are tourists, looking for souvenirs to take home with them, but Christopher knows instinctively two of the people are practitioners of the Magical Arts. The two practitioners, a man and a woman, are shopping for seeds and herbs. They apparently know each other. The man is jovial in appearance. He is dressed simply in casual slacks, and a short sleeved plaid shirt. The woman has extremely white skin, jet black hair, and wears blood red lip stick. The man tells her of a particular spell he plans to cast. She advises him to be careful.

There is a third person who is not a tourist, doesn't seem to know anyone, and doesn't appear to be shopping for anything. She is an old woman with coal black skin, braided hair, and smoky gray eyes that make her appear to be either blind from a cataract condition, or able to peer into the unseen world. She is not blind however. She stares at Christopher. Her eyes follow his every move. Christopher can feel her gaze. He turns toward her and smiles. Her only response is to raise her left hand, and place it palm down on her chest. Christopher turns away. On a shelf is a lapis lazuli stone that catches his eye. He buys the stone and leaves the shop.

It is by now dark outside. Christopher turns on to Bourbon Street where things are beginning to really liven up and thinks to himself: "I have never seen a place so full of life." Young boys tap dance in the streets for donations. Sexy women and transvestites coax men into topless bars, and vendors sell beer everywhere through windows along the sidewalk. The sound of music—jazz and blues, fills the air from every direction.

In stark contrast, there is a small group of people headed by a man who carries a huge, white cross. Emblazoned on the cross in black letters are the words 'Jesus Saves'. Christopher marvels at how safe and lively he feels walking down this street of 'sin', and how much different it is to walking down some of the streets of Los Angeles where one can not avoid feeling fear and apprehension. He wonders why these cross bearers do not practice their trade where life and limb are at greatest risk, and therefore needed most.

Christopher continues his stroll along Bourbon Street until he reaches a point where the nightlife dies. He figures he will cross the street at the next corner and head back to Du Bois' house. He reaches the corner and stops dead in his tracks. Standing before him is the same old woman he had seen in the voodoo shop. Christopher feels certain her penetrating eyes, opened wide like saucers, glow in the dark. Again, she brings her left hand to her chest. With her right hand she points to Christopher and says, "There is a light that shines about you. Pray to the East twice a day, once in the morning, and once in the evening. God will not let you down."

"I thank you for your insight and for your advice." replies Christopher. He reaches into his pocket, pulls out the lapis lazuli stone, and gives it to her to show his appreciation. The old woman closes her hand over the stone and smiles. Christopher goes back to the house and easily falls asleep.

The next morning Christopher awakens to the satisfying aroma of bacon frying in a skillet. He washes and grooms himself before going to the kitchen where he finds Du Bois busily preparing a hearty breakfast. "Good morning, Mr. Du Bois."

"Well, good morning Christopher, but please, call me Stanley. I heard you leave last night. I guess you weren't as tired as you thought you were."

"I guess I had a lot on my mind." Christopher sighs.

"Yes, I can imagine. It does take a little bit of getting used to."

"I'd like to help. What can I do?"

"The cups and glasses are in that cabinet, and the silverware is in that drawer." Once the table is set, the two men start their meal. "Are you familiar at all with Akhenaten?" Du Bois asks.

"Somewhat. I admire his attempt at religious reform but I always thought he was a fanatic."

"Yes, I agree. If only he had given his ideas time to take root gradually and naturally, things might have turned out differently. Over the years I've devoted much time to the study of Akhenaten and the Amarna period. I even traveled to Egypt and Ethiopia many years ago in search of clues to help solve the riddle of the sphere."

"Ethiopia? Why Ethiopia?"

"Oh . . . I forgot to tell you. On the back of the tablet there is an inscription written in an old Ethiopian language called Ge'ez. The inscription is so faint I didn't notice it for some time. It identifies the tablet as once belonging to Zera Yaqob, a fifteenth century Emperor of Ethiopia. From there, the tablet most probably found its way to Europe, and then from Europe to here."

"Were you ever able to find out anything at all?"

"I'm afraid not. Through all my travels I was not able to turn up a single clue. You might have better luck."

"Me?"

"Certainly. Why not? Even if you don't, the trip might do you good. You would be returning to part of your roots."

The thought of traveling to these lands excites Christopher. "That's something to think about." he replies.

"In Egypt you'll want to go to the Amarna ruins naturally, and possibly Luxor, which would put you in the vicinity of Karnak. The museum in Cairo might be helpful. As for Ethiopia, you might try Shewa. That was the seat of power in the fifteenth century—then there's Axum, the earlier seat of power. You might even find something in Addis Ababa, but I doubt it, the city is not very old. There are all kinds of possibilities."

In the days that follow Du Bois and Christopher pour over maps and books. Du Bois covers many subjects. He teaches Christopher something of the history of the two lands, the geography, ethnography, religions, and all the known travel routes, both ancient and modern. The two could have continued for weeks, but Christopher wants to visit Mary's niece, and has a job to return to besides. So Du Bois' whirlwind introduction comes to an end. He gives Christopher a few books and maps for future reference and offers him the clay tablet and sphere. Christopher accepts the sphere, but asks Du Bois to keep the tablet.

The parting is sad for both men. A special bond has developed between them. They feel they have known each other for a long time, and in a sense, perhaps they have. As Christopher departs, he says to Du Bois, "Thank you for everything. I hope you are not offended if I tell you that you are the closest thing to a father I have ever known."

"I am not the least bit offended. In fact, I am honored to hear you say that."

"Good bye."

"Good luck. Try to stay in touch . . . and another thing . . . Don't worry about Mississippi too much. There really isn't anything there for you."

Christopher rents a car for the trip to his birthplace. Mary's niece lives in a rural area on the outskirts of town. As he draws near, he sees children playing on dusty roads and older people standing about doing nothing in particular. Everyone seems distracted by the presence of a stranger. It is difficult to know if their attitude is one of curiosity or suspicion, but irregardless, they have the right to feel any way they choose. These are the hopelessly disenfranchised of the South—the last casualties of the Civil War. They are the discarded accessories of the Dixie glory days.

Christopher finds the house with the help of one of the older boys playing in the street. It is a small shack, badly in need of paint, with a bare dirt front yard and chickens wandering about pecking the ground. To the side of the yard grows a small patch of greens—turnips, collards, and mustards. Christopher passes through a rickety gate and knocks on the door. An old woman answers. Christopher is at first startled, for the old woman has an uncanny resemblance to Mary.

"Hello, ma'am. Are you Sue Willie?"

"Yes, I am." comes the reply. Her voice and her manner of speech has a familiar ring making Mary's presence seem like just yesterday.

"My name is Christopher. You don't know me, but you had an aunt named Mary . . . and I'm . . . well, what I mean is, she . . ."

"I know who you are. Come right in." Christopher steps through the door. The house has only two rooms but it is spotlessly maintained. The aura the interior projects is the ideal of what a home should: free of pretentiousness, warm and soothing, and a refuge from a sometimes harsh and uncertain world. The rich aroma of Southern cuisine permeates the interior.

"Please have a seat." Sue Willie offers. Christopher settles himself into a well-worn upholstered chair and sinks nearly to the ground, Sue Willie returns to her rocking chair by the window.

"That was a very long time ago when you and my Aunt Mary left. I didn't know what happened."

Christopher tells Sue Willie as best he can of her aunt and the time after she departed. She listens intently before suddenly remembering her pots on the stove. When she returns from the stove she urges Christopher to have something to eat. The two enjoy a delicious dinner of greens, corn bread, and ham hocks. She fusses over Christopher as if she was his mother.

After the meal, he asks her to show him the place where his mother's house once stood. She rides with him into town. They reach the neighborhood and pass slowly down the street as Sue Willie points out the house that has since been rebuilt. A woman is out front tending a rose garden.

"That would be your cousin." Sue Willie discloses.

"Really? I'm going to stop and talk to her."

An expression comes over Sue Willie's face similar to one Christopher has seen before. It is a peculiar mixture of fear, embarrassment, and hesitation—reminiscent of the expression on the face of Mary's apparition in the cemetery during the Rite of Resurrection when he inquired about things he was not meant to know. Sue Willie responds by advising, "Things have changed since those days, but not *that* much . . . I can understand how you must feel sugar, but to them you are still one of us . . . no more, no less."

Christopher knows her words are true so he does not pursue the matter any further. Instead, he drives away wondering how he could have been so naive. The answer is: he firmly believes he is equal to anyone. With such an attitude he tends to forget the narrow-minded rules society expects him to follow.

They return to Sue Willie's house. She does not want Christopher to leave, and in a way, he does not want to leave either, but he must. As he departs they give each other a hug and she tells him, "You are family. You come back anytime . . . anytime at all." Walking to his car he now understands the meaning behind Du Bois' words when he told him there really isn't anything there for him. That is not entirely true however, for just as with Stanley Du Bois, Christopher and Sue Willie connected in a very special way during this brief visit.

Christopher drives to Vicksburg where he turns in his rented car and heads home, renewed by a life filled with possibilities. He spends his time on the bus reading the books and studying the maps Du Bois had given him. He has also committed himself to keeping a diary. The diary begins as a record of everything he can recall Du Bois telling him, then it continues as a day to day record of his thoughts and ideas. These activities keep him thoroughly occupied.

By the time Christopher arrives in Los Angeles, he is certain he will make the trip to Africa. He will need money—more than he has to take such a trip. To get it will require plenty of hard work. He resumes his hectic work schedule of twelve hour days, seven days a week. Taking the advice of the old lady in New Orleans to heart, he prays to the East twice a day.

One weekend however, Christopher decides to take off from work. He goes down to the military surplus store and buys fifty lightweight thermal blankets and army c-ration kits, consisting of food, candy, and cigarettes. These items he takes down to Skid Row and distributes to the homeless. Some of the people there recognize him and seem pleased one of their own has risen above the level of destitution. A woman walks up to Christopher and says, "Hello, do you remember me?"

Christopher has trouble placing her. She is now a cleaner, better kept version of the person he knew. Suddenly it dawns on him that she is Rose, the woman he once saved from the rapists. "I sure do. How are you?"

"Better than before."

"Yes, I can tell, you're looking a lot better."

"So do you." They both smile and she continues. "I just want to thank you for helping me when you did. It made me feel like there was hope. I don't do the drugs anymore. I even visit my daughter now, but I still have a long way to go. It's so hard trying to get back on your feet."

Christopher listens to her words, then comes up with an idea: "I'll tell you what. Meet me here at the same time in three weeks. I might be able to help you." Rose agrees to this and they say their good-byes for now. Driving home, he reflects on his homeless days, and finds in them a certain fondness or nostalgia that can only come after the passage of time. "Maybe it was all meant to be a part of my great journey on earth." He thinks. "Maybe I needed to see and experience the depths of human misery in order to understand more fully the great order of things, from lowest to highest. Even the lowest man has special qualities lacking in the highest animals. A dog or a cat might receive greater kindness than a human being of the wrong circumstance. Any person, regardless of his circumstance, is nearer to the top than the bottom, and all people are interconnected in some way. Even the junkie in the common-use bathroom of the flophouse contributed in some small way to the greater scheme of things, for if nothing else, he impressed on me an image I will never forget. I in turn will have an effect on others. But the unbroken chain of relationships do not end with human beings. They extend throughout the world, and throughout the universe. They transcend concepts and time, flowing into the realms of good and evil, or more accurately, constructivity and destructivity; chaos and order, or more accurately, the possibilities and gravity."

Christopher returns to his room to spend the rest of his day in solitude. He feels lonely, but has no one with whom he can talk. For better or for worse he is a changed person, finding it difficult to engage in normal everyday conversation for any period of time. The things that interest him don't seem to interest others, and vice versa.

As the evening wears on, the telephone rings. Christopher seldom receives calls and can't imagine who it might be. "Hello." he answers.

"Hello. Is this Chris?"

The voice coming through the receiver registers like a distant foghorn from the past. Christopher recognizes it, but can't believe his ears. "Geronimo! Is that you?"

"That's pretty good. You still know my voice after all these years."

"How did you find me?"

"Somebody told me they thought they saw you driving a taxi out by the airport. I called the cab company. They told me you worked there, but they wouldn't give me any information. I was hoping you had a listed number, and I guess I got lucky, but man, you're hard to reach. I've been trying to contact you for almost two weeks."

"I work most all the time. I just happened to be off today. It sure is good to hear your voice. Where are you?"

"I'm at home . . . on thirty-seventh and Normandie."

"Well, why don't you come over . . . or why don't I come over and visit you?"

"Since you've been working so hard, you just sit back and relax, I'll come over there."

Christopher gives Geronimo the address and eagerly awaits his arrival. A little over a half hour passes, when the door bell rings. Christopher scrambles to the door and opens it.

"You want to let an old man into your house?"

"Geronimo . . . am I glad to see you!" Christopher shouts, shaking his visitor's hand and pulling him into the house all at once.

"Long time no see partner . . . How long has it been?"

"Too long."

"So what have you been up to all these years?"

"I don't even know how to begin to tell you. Have a seat." Offers Christopher, motioning him to a chair. "So tell me . . . what about Camille? Do you know anything about her?"

"No man. She left town while you were in the hospital and I never heard from her again."

"I want you to know I realize what things must have been like for you and her. I mean, I know I put the two of you through quite a lot. I know you didn't see certain things the way I did, and I really should not have expected you to. You guys did what you thought was best. Well anyway, I just wanted to tell you that."

"No problem, no problem at all. We've been through some pretty heavy things together, but I'm just a simple guy with simple thoughts. I don't know if I can say the same for you."

"Yeah, I know. I'm the crazy one."

"Well I don't know about that either. I mean, you're crazy, but not *crazy* crazy . . . What I mean is . . ."

"That's all right. You don't have to explain. I think I know what you mean."

"We lived it, good or bad, we lived it, and that's about all there is to it." reflects Geronimo.

"Yes, we sure did. I wanted to apologize to you a long time ago, but when I got out of the mad house you guys had already disappeared."

"I felt like I needed to get away for a while, so I moved out to Lancaster. When things dried up there, I moved back down here."

"Speaking of getting away . . . I'm planning to take a trip to Africa."

"Africa?"

"Yes. I have some personal reasons for going. Why don't you go with me?"

"Oh man, you gotta be kidding. I don't know anything about Africa."

"I don't know much about it myself. Look, don't worry about the cost. I'll pay for it. We'll only be there for two weeks at the most. It would mean a lot to me if you come."

Geronimo thinks about it for a bit, then shakes his head and lets out a dry laugh. "Man, I get into some of the damnedest things with you."

"So does that mean you'll come?" asks Christopher eagerly.

"I imagine you'll keep working on me until you talk me into it."

"You know I will."

"When are you planning to leave?"

"In about three weeks."

"What the hell. I might as well go."

"Good then! First, we'll fly to Asmara, Eritrea . . ."

"Where?"

"It used to be part of Ethiopia. There was a civil war and they won their independence not too long ago."

"Man . . . I don't know. They might still be shooting at each other."

"I'm told it's very peaceful there now. We shouldn't have anything to worry about. The only reason we're going there is because it makes a better starting point for us. We can rent a car or take a bus from there southwards to Axum."

"Well . . . if you checked it out and say it's okay, I guess it is."

"Don't worry. It'll be okay. Trust me."

The two friends spend the rest of the evening talking about the old days. When Geronimo leaves, he takes with him a list of things he needs to do in preparation for the trip—passport, visas, and the necessary immunizations.

Three weeks pass and Christopher has not forgotten his appointment with Rose. He goes to skid row to meet her at the agreed upon place, and finds her there as she said she would be.

"Do you drive?" Christopher asks her.

"Not lately, but I used to."

Christopher gives her some keys and motions her to the car. He helps her in to the driver's seat then takes his place on the passenger side. Rose starts the car and pulls away from the curb. She talks mostly of her little girl as Christopher gives her directions to his apartment. Her greatest wish is to get on her feet and get her little girl back. Christopher explains to her what he has in mind:

"I'm leaving town for a couple of weeks. I'd like you to take care of my car and room while I'm gone. The rent and utilities are all paid up. In that time, maybe you'll be able to find work, then you'll be a lot closer to getting your child back."

"You must be some kind of angel." declares Rose shaking her head disbelievingly.

Christopher laughs. "I might be a lot of things, but I am far from an angel. It's just that I know how hard it can be, and I can only imagine how much harder it must be for a woman. People helped me to find myself, so now I'm helping you . . . It's up to you to help your daughter. I know you can do it."

"Yes. I can do it . . . and I will. That much I can promise you."

When they arrive, Christopher packs some belongings into a backpack. In the rear of the bottom drawer of the dresser he sees three skeleton keys. He had never noticed them before. Such keys are not commonly used these days. On an impulse he scoops them up and puts them in his pocket. After he finishes packing he turns to Rose and says "Here's something to help you get started," as he hands her some money. "Now I need to ask a favor of you."

"I'll do anything. Just name it."

"Take me to my friend's house, then come back at eleven o'clock tomorrow morning and drop us off at the airport."

Rose takes Christopher to Geronimo's house to spend the night. She comes back just as she promised the next morning and drives them to the airport. She gives Christopher a kiss on the cheek as she bids them farewell. Inside the terminal Geronimo comments, "She seems like a nice person, but I wouldn't think she's your type."

"She's just a friend I'm trying to help."

"I see. You really have changed. I remember a time when a woman only had one purpose for you."

"Do you think it's a good change?"

"I think it's a very good change."

Geronimo passes through the security check point with no problem. When Christopher tries, the metal detector alarm sounds. He places the items in his pockets in a small bowl, noticing he has only one skeleton key. "The other two must have slipped out in the car . . . Oh well." thinking to himself. He now passes through the metal detector with no problem. The two travelers continue on to the departure gate where they wait for the airplane that will carry them away to a world different from any they have ever known.

13

THE FORBIDDEN FRUIT

The time nears to board the airplane. Christopher wakes from a nap to find Geronimo sitting erect, staring into space. The boarding attendant begins calling passengers by groups of row numbers. The two soon to be world travelers board the plane when the attendant calls their group. Geronimo has been assigned a window seat and Christopher has the seat next to his. As the jumbo jet fills with passengers Christopher tries to make conversation, but Geronimo is not very talkative.

"What's the matter with you?" Christopher asks.

"Nothing." The plane begins to taxi away from the terminal. Geronimo clasps his hands tightly together and his body is rigid.

"Oh come on, don't tell me . . . " teases Christopher.

"Man . . . I've never been on one of these things before!"

"I haven't either."

"Yeah, but you're crazy! That's the difference." Geronimo emphasizes.

The plane builds up speed down the jetway and lifts off the ground. Geronimo can't help taking little peeks through the window every now and then. Each time he does, he turns away with a quick, nervous jerk. Christopher does everything he can to contain his laughter. After they have reached cruising altitude the flight attendants begin the beverage service. Christopher wonders if maybe a drink would help to relax his nervous friend, but thinks twice about it when he recalls Geronimo's proneness to boisterous behavior while under the influence. In the end, he decides maybe a little won't hurt.

"Why don't you split a beer with me?" Christopher offers.

"Yeah. Yeah." answers Geronimo with slight enthusiasm. He has three beers in the course of an hour. He now begins to relax and assumes a more mellow composure.

"Eureka!" Christopher thinks to himself. "I've found the cure for Indian fever."

Nevertheless, the plane's landing in Frankfurt brings Geronimo great relief. They now find their way to the connecting flight, going through a passport checkpoint along the way. The next terminal is small, dark, and not nearly as luxurious as the one they left. In a sense, they have already entered the third world. Over the course of their three hour wait, they watch as the passengers for the next flight gather. The people are mostly Egyptians, and East Africans—businesspersons, and families perhaps returning from vacations.

Geronimo boards the next flight with more confidence than the first. The plane makes a stop in Cairo to let passengers off, leaving the aircraft far less than half full.

"The plane is almost empty! Do you think we're doing the right thing?" deplores Geronimo, with the concern of one doomed to a no-man's land.

"Don't worry, Cairo is a big city. It's only natural most of the people would be getting off here." Christopher speaks in the most casual tone he can manage.

By the time the plane lands in Asmara, twenty-three hours have passed since they started their journey. After a longish wait for their baggage they pass through the customs check of the small airport. They attempt to find a taxi to take them to the main part of town, but it is nearly midnight, and none are available. Instead, they happen on a private individual who is willing to take them for a price.

The hotel Christopher has chosen is conveniently located on the main street, but there is one catch. They have to walk up three flights to get to it. Once there, a sleepy-eyed night clerk who has been napping on the floor behind the reception desk greets them. The rewards for this minor feat of physical endurance are clean, well-furnished rooms, complete with cable television and telephone. Such modern conveniences are not their immediate concern, however. They feel tired, and terribly jet lagged. Their plan is to simply rest here for a day or two, and adjust a bit to the eleven hour time change before continuing their journey.

By the following morning, Christopher and Geronimo are starved. They walk down to the street level to find a bustling mini metropolis, built by the Italians years ago. People go to and fro in their daily routines dressed in styles of clothing ranging from business suits to traditional garb. Directly below the hotel is a shop which serves coffee and cakes. Before they can enter the restaurant, a man stops them on the street, trying to sell them coins purported to be silver, but tinged with green—a telltale sign of copper corrosion penetrating through a thin silver plate. They motion the unscrupulous salesman on, then make their way into the nearly full coffee bar finding seats at a small table. They order coffee and bakery items they see displayed behind a glass enclosure.

As they sit sipping espresso type coffee and munching on delicious gourmet style cakes and pastries, a man approaches their table. Sensing that Christopher and Geronimo are foreigners, the man asks in thickly accented English, "Is this seat occupied?" pointing to the third seat at their table. Christopher informs him it is not. The man sits down and orders coffee. As he waits for the coffee he stares out into space, as if he is a million miles away. He is of compact build, probably in his forties, with brown skin, tightly curled hair, fine features, and a look in his face that seems to echo the memories of troubled times past. Both Christopher and Geronimo know the look quite well. Abruptly the man returns to the world of the here and now and asks, "Where are you from?"

"We are from the United States." replies Christopher.

"So you are here on business?"

"No, not really. We are just passing through. We plan to continue on to Axum."

"That is a very long drive. Do you know how to get there?"

"I have maps, but I was thinking we might hire a driver."

"Should you desire, I would be happy to drive for you . . . forgive me, my name is Brahana, I work for the government, but I am free to take time off almost anytime I choose."

"I'm Christopher and this is Geronimo. We just might do that. Where can we find you?"

"I am here every morning at this time. Or you can ask for me at the doctor's office down the street. I will show you."

"Maybe this guy is on the level." Christopher thinks to himself.

"I have one question." begins Geronimo, "These cakes are fine, but I was wondering where we might be able to get something a little more substantial." patting his stomach as he speaks.

"I know a place." Brahana says as he finishes his coffee. He takes them down the street and around the corner to a small restaurant. They seat themselves at a table. Brahana speaks to a waiter in Tigrinya. Soon the waiter returns with a plate of bread and two bowls of 'ful'—a tasty concoction of beans, olive oil, herbs and seasonings. Geronimo is skeptical at first, but has no reservations after the first bite. They finish the meal, and Brahana insists on paying for it.

"Thank you for everything. We'll probably want to leave for Axum tomorrow. If that is too soon for you, maybe the next day if that's possible." Christopher says.

"Tomorrow is not too soon, but no trip to Asmara is complete without going to Massawa." declares Brahana.

"Massawa . . . isn't that on the coast?" queries Christopher.

"Yes. You can see the Red Sea."

Christopher is not really interested in straying away from his original travel plans, but Brahana is obviously enthusiastic about showing what his country has to offer. Christopher turns to Geronimo for his input. Geronimo throws his hands up, willing at this point to go along with just about anything. Christopher, not wanting to offend his new found friend, agrees to take the trip.

Brahana takes his new friends around town showing them the sights. They pass the Grand Mosque, then turn eastwards toward Saint Mary's Cathedral, a Coptic church. They come back through the outdoor produce market and jewelry district where silversmiths busily practice their age old art. Beautiful sweaters knitted from Italian yarn are on display in the many sweater shops scattered throughout the area.

In the evening, Brahana takes Christopher and Geronimo out to have a traditional Ethiopian meal. A waitress serves them various deliciously spiced meats and vegetables on a large platter covered with a flat, thin bread called 'angela'. There are no utensils, and everyone eats from the same plate. Brahana demonstrates the proper way to pick up the food; between the fingers with the 'angela'.

Three low key individuals enter the restaurant and receive special treatment. Brahana explains, "They are Israeli diplomats mourning the death of their assassinated prime minister." Later on, a man with no legs is escorted to a table. He receives the same special attention as the diplomats. Brahana says, "This man was a fighter in the war for independence." After the meal, they make plans for tomorrow's trip. Christopher and Geronimo return to the hotel.

The first traces of daylight are barely perceptible when Brahana arrives the next morning with the vehicle Christopher has rented for the trip to Massawa. By the time the first rays of the sun emerge, they are traversing the vast, mountainous, sparsely vegetated countryside eastward. Rural people carry bundles of wood on their heads, returning to their round, thatch roofed huts to make the first fire of the day. Occasionally they see an abandoned, rusty battle tank in the middle of an open field. Brahana explains, "Not very long ago during the fight for independence, dead bodies could commonly be seen lying on the ground along this roadway."

"I guess you didn't come around here too much back then." Geronimo comments.

"I was a soldier fighting in these very hills and elsewhere for nearly twenty years."

"Twenty years?" questions Christopher.

"Yes. It was very hard. We would sometimes go for days without food and water. We had no aid from the outside. These same country people you see here kept us alive by bringing us whatever they could."

"You must have had some kind of help." comments Christopher.

"A little, but mostly we won with our hearts, and with whatever weapons we could manage to take from the Ethiopians. We would take a forty barrel Russian artillery gun, and break it down to make many guns . . . then mount them on small boats, four wheel drives . . . whatever we could find. When they dropped air bombs, we would hide in holes dug in the ground, covered with ties pulled up from our own railroad tracks. We are in the process now of collecting the ties and rebuilding the railroad. You can see a stack of them over there." says Brahana, pointing just ahead to the right.

"Do you think you will ever become one country again?" asks Geronimo.

"Such a thing is hard to imagine. They are our brothers, we have much in common, but it was a long and bitter war. We have sacrificed too much. Maybe it will be possible for our children, or our children's children."

There is much in Brahana's manner to make Christopher and Geronimo feel at ease in this country of such recent turmoil. Brahana is obviously a man of honor and high integrity. The two adventurers feel fortunate to have befriended such a person. His story makes their problems seem trivial in comparison.

As the three edge farther on, they ascend to the thickly wooded upper elevations. Here, they stop at a restaurant, where they relax in a cool, shaded patio and have refreshments.

When they descend on the other side of the mountains, the climate changes again. It is now several degrees hotter and barren of any vegetation whatsoever. There is nothing but rocky soil for as far as the eye can see. The farther they go, the hotter it gets, until finally they reach Massawa.

Since the city is the home of an important shipping port it was one of the most heavily bombed areas during the fighting. Brahana tours them through the residential area. Most of the buildings suffered badly from damage caused by bomb shells. The residents, for the most part, are high spirited, making do with what is available. They see a woman in front of her dilapidated dwelling, smiling contentedly, enjoying the morning air and preparing her coffee in the traditional manner—first roasting the green beans in a pan over a fire, then boiling the ground product in a pot.

Moving on, they stop at a famous or infamous sight, depending upon your perspective. It was the summer palace of Haile Sellassie, the former Emperor of Ethiopia; now bomb shattered and in a state of ruin. The three visitors slip through a chain link fence surrounding the former royal residence, and climb the still intact palace stairs leading up to the main entrance. Chains prevent intruders from entering through the huge double doors of the palace, but they are able to peep in and observe the interior. They see a grand room apparently ransacked earlier, save for a few pieces of furniture strewn about on the floor. Christopher notices an arm chair finished in red leather lying sideways, and imagines the emperor once relaxing in it.

Just beyond the palace is the harbor, and south of the harbor is the beach. The three take time out to enjoy the warm, peaceful waters of the Red Sea. For Christopher, it is a ritual cleansing. For Geronimo, it is a fairy tale come true. After two or three hours' time, relaxed and rejuvenated, they have a hearty meal of fine Italian cuisine at a recently restored hotel on the harbor. They then begin the journey back to Asmara before sunset.

Brahana picks Christopher and Geronimo up at about the same time the next morning for the trip to Axum. Christopher is not certain when they will return, so he and Geronimo check out of the hotel, taking their meager belongings with them. They make one stop for gasoline near the edge of town, then continue on, passing several villages in the lowlands before winding upward through seemingly endless stretches of mountain road. They cross a river bridge, and are now in Ethiopia. The border checkpoint some distance ahead is highly militaristic and wrought with delays, but the time passes more easily by taking advantage of a nearby tea stand. Undoubtedly, the whole thing is a ploy to extract money from passersby. The process is otherwise trouble free.

The character of rural civilization on the Ethiopian side is similar to that of the Eritrean side, but there are differences. Whereas the round, thatch roofed huts are generally scattered across the countryside in Eritrea, they tend to be more densely packed, forming villages in Ethiopia. By late morning, they reach Axum. The main street is a dirt road accommodating a curious assortment of dwellings, shops, and a couple of hotels. Everywhere, there are hordes of children trying desperately to sell overpriced trinkets.

Axum is a place where, if the locals have their way, you pay every step of the way. Christopher pays a fee to see the monuments, and archeological sites, and an additional fee to enter the Saint Mary of Zion Church, but finds nothing that relates to the

Aten religion. He feels his best hope might be to find an area with people less concerned about commercial interests. People whose minds and hearts are bound to ancient traditions preceding the advent of Christianity and the Axumite Empire—people who might still practice animism in some form, such as the worship of snakes. Brahana suggests an area near Gonder, several hours drive to the southwest. Christopher consults his maps and finds it to be a reasonable choice. Gonder is near Lake Tana, the source of the Blue Nile—forming a continuous thread between Ethiopia and Egypt. Possibly there he will find people whose folklore can provide glimpses into a now forgotten past. They spend the night in Axum and continue on the next morning.

Before leaving Axum it is necessary to stop for gas, but the station has none. They must resort to purchasing the desperately needed fuel from black marketers at an inflated price. There is a store nearby that sells such gas. Brahana finds out the price per liter, then quickly calculates the amount of gasoline needed to complete the trip, and the total price in US dollars as well as the Ethiopian birr. Christopher has no choice but to give the okay.

"You're pretty good with numbers." comments Geronimo.

"I have a degree in engineering." Brahana replies.

"Is that what you do for the government?" asks Christopher.

"No. I'm afraid not. These days I do clerical work."

"Why?" asks Geronimo.

"Soon after graduation I joined in the fighting. That is all I know. People like me have much catching up to do."

Men bring gas out of the store in plastic containers and fill the tank. Christopher pays for the gas and they head out on the road to Gonder, arriving before nightfall. Tired and weary from the long day's travel, they have dinner and relax for the rest of the evening.

The following morning they go to a government building to inquire about tribes that maintain the old beliefs. An official tells him of the Qemant, a tribe living in a remote region to the west of

Gondar. Christopher is familiar with the Qemant from his studies. He knows their beliefs are Hebraic-pagan in nature. They might be his best hope, but to his knowledge they do not worship the snake and he doubts they would be able to help him much. The official responds by saying there are many tribes in the southern part of Ethiopia who worship the snake. He goes on to explain they still wear no clothes. Christopher doubts these people would have any affiliation with the high culture of ancient times. He needs to be looking for people more akin to the Qemant who still include the snake in their traditions.

Frustrated, Christopher decides to follow his instincts. He knows that over the centuries, cultural influences have repeatedly passed into the area by way the Blue Nile, Atbara, and Tekeze rivers. This infers the older traditions have been repeatedly replaced by newer ones. He seeks an area relatively unaffected by these constant influxes. He takes the official's advice in part—to explore the areas south of the lake, but not so far south as the official suggested. They take the main road bound south of Lake Tana until they come upon a man herding goats. "Why don't you try talking to that man Brahana?" Christopher asks. Brahana stops, gets out of the vehicle and approaches the man. After a brief conversation he returns to the vehicle.

"He has heard of a group of people who worship the serpent. They live farther south in an isolated area away from the roads. He says they keep to themselves. Even if we find them, they might not want to have anything to do with us . . . but we can try."

"Did he tell you how to find them?" Christopher asks.

"He told me where he thinks they might be, but he isn't sure."

They continue driving southward, then turn east onto a dirt road, and drive as far as they can until the ground becomes too rocky and uneven to go any farther. They must now journey on foot, walking for miles, but finding nothing. They become tired and weary, doubting the accuracy of the goatherd's claim. Brahana and Geronimo take a rest on a large rock as Christopher stands looking out over the wide expanse. He has a strange feeling he is on the right track. His eyes single out a stand of trees that seem a bit out of character with the rest of the surroundings. "I think we should go over there." he says, pointing to the trees in the far distance. They continue their trek towards the trees and as they approach they all feel a subtle mystery about the place.

"Look at that tree over there!" exclaims Geronimo, pointing to a huge tree that appears ancient. It has countless strips of leather dyed in bright colors streaming down from the lowest branches. Arranged around the tree in circular fashion are various foodstuffs, mysterious looking stones, and jars of liquid.

"This is a sacred grove." remarks Christopher. "We'd better respect it and keep our distance for the time being."

"I think it is too late." says Brahana, referring to a band of men approaching cautiously. They wear simple cloth robes and carry staffs. Their racial characteristics are hard to categorize. They appear to be in some respects African, and in other respects Arab. They could be both or neither, or maybe a prototype for all that came after them. One of the men speaks.

"What's he saying?" Christopher asks Brahana.

"He is difficult for me to understand, but I think he wants to know why we are here."

"Tell him we came to speak to the one who holds the knowledge of their people, and of the past."

Brahana passes this on, then interprets the reply, "He says that is not possible. We must leave."

"Tell him it is important . . . we have come from far away."

Brahana tells the man, hears the answer, then turns to Christopher and states, "We must leave."

"We'd better do what they say before they start using those sticks on us." cautions Geronimo.

Christopher is disheartened, but not in a position to argue. "All right, we'll leave then." he says.

As they walk away, a thought comes to Christopher. He reaches into his back pack, and pulls from it the luminous sphere.

He turns to face the tribesmen, holding the sphere high in his hand, and as he does, the reflected sunlight causes it to glow magically. The tribesmen, at first somewhat startled by this act, become curious. One of them comes forward from the rear of the group and beckons Christopher to return. He does so, while motioning Brahana and Geronimo to follow him.

"Have you ever seen anything like this before?" Christopher asks.

Brahana relays the question, then delivers the answer. "No, but he has heard legends of such things coming in the merkaribah."

"Merkaribah? Ask him if this is the Hebrew word meaning 'Chariot of World Formation'."

Brahana does so, and tells Christopher. "No. He says it is a word in the language of the People of the Sky."

"Who are the People of the Sky?" inquires Christopher.

The tribesman searches for another word, then says, "Zulu."

"What does merkaribah mean in the language of the Zulu?" probes Christopher.

"It means *space vehicle*. Many Zulus believe they came down to earth in a space vehicle, while others believe the first man fell from the sky attached to a navel cord." comes the tribesman's interpreted reply.

"Are you related to the Zulu people? asks Christopher.

"All men are related to us. We have been here since the beginning of man . . . since the days of paradise."

"What can you tell me about the days of paradise?" asks Christopher, intrigued.

"We all lived around the Sacred Lake." pointing towards Lake Tana. "Life was rich. Everything was plentiful. We scattered seeds on the ground wherever we chose, and would return later to reap a bountiful harvest. If we wanted fruit, we had only to reach out our arms and pick it from the trees. Life was perfect. We ate no meat. God, who resided on the great island in the Sacred Lake, had forbidden it . . . then there was a seven year period of drought. The fields did not yield crops and the trees did not bear fruit. People, rather than starve, began eating meat. This made God very angry. He caused a Great Flood to come. It washed away all the soil and killed the trees that bore the fruit. Most of our people scattered to other parts of the world. Many left by way of the Gihon River, while others found their way to the sea, then on to the land of Canaan, and beyond. The same weapons they made to hunt the animals for food were then used to drive out the ape men and occupy their lands."

"Does God have a name?" asks Christopher.

"His name is Yehavahe."

"And Yehavahe caused man to fall from paradise?"

"Yehavahe tempted man with the forbidden fruit. Man dared to taste from the highest fruit on the tree of life, and with this daring came the knowledge of godlike ability, but the price for this knowledge was to fall from paradise."

"But what of the serpent? We were told you worship the serpent."

"The serpent was the first meat our ancestors tasted. After the fall from paradise, Yehavahe left the great island in the Sacred Lake. The serpent remains as a reminder of our original sin."

"I need to know exactly where this sphere came from. Will you help me?" Christopher asks.

The tribesman stares into Christopher's eyes and sees in them an uncommon mixture of desperation and ageless wisdom. He realizes he is in the company of a man on the road to enlightenment—a lost brother attempting to find his way back through the wilderness of the archaic past. He responds by saying through Brahana, "Come with me."

The tribesman gives instructions to one of his fellows who immediately departs, then directs everyone else to sit in a circle around the great tree. Christopher sits within the circle close to the tree. The leader of the tribesman begins to chant softly as the others clap their hands. Soon, the other tribesman returns with a horn cup filled with a liquid, and gives it to the leader. The leader prays over the cup of liquid, returns it to the other tribesman, who then carries it to Christopher. Christopher drinks the contents at the direction of the leader.

Time passes and Christopher begins to feel the effect of the liquid. The chanting and clapping seem to reverberate in his head. He feels himself being carried off to a place where the land is white and completely barren. The ground beneath him swirls, opening up to reveal a tunnel. He is sucked in to the intense swirl and plummets to the depths, passing through a series of mystical abstracts: the house of Kheper, the house of Ra, the house of Un, and then on to the glorious light that is the house of Aten, where Amen sleeps on the horizon. He plunges into a pool of water, where time suspends, and the sensation brings him back to the here and now.

The chanting and clapping subsides. Christopher comes out of the trance with a look of awe and wonder on his face as Geronimo asks, "What happened?"

"This place holds many wonders. It is the very gateway to all human understanding, but the thing I seek is not here. It is in the land of Egypt." answers Christopher, who is not surprised at this conclusion, but has trouble interpreting the details of the vision.

Christopher thanks the tribesmen, giving them money and the luminous sphere as gestures of his appreciation. They graciously accept the gifts and bid him farewell. Christopher and the others have not walked far before Christopher turns around to pay the tribesmen a glancing farewell, or perhaps even to return and ask their name. He is amazed to find they have disappeared—even the offerings and strips of dyed leather about the tree are gone—almost as if vanished into thin air. Christopher figures it is just their way of remaining unknown to the world—an attempt to preserve their very special way of life. He admires them for their commitment to the old traditions. He appreciates the fact that they are even here, but he is afraid their total commitment to the past will contribute to their demise. Such is life with all its varied benefits and contradictions.

The Forbidden Fruit

Christopher begins the journey back to Asmara with his friends, satisfied with the insights gained in Ethiopia that in some respects are more than he expected. He reasons that perhaps some time in the remote past, the island in the middle of the Sacred Lake might have been infested with snakes. The drought forced men to pursue this relatively easy prey for the sake of survival, and the snake became their totem. A terrible flood washed away the snakes, destroying their food supply. The snake spirit had retaliated, and consequently, eating them was made taboo. In time, the snake spirit would attain the status of a full-fledged god, Yehavahe.

Another insight came by way of the glaring inconsistencies in the Book of Genesis. For instance, the four rivers that supposedly flow from the Garden of Eden don't seem to have much in common from a geographical standpoint. Now, as he returns, he thinks through the matter. Winding upward on the mountainous road, he recalls the things the tribesman said—that people, cursed by God for eating the forbidden meat, suffered a great flood, then scattered to other parts of the world.

Undoubtedly, he reasons, they took with them their language, customs, and myths, together with the hope of finding a second paradise. Many of them did manage to find a second paradise, settling along the Nile as far north as the delta. They had only to throw the seeds on the ground, and nature took care of the rest, as the irrigating floods came reliably each year. About the same time, others reached a land beyond Canaan we know as Mesopotamia, and found a similar paradise.

During the latter parts of the same wave of migration, people found their way to the Indus Valley in present-day Pakistan. After establishing roots there, they migrated north, settling along the Amu river in the Hindu Kush Mountains of modern-day Afghanistan. Here, they found rich deposits of lapis lazuli, and became renowned throughout their known world as suppliers of the rare and highly coveted stone. They traded extensively with the inhabitants of Mesopotamia, Egypt, and Ethiopia. The people of

241

biblical times knew this land as Havilah, and the Indus River as the Pishon.

Each group modified the story of the 'garden of paradise' over time to suit their own perspective. The version handed down to us today is a combined version as told from a Mesopotamian perspective.

Also, the tribesman referred to the highest fruit on his 'tree of life' as the forbidden fruit. Most certainly there was a time when man, or the ancestors of man, ate no meat. Even today, his digestive system resembles that of an herbivore more so than a carnivore. Man's health in all likelihood suffered as he adjusted to the new diet, just as it still suffers today to some degree, but the reward was higher quality protein to feed the brain. This allowed for enhanced mental development, and with it, the ability to devise better tools and weapons to hunt bigger game, to get more protein—and so the cycle has continued. To this day, the most technologically advanced societies also tend to be the most voracious meat eaters.

The story of Genesis mentions two trees: the Tree of Life, and the Tree of Knowledge. The mysterious tribesman only mentioned one tree, but this is purely academic. One can think of the Plant Kingdom, and the Animal Kingdom either as two separate family trees, or as a hierarchy on a single, great tree of life. The family tree of the Plant Kingdom was the Tree of Life, and the family tree of the Animal Kingdom was the Tree of Knowledge. According to Genesis 1:29-30 God told man plants and fruits should be used as food by man and animal. Later, in Genesis 2:17, God reinforced this rule by strictly forbidding man to eat of the Tree of Knowledge. In other words, meat, the fruit of the Tree of Knowledge was the forbidden fruit.

The tribesman's story seems also to have elements eerily matching the flood of Noah. If the father Noah is taken to represent the fatherland Ethiopia, then Noah's three sons—Ham, Shem, and Japheth can be taken to represent the migrating children of the fatherland to Egypt, Mesopotamia, and the Indus Valley respectively. The less advanced, indigenous populations of these areas regarded the newcomers as 'divine beings'. These divine beings found many of the 'daughters of man', that is, the daughters of the indigenous people, pleasing to the eye. They intermarried, then new cultures and myths evolved based upon the old.

Christopher's mind plays with the concept of forbidden fruit further. He considers that hallucinogenic chemicals are taboo, just as meat once was. Their use carries with them possible health risks, and they have an effect on the brain, just as meat does.

Then, in a single, bold sweep of thought, he wonders if somewhere within the chaos of abuse, and misuse of hallucinogenics, if man might someday realize a benefit in their use as a tool to explore the frontiers of consciousness. Just as the ancient's daring to taste the fruit of higher knowledge exacted the price of falling from paradise, at least according to legend, he considers his daring as the cause of him falling from his own peculiar brand of paradise. He wonders if this contemporary taboo is not the modern day forbidden fruit.

*   *   *

In two day's time, Christopher and Geronimo depart Asmara for Cairo. Brahana sees them off at the airport, telling Christopher "I felt there was something different about you when I first saw you. Be careful in Egypt. It is different from here."

The plane makes a stop in Addis Ababa before heading north to Cairo. As the plane approaches the great city, Christopher and Geronimo are struck by the fact so little of the total land of Egypt is inhabited. Cairo itself is barely visible through a thick, brownish gray blanket of air pollution.

After the plane lands they make their way haphazardly through the airport. A man dressed in a suit and tie approaches them, looking a little puzzled at first, but then introduces himself as Moustapha an official hospitality representative. Moustapha welcomes them to Cairo, and goes on to explain he didn't realize they were foreigners at first. He offers to help them find a hotel and provide free transportation to the hotel. He assures them the government regulates his operation and he will provide them with the highest level of service. As the man speaks, he points to an official looking badge pinned to his coat. Christopher agrees to follow him to his booth just outside the airport entrance and find out more, explaining that he wants to visit the museum. After making a telephone call from the booth, Moustapha offers his prospective clients a room at a reasonable rate near the Museum of Egyptian Antiquities. Christopher accepts the offer.

A Nubian driver takes them on a forty minute drive across town in a shuttle van, accompanied by another representative. The representative's conversation starts out on the subject of family and children, but quickly switches to a description of the tours they offer, he quotes prices starting at a hundred and fifty pounds.

"No, thank you. We are not interested in tours right now." Christopher answers politely.

"I give you special deal. Driver take you on his day off to Giza and many other places, including Old Cairo for only seventy five pounds." the representative continues.

"All we want is a room, and to go to the museum." replies Christopher.

"Today you walk to museum. Driver pick you up tomorrow and take you on tour. It is very good deal." The representative insists.

"Look man. He said he wasn't interested. Can't you understand that?" Geronimo adds, by now agitated.

"Okay. Driver will pick you up tomorrow and take you for only fifty pounds."

"JUST SHUT UP AND TAKE US TO THE DAMNED HOTEL!" Christopher shouts. The representative seems hardly affected by this display of explosive emotion, and barely manages to honor the request.

They arrive at the hotel. It is a decent establishment. Beautiful red and black carpet covers the floor of the lobby. The reception desk, banisters, and wall trim are of rich, dark wood. The fixtures are brightly polished brass. Christopher asks the hotel clerk for a room for one night.

"You have to stay for at least three nights or you pay fifteen pounds more, and we can not collect our commission." warns the representative.

"But you didn't tell us that before." replies Christopher.

"It is standard policy." states the representative.

Christopher considers finding another hotel, but the clerk is nice and cooperative, seeming even to despise the representative. "Okay. I'll stay here for one night at the standard rate." He tells the clerk, then turns to the representative and thanks him for his services.

"That will be thirty five pounds for bringing you here." demands the representative.

"You said there would be no charge for the ride."

"That is only if you rent room for at least three nights, and pay for tour." explains the representative.

"Look, I am not paying you anything! Do you understand?" intones Christopher, moving close into the representative's face.

Geronimo grabs hold of Christopher and pulls him back, telling him, "Come on now Chris, we're in a strange place. We don't need any trouble, even if it is their fault."

"I need to make phone call. You wait." urges the representative. He goes to the operator's booth on the other side of the lobby, has some words with the operator, and takes the phone. After a brief conversation, he motions Christopher to come.

Christopher comes and takes the telephone. The man on the other end of the line tells him, "You received a service and you must pay for it."

"I'll tell you what. I'll pay the thirty five pounds, but I want a receipt, then I'll report you to the proper authorities. We'll find out how ethical you really are."

"A receipt?" comes the feeble reply.

"Yes, a signed receipt." demands Christopher.

"Put the other man back on please."

The representative has a few words with the man, then hangs up the phone. Turning to Christopher, he says "All right. You don't pay anything. She needs a pound and a half for use of telephone." referring to the operator.

"You're joking, right?" asks Christopher impudently.

The representative pays the money to the operator, then walks out, angry and disappointed.

Christopher and Geronimo finally check in to their room. After relaxing for a bit they decide to leave the hotel for a bite to eat. On their way out, a bellhop they had not seen before asks them "Do you need a taxi?"

"No, thank you. We're just going to take a walk and get something to eat." answers Christopher.

"I know a good place just around the corner. I can take you there." Christopher and Geronimo take him up on the offer. The bellhop takes them around the corner into a perfume shop and says, "Please, have a seat. I will have food brought to you."

"How much will it cost?" Christopher asks.

"For the two of you, less than ten pounds." the bellhop answers. He summons a boy from the rear of the shop and gives him instructions in Arabic. Christopher hands over ten pounds and the boy goes off on his errand. The bellhop explains his cousin who owns the shop is not in right now. He begins taking bottles of perfumed oils down from the shelves for his two prospective customers to sample.

"Not again." Geronimo sighs with disbelief.

"So which one do you like?" asks the bellhop.

"They all smell very nice, but we only want to eat." responds Christopher.

"I tell you what. You take a bottle of this, and a bottle of this. I give you a special price." The bellhop then pours from large bottles into smaller ones. Christopher and Geronimo say nothing. The bellhop places the smaller bottles into a bag, certain he will complete the sale. Christopher and Geronimo sit quietly until the boy returns with the food—two generous plates of vegetarian fair. Christopher and Geronimo eat as the bellhop proceeds to sell them other items. When the two finish their meal, they get up and walk out of the shop, as the bellhop continues to pitch his cousin's wares.

With the aid of a map they find their way to the museum a few blocks away. After paying an admission fee they enter and pass down the center corridor. Christopher stops at two giant statues. They are likenesses of Amenhotep III and Queen Tiye.

"Would you believe me if I told you I was related to them?" Christopher asks.

"I'd say the smell of those perfumes has gone to your head." answers Geronimo.

They continue down to the far end of the center corridor to the Amarna section. Christopher stops before a colossal statue of Akhenaten.

Geronimo continues to the middle of the area, stopping at smaller busts of the Pharaoh's daughters enclosed in a glass case. Glancing toward Christopher, he is struck by the resemblance. The face on the statue seems a caricature of Christopher's.

Nothing is found that might provide clues to the mystery of the luminous sphere. They spend the remainder of the day wandering through other parts of the museum, but the time remaining before closing allows them to cover only a portion of the seemingly endless displays. Exhausted from the long day, they head back to the hotel to rest. Along the way a vendor tries to sell them imitation papyrus drawings painted on rice paper and a taxi driver tries to sell them another 'bargain' tour.

Later that evening they go out for dinner. This time they are wise enough to refuse any offers of help. It is now dark. The rush hour traffic moves down the main street in a heated frenzy, with horns blowing incessantly. They find a narrow street frequented by the locals. Turning down this street, they pass fabric shops, and brightly lit jewelry stores. Farther down, food is sold from several small shops and long rows of sidewalk vendors. Geronimo is by now famished. The absence of meat in the previous meal does not help matters. He sniffs the air and says, "That meat cooking over there smells pretty good." referring to a cart where the rich aroma of spices and sizzling meat rise above glowing coals.

"It sure does." agrees Christopher. They approach the cart and order two servings of the meat on pita bread and two sodas.

"Man, this is the best thing I've had in a while." proclaims Geronimo, chomping and swallowing as if his life depended on it.

They finish the meal, washing it down with the remainder of the sodas, then go back down the street in the direction from which they came. A truck coming toward them causes them to veer off the street, behind the row of food carts. Christopher happens to look on the ground to his right, behind one of the carts and sees the skin and head of what appears to be a cat. He moans.

"What's the matter?" Geronimo asks.

Christopher, figuring that ignorance is bliss, chooses to spare his friend, and answers, "Nothing."

Geronimo burps, then pats his stomach and says, "We've got to remember this place."

"Yes, we do."

They stroll down another street, window shopping until they come upon a large, brick building where they hear the screams of cats. "That's about the third time I've heard that. They need to do something about all these damned cats." Geronimo complains.

"Let's not talk about cats."

Christopher and Geronimo return to the hotel and relax for a while in the front patio area. The keeper of a souvenir shop next door tries repeatedly to lure them in to sample his wares. They decide now is an excellent time to turn in for the night.

They check out of the hotel late the next morning and take a taxi to the train station. It is difficult going there. The posted schedules are in Arabic and impossible to decipher. A guard directs them to the proper track where an English speaking passerby helps them to buy tickets to El Minya—the nearest town to the ancient site of the City of the Horizon that offers overnight accommodations.

The train is perhaps the greatest bargain of all for the adventurous traveler in Egypt—a whirlwind tour of the Nile country for a few dollars. The gentle, rocking vibrations of the train causes Geronimo to doze off to sleep. Christopher alternates between taking in the sites and making diary entries. They pass through the outskirts of Cairo into the smaller rural towns where the peasantry go about their daily business. Everywhere there are carts drawn by mules. To the east, running parallel to the railroad tracks is the Nile. The intensely cultivated land along the river gives way occasionally to palm trees. Christopher imagines things here must not have changed much since the days of his father.

Geronimo comes out of a doze as the train makes a routine stop. He peers out the window and sees a crowd of people waiting at the railroad crossing for the train to pass. An eerie feeling overcomes him. He looks into their faces and he sees Christopher.

After about three and a half to four hours, they reach their destination. Stepping out of the train station at El Minya, they come directly upon a town square. Christopher cautions Geronimo, "As things stand, they think you are Nubian, and I am maybe Middle Egyptian. We should try not to let anyone hear us speak, or we will blow our cover."

Located in the center of the town square is a circular water fountain, beyond that, many shops, including a hotel. The two travelers attempt to get a room in the hotel, but there are no vacancies. The inn keeper advises them to try another hotel down the street. They find the hotel. A bespectacled mulatto-looking man, bearing a smirkish smile, revealing badly stained teeth, greets them. Christopher inquires about a room for the night. The man offers a room for fifty pounds.

"Fifty pounds? That's outrageous!" Christopher replies.

"That is all we have. What else will you do?" asks the inn keeper.

"We will look somewhere else."

"There is nothing else available."

"If we don't find anything else, then maybe we will come back."

"What is your final destination?" asks the inn keeper.

"We want to take the train to Mallawi in the morning, and from there visit the Amarna ruins."

"But we have the tombs of Beni Hassan here. It is much better."

"We want to go to the Amarna ruins. That's why we came here."

"Just one minute. I will try to help you." The inn keeper makes a telephone call. His lengthy conversation causes Christopher and Geronimo to grow impatient. Finally, the inn keeper gives the telephone to Christopher. A man tells Christopher he can not go to Mallawi—it is a bad place. Christopher is by now familiar with the Egyptian hustle. He refuses to believe the man's words and hands the telephone back to the inn keeper. The inn keeper has a few words with the man before hanging up the telephone. "You can stay here, and then go where you choose. If you are hungry, I can get you a kilo of kabob for fifty pounds." the inn keeper continues.

"'Fifty' must be the magic number around here." Christopher thinks to himself.

Meanwhile Geronimo notices two unscrupulous looking men sitting in the lobby. One is fat, the other is thin. They are both dressed in tunics. The fat one wears a turban. They each stare through mean looking, narrowly slitted, calculating eyes. Geronimo, sensing trouble, turns to Christopher, "Something's not right with this place. Let's get out of here."

Christopher takes heed of his friend's advice and they leave the hotel. They walk east for a while hoping to come across another hotel. Christopher instinctively turns around. "They're following us!"

Geronimo turns to take a look. Some distance behind he sees the two men dressed in tunics from the hotel, now joined by a third. "They must be the innkeeper's henchmen or something. I guess they can't stand the thought of losing a dollar. Let's just keep on walking." Geronimo advises.

Soon they are on the bank of the Nile. To the south they can see a bridge that crosses the river. They head for the bridge, but before they can reach it, one of the henchmen has managed to circle around them, and gets there first.

"It's time to start acting crazy." Christopher says.

"I think you're right." answers Geronimo.

Christopher charges towards the henchman at the bridge, hitting him in the face and knocking him to the ground. Geronimo has by now caught up with him, and the two of them begin to run across the bridge. Geronimo has trouble maintaining his speed. Soon, the other two henchmen are close behind. Christopher stops halfway across the bridge to face them. He raises his arms in the air and yells a curse at the top of his lungs. He waves his hands wildly while reciting a spell in deep, guttural tones. The henchmen stop dead in their tacks. Fear prevents them from advancing further. Christopher completes his spell, then continues on to the East bank.

It has been a hectic day for Christopher and Geronimo. Wanting only peace at this point, they head out beyond the East bank to an isolated area in the desert. They travel in a southerly direction until nightfall comes. The combination of pleasant weather and peaceful serenity afford them few problems in sleeping on the open desert. As Christopher lies on the ground, head resting on his back pack, staring up at the night sky, he tries to come to terms with the fact that these people were once at the height of culture and civilization.

About seven o'clock the next morning Christopher and Geronimo are both still asleep when the ground rumbles. They wake up at the same time and simply look at each other. Having lived in California, they are both well aware of earthquakes. After several seconds the quake subsides and Christopher laughs aloud.

"What's so funny?" asks Geronimo.

"Nothing really." answers Christopher, but inwardly he is thinking "How dramatic. I visit the land of my forefathers and the ground shakes."

"Man, I swear . . . here we are in the middle of nowhere . . . an earthquake hits, and all you can do is laugh. I'm beginning to think you really are crazy. We have to get out of here!"

"Let's try going south for a while. That's the direction we need to go anyway. Maybe we'll run into something along the way."

Christopher and Geronimo gather themselves up and strike out on the open desert. The day wears on with no food or water, and no sign of people. They cover endless stretches of colorless, dry, barren land that relentlessly rises at times, then mercifully falls at others. The day nears an end and they feel they have gotten nowhere. Circumstance forces them to spend another night on the open desert, though not as comfortably as the first.

They continue at the very break of day of the following morning to take advantage of the hours when the sun is low. The day edges slowly on with no signs for the better. Hunger pangs have come and gone. Their lips are parched and their mouths have the feel of plaster. Christopher starts doubting himself, he reasons that Geronimo might be right, "Here we will die!" he worries. He reassesses events in his life: the wild imaginings of a child lying in bed at night, and how he lost faith in God. Then later when Brim introduced him to the hallucinogenic drug Infinity, and the world that seemed to open up to him. He recalls how completely it ruptured the membrane between his subconscious and conscious self, and how it released the demons of a primitive past, a past common to all men. Then, how completely and beautifully he was able to reorder his thoughts in the insane asylum. And now here, on a hostile desert, perhaps near the end of his life. "Was there ever anything to it, or was it all just some silly game?" he asks himself, then recalls the old woman in New Orleans, a complete stranger, who saw something in him and gave assurance that God would not let him down. Pulling himself together a bit, he concludes they must have gone in a southeasterly direction, taking them farther away from civilization. He thinks of the old Hollywood cliché where the hero crawls on his hands and knees, tongue hanging out of his mouth, dying of thirst, gasping with his last dying breath the word 'water'. The thought causes him to laugh hysterically.

Geronimo, taking notice, is not amused, "SHIT! I don't know how I ever let you talk me into this. It's Thanksgiving Day, and look where we are. We're going to die out here, and here you are, laughing again like a madman. How did I ever get mixed up with you? How?" he shouts.

Christopher hears little of what Geronimo is saying. Instead, he focuses on a word—a key word—the word 'water'. Then a memory comes to him, and he says aloud the phrase "I wish I had some water . . ." then again ". . . I wish I had some water. . ." then again, and again, and again.

Geronimo looks at him disbelievingly, and says "Look man, this is no time for some bullshit your grandmother told you when you had snot running out of your nose!"

Christopher continues to repeat the phrase over and over and over, as he wanders aimlessly. Geronimo, frustrated and agitated has no choice but to follow. By mid afternoon Christopher comes upon the edge of a low cliff, with Geronimo not very far behind. Christopher studies the terrain leading up to the cliff's edge. When Geronimo reaches the edge of the cliff he looks out into the distance, and what he sees causes him to rejoice.

"You did it! You got us back! I can see the river, and trees, and plants, and a little village. Can't you see it?"

"Yes. I see it." answers Christopher, somewhat preoccupied.

"So what's the matter? You don't seem very excited."

"I'm excited, but I'm just not showing it. This is just where we want to be. We are overlooking where the City of the Horizon used to be. I can tell because it fits all the maps I've seen, and descriptions I've read. That little village you pointed out over there is El Till."

"So there used to be a great city here, huh? Well, it sure is gone now. Hardly anything, but open space."

"Yeah. You can see a lot of horizon from here. I can appreciate how it might have gotten its name. I think we can make it down this cliff. I'll go first."

Not very long after they begin their descent, something catches Christopher's eye. There is a small opening in the side of the cliff. Christopher removes some loose rocks and gravelly soil to make the hole larger. "I think this might be a cave. I'll find my flashlight and take a look." He takes off his back pack. With flashlight in hand, he sticks his head and upper body into the hole.

"Do you see anything?"

Christopher withdraws from the hole and says, "It's a tunnel. It seems to be pretty long, and it slants downwards, maybe at a forty five degree angle. I'm going to crawl in and see if I can follow it."

"Man, we need some food and water. We can do this later."

"It's still a long walk to the river. This tunnel might be nothing. If that's the case, then we don't have to bother about coming back to this cliff. Hold my flashlight for me while I climb in."

"Be careful." Geronimo cautions.

Christopher climbs into the hole feet first. Standing inside in a crouched position, he says, "You can hand me the flash light now." He turns for the flashlight, but as he does the gravelly soil beneath his feet gives way, causing him to lose control and slide downwards through the tunnel. Geronimo is left with the flashlight in his hand, and the sound of Christopher's screams trailing away from him, then there is silence.

"Oh shit! Chris! Chris! Can you hear me?" There is no answer.

"Chris! Can you hear me!" Geronimo demands.

"Yes. I can hear you."

"Are you all right?"

"Yes. I'm fine . . . but it's dark down here. I can't see a thing. All I can say is that I'm on a smooth floor. Put my flashlight in the back pack so it doesn't break, and just throw the whole thing down."

Geronimo does as asked. Christopher manages to retrieve the flashlight. He finds himself in an odd shaped room. The wall nearest to the tunnel curves inward. The two side walls come closer together at the far end to form the corners of a narrower wall—almost a pie shape. There is a closed door at the far wall. The entire room is made of a metallic material that reminds Christopher of the luminous sphere.

The walls are decorated in typical Amarna fashion—the sun, with rays radiating down, terminating with little hands that caress likenesses of Akhenaten and his queen. On the floor, neatly arranged against the walls are clay jars, furniture, and various other objects made of wood and metal. In the middle of the room is a table that reminds Christopher of a medical examination table. On the table, Christopher sees a box that on closer inspection turns out to be a coffin.

Christopher goes to the end of the tunnel and calls, "Geronimo. Come on down and see this. Just be careful and don't start sliding like I did."

Geronimo crawls through the opening at the mouth of the tunnel, and inches his way down with more sure footedness than his predecessor. When he comes out on the other end he is amazed. "My goodness! Look at this! Is this what you've been looking for?"

"It must be. Would you help me take the cover off this coffin?"

Geronimo hesitates, but knows Christopher will keep at him until he gives in to the request. Rather than attempt futile resistance, he says, "All right. Let's do it, but let's hurry up and get it over with."

The two men lift the cover and place it to the side. Inside the coffin is a well-bandaged mummy. The arms are crossed over the chest. The hands grasp royal scepters. Two gold bands run down from the shoulders like suspenders. The bands, engraved with closed cartouches bear the name Akhenaten in hieroglyphic script. Christopher carefully lifts the wrappings away from the face. He is solemn and overwhelmed with emotion. Speculation about his father floods his mind. "How difficult it must have been having ideas different from most others around him—for seeing the energy contained in the sun as the single god of creation." It occurs to Christopher that he took his father's belief and elevated it to the universal level, expressing the universal energy as a relationship between the complimentary forces of the infinite possibilities and gravity. "How I wish I had known him, the thoughts we could have shared." Christopher sighs inwardly.

"What are you so worked up about? It's not like you knew this guy."

"You're right about that. I never knew him." Christopher places the wrappings back on the face, and says "All right. We can cover it up now."

When the coffin lid is back in place, Geronimo surveys the room with his own flashlight. "I wonder what's on the other side of that door." With some effort he manages to slide the door open, and peer in, becoming excited, but unable to discern the contents. "Come over here and see this."

Christopher is still standing over the coffin, deep in his thoughts. Finally he turns to acknowledge Geronimo, beckoning him to come. They enter a circular room. In the center of the room are three clear, egg shaped vessels, about four or five feet in height. Next to each vessel, is a control panel with little squares representing keys. A robe hangs on the wall near each of the vessels. Christopher recalls a vision he had several years earlier that was almost identical to the scene before him.

"What is this?" wonders Geronimo.

"We are in the merkaribah."

"You mean that Zulu space ship business the Ethiopian was telling us about."

"Yes. I know it sounds far fetched, but I once heard a story about a computer chip the government claimed to have developed. I say 'claimed' because they had to call on private industry to help them figure out how it worked. It doesn't add up. If the government really did develop it, why would they need someone else to figure out such a thing for them?"

"I don't know, why would they?"

"Rumor has it, the chip was taken from an alien spaceship that was reported to have crashed in Roswell, New Mexico back in 1947."

"That sounds interesting, but its just a rumor, this is real. You don't mean to tell me you believe this thing . . . whatever it is . . . belonged to the Zulus, and that they came from outer space?"

"No. I'm not saying that . . . but whoever came down in this vehicle might have had contact with the Zulus . . . and maybe the Zulus included these visitors in their own myths, but I don't want to worry about that right now. It's too many mights and maybes."

"Visitors from outer space. Up until now I would laugh at such a thing, but now . . . who knows? I wonder what they looked like?" asks Geronimo.

"Probably not much different from us, I would imagine."

"Why do you say that?"

"Because I believe there's something divine about the human form. To show you what I mean, let me ask you this: What would you change about the human body if you could to make it better?" Geronimo searches for an answer. "There's not a whole lot, is there?"

"No. I don't guess there is."

"Maybe that's one of the things the pyramids symbolize. The base of the pyramid is large, representing the many possibilities at the beginning of creation. Moving up from the base is like moving up through creation. The pyramid narrows, and as it does, so do the possibilities, until you reach the top where there is only one possibility. A snail or a cockroach starting near the bottom might develop a human form if given enough time under the right conditions."

"A human cockroach . . . now there's a thought."

Cockroaches do not concern Christopher much, though. He is thinking about his same vision from years earlier that relates to the objects before him. He ponders the idea that the figure he saw in the robe could have been him. Using this thought as his impetus, he goes near one of the vessels, strips off his dirty clothes, puts a robe on, then turns to face the control panel. He presses the keys in sequence: first, the lower left corner, then the upper middle, then the lower right, and so on, until he determines the shape of a pentagram.

Suddenly, a low humming sound is heard. The floor beneath the egg shaped vessel glows, bathing the vessel in a soft, orange light. The vessel fills to about one half capacity with an opaque fluid, as a tubular connection raises the top third straight up, opening the vessel.

Geronimo bolts backward, exclaiming "This thing works! How can that be?"

"If all this was designed for deep space travel, then it was built to last for a very long time." Christopher reasons as he peers into the opaque fluid. He recalls the vision he received in Ethiopia where he found himself falling through a tunnel, and landing in a pool of water. He takes his hand and submerges it into the fluid. It is slightly warm. He brings his hand to his nose, and smells it, finding it to be odorless. "I wonder if this is all right to drink."

"We're not *that* far from the river. We made it this far. We can make it there. Why take the chance?"

"All right . . . but before we leave, I want to bathe in it. It might have some kind of healing properties. Do you want me to open one for you?"

"No thanks. I'll pass."

Christopher disrobes and steps into the vessel, submerging his body to the level of his chin. He finds the fluid both invigorating and relaxing.

Meanwhile, Geronimo walks around the perimeter of the room inspecting two additional doors spaced equally from each other and from the first door. He tries to open one of them, but it will not budge. He tries the other door and has the same problem. As he stands before the door, trying to figure out how he might get it open he says, "I owe you an apology. At first, I thought all this was just a lot of nonsense, but now I see it's not. I'm glad I came, and I wouldn't trade the experience of it for anything. We should come back and try to figure out how to get these doors . . ." Just then he hears a thumping sound coming from behind him. He turns to find Christopher trapped in the vessel. The top has come down, and is filling with more fluid as Christopher beats frantically on the inner walls.

"Don't worry! I'll get you out!" Geronimo screams as he runs back to the first room. He quickly scans the room and locates a wooden chair. Grabbing the chair, he rushes back to the circular room. The vessel, now completely filled with fluid, has left Christopher with no more air to breathe. Geronimo swings hard with the chair against the side of the vessel. The chair falls to pieces, while the vessel remains intact. Again, he returns to the first room, this time finding a sizable rock that apparently had rolled down through the tunnel sometime before. He returns to find Christopher struggling to hold his breath. Geronimo delivers a mighty blow to the vessel, but is dismayed when the rock bounces off, leaving the vessel with hardly a scratch. He pounds away again, and again.

Finally, Christopher can not hold his breath any longer. He surrenders to the fluid, and slips into unconsciousness—but Geronimo knows if he gets him out soon, there will still be a chance of reviving him, so he does not lose hope. He continues to pound away, hoping to weaken the vessel. As he raises the rock to continue his assault, he sees something that causes a chill to go down his spine and his body to freeze like granite. Christopher's eyes are wide open, fixed on Geronimo. He moves his head slowly from side to side, as if to say, 'No. Don't bother', then weakly waves his left hand as if saying, 'good-bye'. Christopher's eyelids then fall as he drifts away.

Geronimo stands before the vessel with tears rolling down his face, confused and feeling helpless. He has lost the best friend he ever had and there is nothing he can do about it. Then he notices something peculiar. "But what is this?" he asks himself. Extending up from the bottom of the vessel is a flexible looking length of opaque tubing, about an inch in diameter. Some time during all the commotion, the tubing had attached itself to Christopher's navel. "Attached to a navel cord . . . like in the Zulu story." Geronimo recalls. "And his position . . . he seems to be in a fetal position." Now it becomes clear to him that Christopher is not dead at all, but rather in some other state of life.

Geronimo is tired, hungry, dehydrated, and emotionally drained. He sits on the floor with his hand on the vessel wishing he had allowed Christopher to open another to give him the chance of undergoing the same fate. He rises from the floor, goes to one of the other control panels, and starts pressing keys, but he does not know the code, and therefore fails. Sorrowful and disappointed, he goes to the first room, and returns with Christopher's back pack.

Searching through the bag, he stumbles on the diary. This he opens and reads under the soft light that bathes Christopher's liquid world. What he reads astounds him, but he has no doubts that it is true. He comes to the opinion maybe this is the way it is supposed to happen. This very thought gives Geronimo the fortitude he needs to go forward. He takes the skeleton key from Christopher's pants pocket, and decides to keep it as a remembrance. From his wallet, he takes enough money to get him home, and thoughtfully folds the clothing, placing them in a neat pile along with the back pack and diary.

"Good bye, my friend. May God be with you." whispers Geronimo. He leaves the circular room, and slides the door shut behind him. He stops at the coffin in the first room, the secret tomb of Akhenaten, and reserves a moment of silence in honor of the Pharaoh. Now he gathers up his own back pack and climbs up through the tunnel and out into the open where the Egyptian sun is now setting majestically over the western horizon. Carefully, he places the rocks over the mouth of the tunnel so as to hide any trace of an opening. He finds his way down to the bottom of the cliff, fixes his sight on the village by the river, and trails off into the distance.

As for Christopher, when he was struggling for his last breath of air, he saw his entire life pass before his eyes, for death seemed eminent. He received a sudden flash of insight that revealed to him an untold of number of realities, and in them, all the probable paths his life might have taken. With this same insight came the understanding of how his spiritual journey had set up interference patterns in the plastic time of the quantum realm in such a way as to alter the past, and therefore the future. He saw these subtle manipulations as the source of the signposts that guided into him into the present state of things.

He thought of the little girl who would be his daughter, and felt remorseful he had not risen to the call of fatherhood. At that instant, he came to the conclusion that in reaching so far—in trying to attain some degree of the ultimate—he managed, only too late, to grasp what the simplest farmer or herdsman in the remotest part of the world might know instinctively—that the greatest thing a man can do is to love women and children—and if this is cultivated then life has a chance of blossoming to its fullest—but such would not be the case for Christopher—at least not in this lifetime.

When the lids of Christopher's eyes closed for the last time, it dawned on him perhaps this was not the end—maybe somewhere down the line through another twist of fate he would have another chance at life—a happier life in a world less troubled than the one he was leaving. Maybe by then people will be more receptive to the ranting and raving of a sometimes psychotic, sometimes hysterical madman—but for now, it is a time for rest—a time to feel no pain—a time to lose one's self in a tranquil sea of blissful foreverness.

Little did he know the vision he received during his Rite of Passover was actually a prophecy, the fulfillment of which would come to pass: that planes, and birds, and every manner of flying thing would fall from the sky—while the sky, aglow as if on fire, bursts forth with color—brilliant hues of red, orange, yellow, and blue. Sounds—loud popping, stabbing sounds that sting the ears, signaling the end of one age, and the beginning of another—as the torch of humanity passes on to the new caretakers—and this is the testament from the life of Trikrisaton, the Pharaoh's Son in the twentieth century.